CURTAINS
FOR ROY

A NOVEL BY

AARON BUSHKOWSKY

CURTAINS FOR ROY

Cormorant Books

The publisher gratefully acknowledges the support of the Canada Council for the
Arts and the Ontario Arts Council for its publishing program. We acknowledge
the financial support of the Government of Canada through the Canada Book
Fund (CBF) for our publishing activities, and the Government of Ontario through
the Ontario Media Development Corporation, an agency of the Ontario Ministry
of Culture, and the Ontario Book Publishing Tax Credit Program.

LIBRARY AND ARCHIVES CANADA CATALOGUING IN PUBLICATION

Bushkowsky, Aaron, 1957– , author
Curtains for Roy / Aaron Bushkowsky.

ISBN 978-1-897151-74-7

I. Title.

PS8553.U69656C87 2014   C813'.54   C2009-907175-4

Cover art and design: angeljohnguerra.com
Interior text design: Tannice Goddard, Soul Oasis Networking
Printer: Friesens

Printed and bound in Canada.

The interior of this book is printed on 100% post-consumer waste recycled paper.

CORMORANT BOOKS INC.
10 ST. MARY STREET, SUITE 615, TORONTO, ONTARIO, M4Y 1P9
www.cormorantbooks.com

For my wonderful wife Diana
who's outlasting them all

Nothing happens to moments; things happen at them.
After a moment passes, nothing that happens anymore happens at it.

MARK CRIMMINS

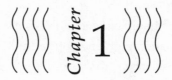

Chapter 1

The moment before, it was just a river. A connection between two bodies of water, a place where fish swim, kids play, leaves float. Now it is where Roy nearly dies.

It's a hot, sunny August afternoon. Roy, nine years old and barely able to swim, makes the mistake of trying to walk across the Swan River in northern Manitoba while a group of other nine-year-old boys scream at him from the other side. It's their theatre.

MOVE IT, ASSHOLE!

WE'RE WAITING!

CHICKEN!

But Roy loses his footing because he's spindly and uncoordinated and isn't wearing running shoes for better traction like us. He does the banana peel slip backwards into the rushing water and smashes the back of his head on a rock. A kid screams HE'S TURNING THE WATER RED. I stumble down the branch-webbed embankment still dripping wet, hit the water like a superhero, and churn toward him, wondering for the first time in my nine-year-old life where the adults are, grab his hand, not his hand, his head, grab his head, the red head, the bleeding head, and pull him up, get him out into the air, before the water curtains him into death and I have to explain this drowning to everyone for the rest of my fucking life, SO DO IT, DO IT NOW, GET HIM OUTTA THERE!

And I do. Yank him up and out of the cold water, his eyes big as saucers, hair standing on end so that he looks like a really shocked paintbrush. Drag him across the rocks to the shore. Drag him like he's already dead.

And Roy sputters and sputters.

And decides to live by coughing all the way into his forties, when the doctors discover inoperable lung cancer.

He calls me from the ferry on the way over from Vancouver Island. You there, he says.

Yeah.

Guess how long I'm going to live, he says.

What?

Six months.

What?

Six months.

Right there it occurs to me that doctors who predict such things should pick odd numbers more often. Why not eight months and eleven days? Or next Friday after lunch?

Roy says, That's funny.

It's then I realize I spoke aloud. It's a bad habit I have, saying the things in my head when they should remain there, behind curtains and ready to perform when called upon.

You're joking, right?

No, he says, his voice pulled thin between transmitters, except for when a ship horn adds bass with a sudden blast.

Oh God.

Are you surprised? I know I am.

I've been holding my cell away from my ear, sitting in traffic on Main and Broadway behind a cop car, waiting to turn left, waiting for the three remaining pedestrians, the goddamn slowest, fattest, dumbest pedestrians, to cross, all three of them on their fucking cellphones and looking up at the sky, walking, no not walking, waddling to the other side to catch their bus or whatever fucking pedestrians do these days. Thank God I'm not one of them.

Yes, I'm surprised, Roy, I had no idea. What happened here? When did this all happen? Are you serious? Please, come on, you can't be serious.

I'm serious, Roy says.

But how?

It's called a two-pack-a-day habit, Alex.

You asshole, you were smoking two packs a day?

Yeah, he says. Two. And a bit.

For how long?

Who cares.

Well, why would you do that?

Then we lose our connection.

The cop car turns. I wait. I don't know why; nobody is crossing the street anymore and it takes a very long honk from a silver Mercedes — why are they always silver? — behind to get me going again.

Where was I going, anyway? I've lost my objective. And a playwright without an objective is just a wordy poet who loves dialogue.

Right?

Right. Comedy.

I have a hangover. I'm broke. Bitter. Lonely. Maybe I was going to a bar. Maybe I was making a run to the liquor store. Maybe I was just looking for a mall. It wasn't much of a day anyway.

Vancouver grey. The kind of grey other cities can only dream of, where the sky sits on the water, skirt lifted slightly, a hint of mountain showing. The promise of better days ahead, but nobody here gives a shit. I guess they're used to broken promises. And heartache.

Roy doesn't call back. My cell eventually goes dead. It does that a lot because I'm lazy and don't recharge it regularly like I should. It's an iPhone and it's my lifeline. Although nobody calls. Not really. Certainly not my ex. May she rot in hell.

I'm pathetic. I know, I know. I'll be better. Soon.

I get home a couple of hours later and he's there on my steps with a case of BC red, wearing all black, including leather pants and his trademark bomber jacket. His outfit looks baggy on him, like a deflated turtle shell, his neck strained from the weight of just sucking air in and out. I'm not making this up. Every breath seems organized: out of his body, next, out of his body, next, and so on. You get the picture. Terrible.

You look terrible, I don't regret saying.

Don't remind me, says Roy, fumbling with the round black-rimmed sunglasses perched on top his thinning light brown hair, a bald spot the shape of Australia spreading on the back of his head. This is the first time I notice his hair loss, and quite frankly I am shocked. In my mind he's still a young man.

His fingers, though. His fingers are witch-bony. His legs have always been Mick Jagger-thin, but now his face is too. It's sunken. It's the kind of face you can imagine on any sinking man — the dread is in the eyes and you want to look away, but you don't.

Jesus, I say.

Six months, he says.

Yup.

Six months.

What are we going to do?

Road trip.

Where?

Roy pulls a bottle from the case, like it's a rod from a nuclear fuel bundle or something. Expensive wine, forty bucks a bottle. He points to the label: The Okanagan Valley. Then he smiles. Toothy, of course, always toothy with him, but in this case I'm thinking, He has something to smile about? Roy, my best friend from forever, is dying. I mean, really dying.

And so the end begins.

Weird, Roy says. Really, really weird.

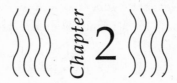

Chapter 2

*L*ights *dim. Some* applause. The actors fade into the shadows, somewhat uncertain. Post-show music comes up. Classical shit. You know — sleepy Canadian Tire-aisle-three-plastic-wrap-and-kitchenware kinda music. A man in the back hoots. He's the only one. The hooter. Probably a really drunk theatre friend. House lights up. I notice nobody in the audience stands to clap. They just stand to leave. Hundreds of them. The city's largest theatre, seating over six hundred, empties quickly, very quickly. The red velvet chairs like tombstones row on row. Some of the people stumble slightly as they file out back toward the light now spilling from the double doors, two sets of them, like blast doors, which is entirely appropriate given the bombs this theatre usually produces.

The stout lady with the black baseball cap and ponytail in front of me turns around and says, Nice job, Mr. Playwright.

Thanks, I say. Do I know you?

I hope not, she says, heading for the doors. Her teenage kid frantically waves her on from the back. Probably skipped out at intermission.

People are leaving pretty fast, says my date, Diana, chewing on her always-broken leather purse strap.

It's Thursday night; people have to work tomorrow.

Well, I think it was good, no matter what anyone says, she whispers, as if we are at the funeral of a close friend.

I search the seats for a friend. Even a lousy acquaintance. Nothing.

A critic passes me. He looks like a cross between Nick Nolte and Beethoven: stoic, unsmiling, white, big head, huge head, HUGE-like-a-Martian head, eyes big and black, absolutely no expression. Apparently I'm invisible even though I'm staring at him. He follows another critic, who is also unsmiling, short, and who resembles my sister Eunice. She quickly checks for litter between rows of seats as everyone motors toward the back of the foyer, the dark side, where they know free drinks and stinky cheese await. Or their cabs.

Was that critic running? asks my date.

That's not funny, I say.

I'm serious, she says, pulling at her long blonde hair. He's running.

I skip the post-show party and take my date home. I also skip the kiss at the door. She doesn't complain.

⌇

The reviews come out two days later. Nobody likes the play, not even the reviewer who likes me, the older woman who always tells me to get a haircut and then winks. She's the last of the winkers. Her father was quite the winker and she's keeping the tradition alive. Her joke, not mine. Anyway, the show closes when it closes. The actors phone me and tell me the experience was interesting and what was I going to think of next.

Bill, the most experienced actor in the company, meets me for drinks and tells me not to worry, comedy is hard and my comedy is especially hard. I'm not surprised the audience isn't laughing, he says, nursing his Chilean Merlot. They're used to sitcoms and this is bigger than that. Irony, right?

Right. I think hard. What kind of irony? I ask him.

Bill smiles. Well, that's where there's some confusion, obviously. Particularly in the second act. Although a lot of people didn't stick around for it.

Oh really, I say. Was it that obvious?

He doesn't smile. Just rubs the top of his shiny head with his palm, then runs a finger along the rim of his wine glass, all while keeping an eye on a zany black-haired chick with monkey-face tats on her forearms sitting at the bar. Normally we'd be sitting where she is but there isn't anything on the TV except cage fighting. We hate cage fighting. This place should know better. It's the kind of bar where nineteen-year-old wannabe actors hang out in clusters, their cellphones lining the small round oak tables like glowing oysters.

Greek tragedies, that's where you should go, Bill says. Read a dozen of them, rethink the life of your play, and then find a cabin in Tofino and write like a madman.

I'm not into the Greek thing, Bill.

Listen, he says, leaning forward, we all lead tragic lives.

After that, I catch the flu and remain in bed for five days, switching between the Golf Channel and MuchMusic. Nothing cheers me up. I try not to answer the phone. I obsess about my email, or the absence of it, and the emptiness of the occasional compliment like, Thank you for a challenging evening of theatre.

⌒

Weeks later I get a call from the artistic director of the big city theatre. Coffee, the AD says. So we pick out the nearest Starbucks and sit inside, sheltered from a slight May drizzle, nursing half-pump vanilla lattes made by our barista, Josh, an aspiring actor who absolutely loved the show even though he couldn't remember the name of it.

How do you feel? says the AD, her eyes narrowing like eyes narrow on TV.

Lousy, I say.

It *was* a good show, she says, it's just too bad we couldn't convince the critics. Who should all be killed anyway.

She pulls off her thick curling league sweater. There are ducks sewn onto it, red and black ones.

Where'd you get the duck sweater? I ask.

They're not ducks, they're Canada geese. And I got it in Hong Kong for twenty-five bucks.

They look like ducks.

A lot of people say that, she says. But they're wrong.

Yeah, funny, I say.

Can we get back to killing the critics? she says. Can we, because I have a two o'clock with my board and I haven't prepared for it at all. I have to explain the numbers for your show.

Great. Wonderful. How were the numbers?

I can't talk about it. I'm worried about your mental outlook.

Josh the barista gives us a wave and points to Jay, a rotund TV actor with jet-black hair and a car salesman moustache, who exits balancing a tray of lattes.

Oh, there goes Jay, says the AD. Jay, you look great.

Jay smiles. I'm doing great, absolutely, he says. Gotta run, I'm doing the coffee run and we're on location.

Where?

We're shooting in the brewery down there on Granville Island. I'm playing the victim who's found dead in the bottom of the beer tank.

Oh, that sounds great, she says.

It *is* great, says Jay.

Have a nice death.

Catch you, he says on the way out.

The AD sighs, as if the whole exchange took tremendous energy, then pushes her coffee cup away with her thumb.

What's that? I ask. Catch you?

He always says that, it's cute, she says, still waving at Jay who wiggles past a woman trying to enter the Starbucks carrying her wiener dog in a wicker handbag, the traffic noise doing what traffic noise does when you open and close a door.

Oh well, I say. We tongue our lattes, or at least the foam.

Seriously, the AD says. Where were we?

Critics.

Oh yes. I know what I was going to say: Ben Jonson killed a guy who criticized his work in public.

Which Ben Jonson?

The one who drank with Shakespeare, she says. In fact, Shakespeare was at his house drinking the night before he died. Maybe he killed Shakespeare too.

I'm no Shakespeare, I say. I think that's clear.

Come on, don't be so glum, chum, she says, wink-wink, nudge-nudge. You're young, you will survive this. I hope. What are you, forty now?

I'm forty-five.

Jesus, she says. I had no idea. You're older than me. Shocking. But good for you, the young women must not be told under any circumstances. Right?

Right.

The AD looks at her watch. Did she do that before?

I shiver and watch a skinny teen, male or female I don't know, wearing skinny black jeans and a skinny tattered blue jean jacket, staple a pink Fringe Festival play poster to a skinny telephone phone. He or she looks around cautiously before firing in the four staples. BANG-BANG, BANG-BANG. Then he or she pulls up his or her skinny pants and makes for the alley, staple gun at the ready.

The AD yawns. God, she says, that kid is really nailing that play. I know, sorry. I'm exhausted, and that's when I'm never funny, I should know that by now. Oh, I've just got my lids done, did I tell you that?

Oh, I say back, looking for lids somewhere on her body before figuring it out.

Look, she says, you should do what I do after a show closes. I take the critic out for drinks. We talk about the show, what he did or didn't like, that sort of thing. She yawns again, like a dog yawn, then watches me look out at the clouds topping a glass building nearby, sitting like whipped cream, like mashed potatoes. Or something. I've run out of similes. A warning sign, I'm sure.

What's out there, what has you thinking? she asks. Alex?

I've never actually thought about killing a critic, I find myself saying aloud to her. I mean, not literally, because I'm a pacifist at heart and I couldn't imagine killing a mouse let alone another human being.

Her eyes narrow again.

How do you do that? I ask.

What?

Narrow your eyes? I mean, they look completely black now.

It's just a thing I do, she says, re-narrowing them. See? Easy. Especially since I got my lids done. Look, I've got to go. Whatever you do, don't kill him for real. Bad karma. And the theatre would look really bad. And please, try to remember it *was* a good production. It was, no matter what anybody said. In the press especially.

So where do we go from here? I say.

Well, write me another play, but make it better. How's that for a start? I can't promise a production on the big stage again, but maybe we can find a small space, something more intimate, a hundred seats or less. A small audience will get your writing. I'm positive.

What kind of play?

The kind where people respond to your humanity. They can laugh only so long, right? Then they want serious life issues to be properly addressed before going for drinks and home to their disenchanted teenagers.

They didn't laugh during my play?

Exactly, she says. Exactly.

I took most of my best jokes out of it though, I say. Because you told me to.

Now why would you do that? she says. It's the best thing about your writing.

I'm confused, I say. Exactly ... exactly what are you saying?

Oh, you are something, she says. Then she gets up and kisses me on the top of my head. Hey, you're losing a little up here, she says. That's tragic, I've always liked your hair. I tell people about it all the time.

Thank you.

No problem.

She gives my shoulder a feeble pat, then heads out toward her Jeep. I notice how short she is, barely taller than the parking meters. But she walks like a big person, huge steps, as if she's carrying two milk pails and needs to empty them into a tank.

At home, I stand on my six-foot-wide balcony, watch the rain pelt the dog owners standing under the big branches of the fir tree. Watch them wait for their pooches to finally take a crap so they can get back to their warm TV sets.

I email the critic, the one I hate the most, Mr. Big Head, and tell him I'm interested in hearing his dramaturgy over drinks at a biker bar downtown. He emails me back suggesting another bar, a gay one. I agree. They have free olives at that bar, just like the bars in Israel, or so I've heard.

I courier him my script because he doesn't want to open any attachments. Wants to read it first before talking, compare what's on the page to what was on the stage. His words, not mine.

⁓

It's another Thursday night when we meet.

The critic waves me to a stool beside him at the giant oak bar, where a scantily clad woman waits behind with an apron that reads I'm Henry, Not Horny.

I'm not sure I get that, I say to her as I sit down. Shouldn't it be the other way around?

You must be straight then, the bartender growls. What'll you have?

A Shiraz, please.

Good start. That's what I'm drinking, says the critic, holding out a thin sweaty hand.

I shake it and sit down on the stool. Thanks for meeting with me, I say.

All part of the job, he says, chewing on the end of a pencil.

You're not writing any of this down, are you?

No, no. I just love the taste of erasers, he smirks.

The bartender slides the Shiraz down in front of me and saunters away.

Cute, the critic says. No?

Sure, I say. Where are the free olives?

They stopped that, he says. People go to the bathroom and don't wash their hands, then come back to the bar and finger the olives. It's very unhygienic, you know, so they got rid of them.

Oh, I say.

But a lot of people ask about them still. It's been months.

What did they replace them with?

Nothing. But they have a new condom machine in the men's room.

I sip the wine. Awful.

So, about your play. The critic leans back as if ready to throw a fastball. I see he's got a pot-belly, the kind you get from a steady diet of tacos and beer, and he notices I notice and pulls down his striped blue-and-yellow shirt with both hands. They are tiny clenched hands that look like they belong on a twelve-year-old girl. A cruel thought, I know.

About your play, he tries again, leaning in closer as if to sip his Shiraz without actually touching it, his perfect girlie hands now shoved deep in his blue jean pockets.

You think it sucks, I say.

Well, that's a little blunt, but no, I don't profoundly hate it.

You said, and I quote, If the actor would have found a gun in his jacket pocket, he most certainly should have used it before the second act.

Did I, says the critic, laughing. That's cheeky. Really cheeky. I don't remember my reviews. Any of them, even the good ones.

Well, I remember, and I didn't laugh, I say, pushing my Shiraz away because it tastes like the bottle was left open overnight. I tell the bartender, who sighs and explains reds need more time to breathe. She doesn't replace my wine. Idiot, I think.

About your play, he starts up again. What do you, as the writer, like about it?

I like it all.

Well, within the context of this play, what do you, as the writer, think you can live without?

It all works. I like it all.

Well, what do you, as the writer, feel most strongly about?

World peace, actually, I say without a smile.

You're very sensitive for a writer, says the critic, again without a smile. You really don't get it, do you?

He pulls down the square-framed sunglasses perched on top his head, licks the lenses, and begins to wipe them on the front of his shirt.

Did you just lick your sunglasses? I ask.

You're not offended, are you?

Well, I say. It's a little —

The critic puts them away. That better, Mr. Sensitive?

About my play, I say.

Look, you can't write about things you don't know, says the critic. You have a play where the central character thinks he's in love. But I don't believe him. I don't know how anyone would. It's clear you're talented, but you don't occupy your characters from the inside out. He takes a long sip of wine, rolling his blue eyes back as if studying the glitter ball above us.

Glitter ball?

Henry the bartender says it's left over from the previous owners. They were from Romania. The critic giggles. Romania is a funny country, he says. My editor is from there. Hilarious. Can't spell worth shit.

Can we get back to my play, please? I say.

All right. Then there's the added problem of your theme, which quite frankly seems to suggest that life is barely worth living. Where's the hope? Where is it?

I think this was a mistake, I say, pulling out a ten dollar bill and sliding it under my glass of stinking red wine.

Don't hate me too much, says the critic, pulling at his hair.

How much do you think is too much? I offer.

The critic doesn't smile. When is your next play up?

I don't know, I say through my teeth, not after this last round of reviews.

Again with the reviews, says the critic. They're just reviews, nobody cares, nobody really reads them anyway. You think I like writing some of the things I write? I'm just trying to sell newspapers, OK?

I've got to go, my back is killing me, I say, and I'm not lying.

And then I leave.

When I get home I find an email from the critic. It says: All good writers should have thick skin. And PS, that Shiraz at the bar was fucking horrible, one of us should have asked for our money back. Are we both sensitive writers or what?

The thing about killing a critic is you can't do it in the press — like my uncle would say, it's like bringing a knife to a gun fight. Or maybe he said don't fight with people who get their ink delivered by the truck. And I don't like the concept of getting convicted and jailed for actually killing another human being, even though it would probably mean a lot of quality writing time.

I get yet another email from the critic: Let's try that again. Let's meet and behave. Can we do that finally?

So I agree.

This time it's a bar at a hotel I know, Vancouver's hangout for film knobs, a bar that lawyers have also recently discovered.

Another Thursday night of rain. The critic sits by himself at a round table by the window. He's eating from a small ashtray-looking dish filled with salted cashews. It's a nice bar. The blue carpet has little silver stars embedded in it. It's supposed to make you feel like you're walking both outside and upside down, with an expensive drink in hand.

Aren't you supposed to be at an opening? I open with.

I was last night, says the critic, patting the padded red velvet chair beside him. You think your play was killed, wait till tomorrow's edition comes out. My first line starts with, Someone call 911. Very funny stuff. Please sit.

So I sit. I feel like a French king in this old chair. I notice how tall I am from the waist up in the mirror across from me. It's nice, but I can barely make myself out from behind Mr. Big Head sitting across me like a miniature Jabba the Hutt, nursing his Australian red like it's vintage port. Idiot.

I order the Riesling because I know they have good Rieslings in this bar: the bartender is German. And this is a good night for a low-alcohol Riesling. No chance of even more blather coming from me.

About your play, says the critic.

Yes?

I could write something over the next, let's say, three days talking about some of the potential of the piece. It actually has potential, particularly the ending, which, if you ask me, is misdirected with all that creepy music. I mean, the man is dying, don't have dying music on top of it.

I didn't write creepy music into it, that was the director's choice, I say.

But you've written Creepy Music in pencil in the margin, what's that about? He shows me my play, sliding it across our tiny table with one of his equally tiny hands.

Not my note, I say. That's what the director scribbled. I keep my stage directions to a minimum, never direct from the page. Nothing in the margins belongs to me. I don't work from the margins. Never.

Oh, that's clever, says the critic. Can I use it?

No, I say. It's been done.

He stifles a smile and says, Of course, this article I'm writing would be an opinion piece. It'll run in our Thursday Arts section.

Why would you do that? I say. Let sleeping dogs lie and all that, right? I mean, the play has come and gone. It's over.

You run a theatre company, right?

Right.

A small, struggling theatre company, right?

Right.

I have this play.

Oh, I see.

I think you should just read it, the critic says, sliding the play across the table, pulling mine away at the same time. Here, I brought you a plastic bag because of the possibility of rain. We're in for it later tonight, you know.

I see the title *The True Nature of Us* and immediately dismiss it as pretentious bullshit. I drop the play into the bag.

Thank you, says the critic. Now I can relax.

And we do. But we don't talk about my play again.

⤳

Two weeks later I meet with Joanna, an actress-slash-director-slash-former relative. She's read the critic's play and hates it more than I could have imagined.

We run a small non-profit theatre company together just to keep us somewhat employed throughout the year. I mean, if you can't find work, make work. And it's all about the work. But we only produce once a year. I write, she directs. It's not the big leagues, certainly not six hundred seats of the big city stage, and certainly not funded enough.

I really hate *The True Nature of Us*, she says, sweeping back her strawberry hair to reveal a giant hickey on her neck. Oh, that, she says. Silly isn't it, at my age too.

She's forty-five but looks forty. I always tell her that but lately she's told me to fuck off so this time I just nod.

Are you going to make a joke about my age? Joanna says, watching my expression. Just let me know now so we can get it out of the way. Yes? No?

I make my face solid. Block of ice. Don't blink either. Not a chance. Did I say that aloud? Did I?

We are sitting in a Starbucks near the hospital. This one has disco music playing. Blondie, of course, followed by Lady Gaga. A young mother waiting for her latte is dancing with — I'm guessing — her four-year-old daughter around the display of purple one-pound coffee bags and new Alanis Morissette CDs. You can't get Alanis Morissette CDs anywhere else now, just Starbucks. The manager, a tall balding man in his late thirties, watches them from a computer-lit backroom, an unlit cigarette hidden in his cupped hand, counting the minutes before his break. He waves at the young mother but I'm not sure whether it's a warning to stop the dancing or an indication to go faster.

Are you in another space? Joanna asks.

Why?

You're not focusing on me.

All right, I'm focused.

Then why don't you look at me? Is there something wrong with my face?

I cock my head like a dog and stare her down. What the hell?

Don't think of children, she says, looking at the blonde child dancing between tables now. You'll just get weird again. Let's not forget you're getting a little too jaded and old for kids anyway.

Thanks, I say. You're too kind.

She smiles, not a nice one either. Now, she continues, this piece, I have to say, *The True Nature of Us* is the worst piece of pretentious crap I've ever read in my life. Nobody cares about a scientist who discovers how to genetically engineer embryos to create artists.

It might be a movie, I suggest. It *does* have a cool premise, when you think about it: if you had the power to genetically engineer embryos to be artists, wouldn't you do it? I mean, isn't that at least interesting?

Joanna laughs. In which fucking theatre? The one in hell?

When she stops laughing, the Starbucks looks emptier. With the mother and child having left for the patio, only two people reading newspapers remain — very old school, no electronic devices.

So what are we going to do? I ask. We have a new production coming up in a few months.

Why don't we *not* invite him?

We need the press, I say. We can't do that.

Why don't we send him an early draft. Ask for comments.

Look, Joanna, I don't have an early draft.

What?

There is no draft. I can't write. I have issues right now.

Come on. What issues?

Well, I say. My recent production at the biggest theatre on the West Coast bombed. I just met with the AD and she wouldn't tell me how bad it was.

Yeah, says Joanna. You don't have to tell me, I was there on opening, remember?

I think I'm a total failure, I say. Not funny anymore.

That can't be the only reason, Joanna says. You've had bombs before. In fact, I directed one. Three years ago. Remember?

There's other reasons, I snap. It's personal. OK?

I think I know, she whispers. It's your voice.

What voice?

Writing voice, idiot, she says, pulling on her red coat. There is no authentic writing voice. Yeah, that's your big flaw. Who are you, Alex?

What?

That's what everybody says: you hide behind your humour. Joanna lightly caresses her hickey. Everybody can't be wrong, can they?

Who are these people?

I'm not going to tell you, she says. Mostly they're our friends, for what it's worth. And your ex. But I refuse to talk about her. She's still my relative and Facebook friend, so get over it.

Great, I say. Thanks. Wonderful.

We sip our drinks as if they've been poisoned.

Here's an idea, she finally says. Maybe you've heard of it before: write what you know.

Yeah. Wow. I'll write that down.

Joanna fake smiles. Please don't miss our deadline. We're going to read the first draft in September. We are on a very tight schedule. Do not slack off on me. You always do that and it's very irritating. You need to be more organized. Write things down. Keep a journal or something.

I need to go away for a while, I say. I can't think about theatre.

What? You can't, she says. No way. Seriously, I'm serious.

So am I, I say.

OK, she says. Suit yourself. Run away from your problems and allow your shit to become pent up beyond control and see if I care.

OK.

Fine.

OK.

Then we sit there, squeak our bums in the faux leather chairs, and listen for the end of the fucking Gaga song.

Then we kill our drinks.
And then we leave.

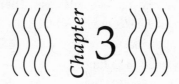

A near-death experience together in early life means nearing
death together in later life. This is Roy's logic.

You owe me, he tells me.

How's that? I say.

You saw me almost die when I was a kid, now you can see me
die again, Roy says.

If anything, I say, you actually owe me.

But he isn't satisfied. Not that he ever has been, not in
twelve years as the artistic director of a small but somewhat
successful theatre in Victoria, making barely enough money to
buy his groceries and feed his bad habits: smoking, drinking,
and sushi.

What a way to go, he says now, coughing on a Player's Light
glowing halfway out of the window of my blue Mazda on a very
warm July night on the way to Kelowna.

Here we go, I think. Here we go.

At first you think, I'm going to live to a hundred, no problem.
Then you get a bad flu that doesn't go away and start thinking
eighty would be OK. Then you start hacking up some blood and

you start bargaining, Come on, sixty-five, sixty — at least let me retire before kicking the can.

Roy, shut up, please, I say. I'm in my forties and I haven't found true love yet and you're depressing me.

Try Internet dating, it's fast and easy. That's how I found Connie. Roy strokes the sleeve of his black silk shirt, part of his trademark outfit of all black, any day of the week.

And what happened to Connie?

She left me for a younger man, he says. What can I say. I would too if I could find somebody younger who just wants to have fun for, let's say, six months.

Stop it.

Maybe I should go back to dating actors. At least they put the fun in dysfunctional, right?

Stop it.

They don't know who they are. They don't care who you are. And they're just a tiny bit co-dependent. But boy do they know how to party. Are we almost there?

Stop that too, I say.

We drive. Down one mountainside, up another, into the Nicola Valley, where Merritt sits baked brown with the July heat, where you can see your life unfold up the Coquihalla Highway ahead.

What a view, says Roy.

And it is a great view, because you can easily see where you've come from and where you're going until you finally get to where you want to go. This is the brilliance of the Coquihalla: six lanes of divided highway where you can break the speed limit and still enjoy the view, especially when you reach the summit and see forever, see the tops and bottoms of mountains, see unreachable clouds that are now just over to your right.

We pull over for a bit to take it all in, and we're soon joined by a bus. It frees its load of tourists, who hit the slopes with their cameras in hand, clicking their heels at the deer gathered in the ditches kicking at the grass poking out of clumps of dirty snow. In the distance, along the treeline curled around the waist of the mountain, movement — maybe a bear — scatters the deer, who move gracefully, like young girls after ballet practice, to cross the road into the thicker forest below us.

Did you see that? Roy gushes.

Yes, I say.

What was that? What spooked them?

I don't know, I say. Something up there.

I wish I had binoculars, he says to the world around him. My kingdom for a good pair of binoculars. Anyone? Anyone?

The tourists turn their backs on us, concentrate instead on the other side of the road, snapping shots of deer shadows as the sun beats down on our backs.

Then we drive some more, winding our way through the mountains, picking our way through the Safeway trucks and RVs to find a better scene. It doesn't take long. One hill, a couple of dales, and we see more deer hugging the side of the road to feed on the grass, oblivious to our speeding blue Mazda.

Aren't they even a little bit afraid? Roy says. I mean, look at the buses and trucks around here.

They're used to it, I say.

Death is right over there, right over there, and they're used to it, he says. What are they? Stupid?

Yes, deer, I say. Then giggle.

He smiles. Good for you. Yeah. Real funny.

We start the descent into Kelowna, the sunniest place in Canada, neatly pressed into the curves around Okanagan Lake. The lake itself is over one hundred kilometres long and full of fast boats and big stories like the one about the mythical Ogopogo, Canada's answer to the Loch Ness monster.

Here be monsters, says Roy, as we cross the bridge in the middle of the lake into the city. On either side, dozens of sailboats lend thin wedges of colour to the sky — red, yellow, green, you name it.

Looks like a competition, I say. A flotilla? No, that's not it. Come on, what do you call that? We have six degrees between the two of us. We're not that stupid, are we? What do you call that, when sailboats compete?

Who cares, he says. Over here, everybody's a winner, my friend.

We wind our way out of the city along Harvey Avenue, the main drag, looking for the bed and breakfast we've booked, near the edge of a winery on the far side of the lake.

Monsters! Roy barks at a couple of older long-haired skateboarders standing by the bus stop reading a *People* magazine together.

They give us the finger. He flashes them the peace sign and says, Yeah, baby, yeah!

What the hell? I say. You're a forty-something-year-old man, not some kid. What happened to demure, intellectual Roy? The guy who reads *Psychology Today* and grows his own fennel?

I'm on vacation. Just drive.

So I do. His skinny body halfway out the car, Roy strains to look back at the lake, one hand braced on my dusty blue dash. His fingers are red at the tips. His watchband is too big for his wrist and he's shaking. Not a lot, but enough for anybody to notice even with the wind whipping his clothes.

Woo-hee! he yells at a passing cyclist talking on his cellphone. Woo-hee! I love the air out here, he says, pulling his face from out the window, the wind catching what's left of his thinning light brown hair, making it stand on end like he's received the scare of his life. Christ, what is that smell?

It's a dry air, clean, crisp finish with lavender notes, I say.

Save it for the wineries, Roy says, then leans over with his head so it lolls. He sucks in the outside, closes his eyes, opens his mouth, balancing himself against the dash with his spindly legs as I turn the corner to move up and away from the lake. Gulps the air, letting the speed of the car force it into his decaying lungs, allowing it to inflate his face until the spit flies. Ah, he gasps. It's fresh air. Fresh, unfettered air. He pretends he's a big dog with a sinus problem, shakes his head in the wind as if trying to get a better whiff. I love this place, he says. Love it. Want to lie down on the beach. Watch the kids stomp on the waves and think nice clean thoughts. What a way to go.

Stop saying that, I say.

Don't be so crabby, please, he begs. We have a few weeks together and we're only on the first day. It's beautiful out here.

I know what he means. It's reflected in the rear-view mirror, the perfect blue sky matching the perfect blue water of the lake, the shiver of the wind sending waves to flash, the sun coming at us in bits and pieces. This is paradise, or as close as you get in a northern country that barely gives us more summer than winter even with global warming.

Along the shores of the lake, gnarls of vineyard promise us untold hours of wine tasting and hazy nights of drunken patter about bad theatre and the assholes who create it. This is what being an artist is all about, because theatre royalty cheques rarely cover the rent and TV always sucks. Forget about productions and fame, it's the gossip that gives us hope, the stories on top of the stories.

Trumpeter Road, that's what we want, I tell Roy. And put out your cigarette. It's very dry out here and the radio station says forest fire conditions are extreme.

Yeah, yeah, yeah, he says, flicking his cigarette out at a passing cop car and rolling up his window.

Did you just flick your cigarette out the window? What did I just tell you? I say.

Regatta, that's what it's called, he says.

What?

A boat race. Roy smiles, his gums white instead of red, the result of his two-pack-a-day habit. He pops a candy into his mouth. His teeth are yellow around the edges, like his gums have been leaking oil. My fucking regatta, he says, and breathes across the car. He has very, very bad breath, a penetrating smell I can almost taste, a mint-flavoured decaying reek that seeps into my pores. Dead flesh around the corners of his mouth. I try to hold my breath, avoid the air of death.

God, are we there yet? I say.

He doesn't answer.

I turn on the air conditioning and gun the Mazda up Lakeshore Road past the winery with the pyramid. The sun is now at our backs, peeking over the brown slopes that surround the city. I drive and drive. Breathe slowly through my nose. Try not to think.

When I pull up to the bed and breakfast, Roy is asleep, slumped against the door, his breathing like air coming out of a tire.

I can't hear it going in.

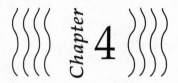

Chapter 4

The first day we went to three different wineries, sampling Riesling and Pinot Gris. Our comments follow — and it doesn't matter who said what because both of us were pretty loaded and my writing got progressively worse:

I like the burnt-match smell of this one.

I like the grapey-ness.

I sense a slight Granny Smith apple in the second one.

Nice mouthy-tongue feel thing going on in here.

I enjoy the balance of fruit and alcohol of number three.

Goes good with bread.

Taste is linen with a look of lemon zest.

You're mixing your metaphors.

What?

What does it look like, then what does it taste like?

Fuck, this is good.

What is that smell, lavender?

Bouquet, asshole.

Bouquet?

Straw?

Fuck off.

Meadow-flower thing going on here.

Like you'd know.

Wildflower kinda thing.

Pansy.

Not quite.

No, I mean you. Stop being such a pansy.

Wanker.

Big wanker, you.

Don't talk to me, you asshole.

I'm not talking, I'm drinking, asshole.

Shut up.

Shut up yourself.

Great dialogue, is this going to be in your next piece?

Not if you're directing.

I'm a great director.

You direct like an administrator.

And you have no conflict.

Boring!

Hack!

Fuck you.

Fuck you too.

That was only the first winery. It got worse from there.

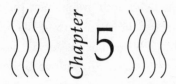

It was Helmut, the co-owner of the B&B we were staying at, who found him with a plastic bag over his head. A Safeway produce department plastic bag that has those thin perforated holes in it. You can barely see them, but they're there and they are the sole reason Roy lived — that, and the fact he doesn't know how to tie a knot. He flunked knots in Boy Scouts and his shoes are always slip-ons or boots. Because his granny-knot had come undone, the plastic bag was too loose around his neck. This is just a long explanation that may or may not actually explain anything, because I was convinced Roy wanted to live out his last six months by knocking back Cabernets and metaphorically killing bad actors — not killing himself. This was the worst suicide attempt ever attempted. I'm sure of it.

We had been looking for about an hour, scouring and poking around the nearby vineyards with Helmut's outdated golf clubs, Callaways I think. I had a nine iron but wasn't sure why the clubs were needed until I spotted a snake behind a large rock. A rattler, I was told later. A small one.

What happened was Roy didn't show up the night before. We reasoned that he maybe got lost walking home from the local pub — he had done it before, twice, in fact, the first week of our stay. Both times we found him nearby, just down the long road that was lined with grapevines, the one that wound toward the grey-and-white B&B sitting like a cake ornament on top of the hill, with another bigger hill just behind it that led to yet another B&B also surrounded by vineyards, and so on and so on. There's a pattern to it out here, and sure, you can lose yourself. This might be a good thing for city folk, as Helmut would say, although it's not so good to lose yourself overnight considering the snake issue.

Helmut says, Yes, we have the bad snakes here. Some people have been bitten because they do not understand how Canada could have such a threat with the reptiles, but clearly we exist in desert country. Unique circumstances agreed.

Helmut is from some unidentifiable Eastern European country. His wife Katrina is from near Kiev. She is a former Olympic shot putter and her forearms are bigger than Roy's torso. Both worked as nuclear scientists and met during a conference on ground radiation. Happy now to be far beyond that world and operating a bed and breakfast in the Interior, catering to the wealthy, disillusioned, and curious.

We are mostly the latter, considering we barely have enough to cover the two-hundred-dollar-a-night expense of the place. Roy is paying for everything. He insisted. But it's all going on his credit card.

Credit cards are a necessary evil, Helmut said one day over pancakes, sitting on the veranda overlooking the baking vineyards below.

The suicide rate in Belarus is through the roof and this is such horrible tragedy, he said, pouring us some very dark coffee.

But who can blame the women when birth defects are ten times above the normal rate. Ten times, can you imagine such a thing?

Because of Chernobyl? Roy asked.

Yes, of course, Katrina said. So, making a go of it there, well, this would be impossible, because this was our dream and so when we retired we came to Canada, and here we remain, older and sometimes alone without our children, but healthy and surrounded by people like you, and this is welcome.

That is how Katrina talks all the time. She is a hesitant talker, thoughts coming in small, calculated phrases.

In this first week I've learned more about Belarus than I care to know. It's probably a fair bet as to Helmut's country of origin. I've also learned that some very intelligent people with exotic accents can be just as irritating as anybody else. But they are great characters. I want to take notes around and about them. Use them, basically.

During most breakfasts Katrina circles our table, and the floorboards on the second-floor veranda creak under her weight despite the fact that she wears fluffy white slippers with black socks. Are you happy? she always asks, coffee pot in hand. Are you finally happy?

Roy isn't very happy. And he doesn't like Helmut because he is too much of a touchy-feely guy, always punching people on the arm and pinching bums, that kind of stuff.

When Helmut found Roy with the bag over his head, he asked him to come back to the B&B for drinks and a serious talk about the value of human life. They came out of the vineyard along the road, toward the house where I stood with Katrina, who wore outdated Jackie Onassis sunglasses perched on her forehead, her grey hair pulled back into a bun so tight it made her eyes slant a little. I could see Roy was a little pissed off. His hands were shoved deep in his pockets, his head was down, and he was stumbling a little, making sure to keep some space between him and Helmut. He took little steps, the kind used by kids the world over to stall for time, while Helmut followed closely behind, the plastic bag in one hand, an eight iron in the other. Once in a while he would try to land a bear paw of a hand on Roy's shoulder. Sensing this, Roy would scoot ahead, but it still looked like a bit of a lurch.

Life should never be so heavy like you are carrying boulders on your back, Katrina said. Never be so heavy that you forget your friends and family to sleep in the fields without warning them of this tendency.

Sorry, Roy said. Or at least looked like he wanted to.

Katrina again: How terrible it is for those who love and respect you to wonder why you have left without saying the reason, or at least, to give them nothing to worry about.

Helmut finally told her to quiet down and she did, turning quickly and stomping back into the house while us men decided to say nothing.

Roy went to take a shower. Helmut showed me the plastic bag. Your friend is not so interested in living, yes?

⁓

I wait until dinner to talk to Roy, let the wine loosen him up a little. So here we sit at a small table at the 1812 Restaurant on the shores of the lake. Decorated by a bunch of insane grannies, the place is packed with knick-knacks, figurines of blind horses peeking over railings, flightless wooden ducks along the floor, candleholders shaped like bronze roses, and framed letters from 1929. Despite the knick-knacks the place is cave dark, lit by squares of blue light from the windows overlooking the lake. A submarine of lost memories.

Roy hasn't touched his veal, but we are finishing our second bottle of local Pinot Gris. We are in our white zone because it's hot out.

I love this place, one of us says. The other nods. We drink.

He drinks white wine like most people drink beer, two gulps each glass and all gone. What? he says, noticing me stare — and I am staring, have been for the last five, ten minutes. He knows I'm keeping track of the glasses.

Why, Roy? Why'd you do it?

He finishes off yet another glass then gives me one of his famous smirks. Well, officer — it all started with my mother.

Asshole, I say.

Thank you, he says. Let's order more wine. Chardonnay, can we have some local Chardonnay, please. Hey, you. Chardonnay. He waves at the server hugging the wall like a bat nearby, who signals to another waiter along another wall to signal our waiter hidden in the back. Jesus, Roy says. Who's on first here?

Can we talk about what happened this morning, Roy?

I can't talk when I'm ordering. Hey, Chardonnay, OK? He snaps his fingers, like he's Hitchcock moving some actors around the set during a shoot. I know, I know, he says. Hitchcock. Ordering actors around.

I was just thinking that, I say.

What?

What?

He pulls his glasses down his nose and pretends he's my mother. No, Alex, he says, you just said that aloud.

I think we are very, very drunk, Roy.

He holds his glass up to the ceiling, calls, Chardonnay — is there a Chardonnay in the house?

Jesus, Roy, people are looking at us.

He waves at the American couple wearing the red-and-blue cowboy shirts next to us, but realizes they're not merely closing their eyes and trying to block us out — they're praying. Jesus, he says. How embarrassing.

I know, I say. I know.

I mean, praying, in here. Who do they think they are?

Americans. They're Americans. That's what they do. You should see them in Denny's. It's like a revival in there.

He laughs, and bellows in a bad Chinese accent, You so funny.

Roy, please. We're in a nice restaurant and I don't want the Americans praying for us now.

Stop it, you're killing me, he says, waving his napkin in mock surrender. You velly, velly funny.

I put my sunglasses on.

He laughs at that too. You can't do that yet, he says, You're not famous enough.

I'm undiscovered, so shut up.

And according to one critic, thus you shall remain, he guffaws.

Finally our waiter, also named Roy, brings us a bottle of Mitchell Hill Chardonnay, opens it with the flair of a magician, and tells us it's the best wine in the joint. Citrus and apricot flavours with a hint of vanilla-scented oak, he sings, long-pouring the glasses from a foot above the table.

I notice he's all teeth and eyebrows, the kind of waiter who moonlights as a mad scientist.

You two are my favourites tonight, he goes on. I love watching you argue. It reminds me of *Everybody Loves Raymond*.

Piss off, my Roy says, slurping the glass of wine down while other Roy stands stiffly by the table, bottle in hand as if it's a .38.

Excuse me, other Roy says, But I thought you might be interested in the Mitchell Hill winery because of your background.

My Roy blinks, clearly drunk now. What?

Because of the theatre they have in the vineyard. You must see the play there when it opens in a few weeks. Fully professional. Most of the actors are from Vancouver. Shakespeare is the theme, I believe. By the way, I saw your *A Midsummer Night's Dream* in Victoria three years ago and I haven't been the same since. Ask anybody in here.

You liked it? Roy asks.

I didn't like it, other Roy says. I loved it. It's the only reason I still work here. I live in hope.

You're an actor?

I'm an actor. Well, in my head I am. Always will be, thank you very much.

Other Roy refills my Roy's glass, puts the bottle down, does a little fake bow and says something like, You are the maestro, before twirling and skating back to the kitchen. I notice he's wearing purple Arabian slippers. I think they probably slide easier.

We sit there. I put my sunglasses away. Sip the wine. Savour it even. Think of a citrus or two. Or vanilla ice cream. Or butter.

A motorboat roars past the windows.

One, two, three —

A skier appears behind. Big rooster tail. Huge.

Four, five, six —

Why am I counting?

Roy takes off his napkin. Folds it twice then shrouds what's left of his food. He says, Maestro?

That's what he called you, I say. You must have made quite the impression with that *Dream* of yours.

Fuck.

He picks up his steak knife, puts the blade between his teeth like he's a mercenary. I'm exaggerating here because for a long time nobody says anything and it's a little boring.

I fidget. Not well, I might add. I play with my food, what's left of it, parsley mainly, added to my plate to give it a festive feel. I count wooden ducks. Eleven. No, twelve. Finally, I look past the praying Americans, out the window framing them with angelic light, and scan the lake for the monster, as if it might take this moment for it to finally appear. After all, this is the true nature of monsters: to surprise the unsuspecting, to build themselves into myths, and to complicate religion. I will the monster to appear, to pick us, pick this time when my suicidal best friend and I sit at a table in a nice restaurant in the middle of the Okanagan in the middle of a meal that wasn't much of a meal, in the middle of a stuck conversation, in the middle of our gloriously ordinary lives, and come now, devour us, and please end this horrible unbroken moment.

Any monster will do. Please, come now.

A shadow passes. Other Roy darkens the nearby window, waiting and watching us like a vampire.

Roy rasps, I can't believe he recognized me. He leans back into his straight-backed chair and flicks his Zippo. Flame on. Flame off.

We don't talk about suicide again.

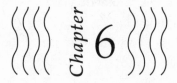

Chapter **6**

This journey — like every journey — begins with the light and ends with the dark, says Susie, our cute, cherubic server, while pouring our first flight of wine. Riesling, in small but deep wine glasses.

We sit at the long tasting bar at the Mitchell Hill Winery, apart from the busload of chit-chattering Korean tourists, gently swirling our wine, pretending to smell burnt match or lavender or whatever Susie told us we'd smell. We don't.

Lovely, winks Roy, before downing his in a quick gulp and grabbing one of the pieces of white cheese, Swiss I think, sitting on white plates perfectly placed along the entire length of the wooden bar like little landmines.

I savour my one inch of Riesling. Let it linger on the tongue as long as I can. Hold it, not yet. Study the white room, with its double-vaulted ceiling, faux Greek pillars, and bright, earthy wood tables and bar. Watch the yappy colourful tourists with their new camera phones taking photos of their wine. Admire the casually dressed hosts in blue jeans and black shirts ferrying in trays loaded with new glasses. Eye the endless rows of wine bottles lining the back wall behind the bar. Feel the sun streaming in through the stained glass. Sink into the music from the tiny speakers sitting like ravens around the top ledge, yes, it's music you can skate to. Now, let it go. Let it all go. Swallow. Swallow it. Yes. Wonderful. Perfect.

What is it I'm experiencing?

Umami, says Susie. Probably because of the cheese you're eating.

What's that?

It's a bit unidentifiable. Japanese word. Our fifth sense of taste beyond salty, spicy, sour, and sweet. It could be interpreted as all-encompassing, or even fishy or meaty.

Ooh, I love meaty, Roy says. More please.

Behind the bar Susie turns her head, bends down, lets her bouncy blonde hair nearly hit the counter. Are you sure? she sings.

Hit me, he says, holding out his glass like a little kid. Hit me, hit me, hit me.

Pinot Blanc, she says. Fantastic with seafood. Susie pours like a robot, perfect little shots in our perfect little wine glasses, holding the bottle out like a model from *The Price is Right*. Crisp and refreshing with lively citrus and pineapple fruit flavours that linger for a delightfully rich finish, she says.

Wow, Roy says, You said that like a robot.

She laughs. Oh, that's funny, I was just thinking that too.

Me too, I chime in, then think to myself, was that really necessary?

Susie blinks as if processing info through her hard drive, which I imagine to be exactly between her two very perfect breasts nearly hanging out of her very perfect blouse, which is black with the first three buttons undone. Are you guys hilarious or what? she says.

Please do not say Or what, I tell myself. Be cool, don't ogle, concentrate on the wine in your glass, who cares if the first three buttons are undone and her bra is red. Who cares, right?

More wine, somebody else says. More wine. And Susie moves away down the line to pour another round of Pinot Blanc, twisting the end of the bottle a little to avoid spillage.

We taste, seriously, as if our very lives depend on it.

Peach, I say. I got peach here.

Perch, says Roy. Fishy. Big time.

Spoken like a true smoker, I tell him.

Are you saying I can't be subtle?

I'm saying you can't taste subtle.

Fuck you, he says. Hit me again.

Boys, boys, boys, Susie scolds, cradling another bottle. Behave or I won't let you taste our award-winning reserve Chardonnay.

We're kinda like brothers, Roy says with a toothy smile, pleading with his empty wine glass. We're always like this. No big deal.

She pours the Chardonnay, again like a robot, but this time a self-aware one. A perfect one-ounce sample of Chardonnay appears in my glass, golden, like liquid hay. I lead it to my nose and immediately think of running through meadows with naked women holding wads of cash. Exciting. Exotic. Rich. Yes. Yes. Yes. And just a little bit crazy.

Susie bounces her hair on the bar with each response. She has the hair to do it and she knows it. I decide I'm madly in love with her.

I smack my lips. What is it, what is it I'm experiencing?

Wine and women, mirth and laughter, says Roy. Sermons and soda water the day after.

Oh, Shakespeare, right, gushes Susie, her eyes widening. I'm an English major.

Byron actually, he corrects, holding his glass out again.

Byron who? she asks.

Try Wikipedia. Under Lord Byron.

OK. I will.

She bobs and weaves toward the end of the bar to hide behind her computer screen. Her face, of course, glows. Roy says, She's cute. Very, very cute.

And then he ogles her.

I've never really seen Roy ogle a woman before. In fact, I've always been somewhat unsure of his sexuality. He was married once to an Amazon woman, a giraffe with big hair and a plan to be in control of the West Coast theatre world before she turned forty, but they eventually split up over another man. It was never clear who had the affair.

Are you bisexual? I ask Roy now.

I could be, he laughs. Who's the guy?

I'm serious.

So am I.

We drink.

No, really, I say. Are you?

No, really, he says. Who fucking cares.

We drink.

I just thought I'd ask because I've rarely seen you with a woman, I say. I mean, in a serious relationship.

Well, not lately, he says. But then I've rarely seen you with one either. In a serious relationship. Not since your marriage ended so horribly. And wow, people are still buzzing about that one — one for the history books, that's for sure.

Do you mind, I say. And just so you know, before that one, it was endless, my friend. Endless.

Endless what? Misery?

An endless number of very nice women, I snort. I was a dating machine.

Like when?

In my twenties, I say. In my fond and distant twenties when the world was a summer of bikinis and bliss, margaritas in water bottles, and condoms in my wallet.

Very poetic, Roy says. Cheers.

Cheers.

I'm noticing a buttery aftertaste with a slight honey melon something something.

Then he says, I think this is a show wine.

Like you'd fucking know, I say.

Well, I know you're hopeless with women and will continue to be hopeless with women until you find your humanity.

I have tons of humanity, I say. Tons. Anyway, women don't care about that. They want intimacy and that's what I know.

Uh. What's that?

Talks about feelings, I offer. Detailed discussions of fears and wants. You know — intimacy.

You never talk about that, Roy says. But you love writing about it, which brings us back to your big problem.

I don't have a problem, I say.

Oh, you've got problems, he says.

We drink, but somewhat faster, as if looking for a way out of the tasting room.

How about my ex-wife? I finally say.

How about her? he says.

Doesn't she qualify? I mean, isn't that an intimate relationship?

You forget I was your best man at your wedding. She was a control freak. A drama queen. And a diva. A medicated one, at that. And you married her because she was the least intimate person in the world. Roy throws a glance or two at Susie. I love that girl's personality, he says. Look at her work the room. Now there's somebody who couldn't be miserable if she tried.

She's supposed to work the room, Roy, that's her job.

He waves at her. Hey, sweetie, what else you got over there?

Susie pulls out a red on her way to us, pulls it out neck-first from the huge supply of bottles sitting neatly in their nests like cormorants along the wall behind the bar.

Pinot Noir; we're really nailing them now, she says while machine-gunning our shots. Global warming is on our side with this one. Burgundy has issues with rain, too much actually, while we have the perfect growing conditions, twelve to four-teen hours of sunlight a day most of the summer. Think black cherry or wild strawberry. It's very balanced.

Unlike me, Roy says.

Oh, you look perfectly balanced to me, she says, poking him with the butt end of the corkscrew.

Roy pulls his head back and lets the last of his Chardonnay slam into his mouth at full speed. A bold, bold fruit with a touch of honey, he says.

Wow, she says. I'm shocked you got that from slamming it.

Short and quick, he says. That's life.

Try the Pinot Noir, please. Think of it as a white disguised as a red.

Why would I do that? says Roy.

It's just what they tell me to say here. Harry is my boss, that's him with the ponytail over there talking to the bus tour. He's a sommelier, graduated last month with the certificate and every-thing. He can work anywhere he wants, even Ontario, but he's staying here because he thinks this winery has even more poten-tial. A world-beater, he thinks, because of our Pinot Noirs and Chardonnays. But the real winner will soon be our Merlot. It's just not there yet one hundred per cent. Next year for sure, dude.

Very interesting, but can I have some really expensive wine, please? Roy holds his glass out as if it's a knife.

Look, Susie says. Why don't I leave you with this bottle and you can taste as much as you want? I have to help with the bus tour. And with that, she glides away, no more bounces. Not for us. Not anymore.

You're being an asshole, I say to Roy.

Yeah, I know, he says. And it only took three glasses this time.

I'm not talking to you, I say. You're irritating the hell out of me.

So we sit there and drink the Pinot Noir. Think about wild strawberry patches hidden under bridges. Black cherries rotting on the window ledge. Balance on our stools. Drink. Think. Dream. Balance. Watch Susie have fun with the Koreans. Watch her bounce for them. She serves the oldest first, all down the line to the happy young women with their designer handbags and matching cellphone cameras. All so beautiful, someone sings. All so beautiful. And Susie giggles and starts pouring from the beginning again.

Tourists, she says in our general direction. I love tourists.

They all snap photos of her teeth. They are perfect teeth.

∽

With a shake, rattle, and wheeze of air, Roy satellite-dishes his head back and forth to fine-tune the sun rays beaming down on him from between distant thick pillows of clouds. A thin layer of sweat turns into a white equator around the rim of his black baseball cap. Sunglasses are perched like night vision goggles on the brim.

It's later now. Four o'clock. Hot, hot, hot. A dry heat. Because we're a little drunk we've moved outside to soak up the sun, sitting under the archway on a stone bench to admire the lay-out and architecture, the Romanesque columns and Stonehenge reproductions that give the sprawling winery its sci-fi feeling.

Stargate, Roy insists. A series that ran for ten years which every actor in Vancouver coveted because it paid two grand a day with catering to die for — perfect little roasted potatoes and venison sandwiches for lunch, free Pellegrino with wedges of lemon.

Roy says, They wanted me to direct for them but I said fuck that, I'm an artist. Said I didn't even own a TV.

That's honest, I say.

It's a complete lie, he says. I have a flat-screen plasma in my bedroom. Fifty-two inches, high-def and 3D-ready. I love it. Life's too short, right? But don't spread it around.

Wow, I say. Plasma.

We sit on the stone bench and let the sun do its thing. Nerve endings melt slightly. Foreheads warm like Teflon frying pans. Backs of eyelids movie screens of melted butter.

Loving it. Just loving it.

Beyond the brick and stone buildings, endless rows of grapes march down toward the blazing blue lake. Beyond that, on the other side, more vineyards, and our bed and breakfast in the hazy, lazy distance.

Roy asks, Are we in heaven? Are we?

These are not the kind of questions one expects from him, drunk or not.

No, I say, noticing Roy has smuggled out his tasting glass, holding it between us on the bench like a lit candle. If we were in heaven we'd hear harps and all I hear are seagulls.

He sneaks a sip of his wine, then decides to pull off his ball cap. His hair looks like the nest of some deeply disturbed swallows. Is that a bell tower? he asks, pointing to the sand-coloured tower overlooking the winery courtyard.

Yes, I say. It is indeed.

Wow, are those actually slots to fire arrows down upon our heads?

It's retro, I say. And even if they could fire arrows from there, we're out of range.

What are you, a bow-and-arrow expert? He coughs and lights up a smoke.

First one in a long time, I figure.

My first one in a long, long time, so shut up, Roy answers.

Am I saying things aloud again? I ask.

He says, Yes indeed, asshole. You are. He arranges his cap to sit on his head loosely and askew, like the kids wear them.

At that very moment, a woman, a beautiful red-haired woman, walks past us wearing a seventeenth-century dress, or a reproduction of one. The dress sweeps behind her along the perfectly manicured lawn, all purple and gold, the ends frayed and knotted. She's also smoking, waving the cigarette smoke away from her gigantic wig and talking on her cellphone.

This is what I overhear: Yeah, yeah, it's great, I know. I know. I love this piece, it really speaks to me ... look, I'm going to give it a try, OK, so just fuck off —

Roy pretends not to notice. He sips his wine, then hands it to me. I feign a sip and hand it back.

The woman is followed by a man wearing a fairy king cape, gold too, with orange-and-green New Balance running shoes and black tights. He's eating from a can of smoked oysters. Hi, guys, he growls as he passes.

We aren't sure, but we might know him. An actor from Vancouver.

Roy turns to me. OK, exactly how drunk am I?

Then it happens. One of those life-defining moments you only see in movies. I see the AD — the one who produced my last big bomb — trudging towards us with an assistant stage manager trailing behind. Are they in the middle of a heated discussion about props or something? Or maybe music cues?

Some temperamental actor named Allan? What's going on here?

Roy doesn't see the AD, she doesn't see Roy. And when he stands up to steady himself against the side of the archway, he misses and falls into her face first.

The assistant stage manager, a lesbian I once mistook for a man, steps aside nimbly. That was close, she says.

Sheila, I say.

Sandra, she says.

Alex, I say.

Alex?

Yes.

No way. No.

Some nervous laughter all around.

Are you OK?

The AD is first off the ground. She's shorter, her legs are stronger, and she's wearing brand new black Nikes, the kind made for old ladies or basketball referees. Brushing her tights off, she says, Roy, Roy, what the hell —

Howdy, he says, still lying on the ground, still holding a half-full wine glass in his right hand.

What the hell are you doing here, she continues. What?

Tasting wine, he says, pulling himself up with my help. How about you?

I'm directing, of course, the AD smiles. You must have heard. It's a great gig. Practically everybody wanted it. And you, Mr. Playwright, how's the writing coming along?

It's coming all right, I stutter. Really sorta interesting in places now. Two great characters from Eastern Europe. They talk funny.

Wonderful. I can hardly wait. She hugs me. Nice to run into you, Mr. Playwright. It's a big, big hug. Vanilla, I smell vanilla.

Oh, it's my new scent, she says, pulling away from under my chin. Doesn't it make you want to run out and buy a gelato? She giggles at her joke, if it is a joke. I decide not to go any further than a guffaw.

Roy won't match me guffaw-wise. Instead he studies the bell tower, takes a slow deliberate sip of wine, then sits back down on the stone bench, crossing his legs like a politician.

The AD waves the ASM away. Roy, ROY, how are things?

Fine. You?

Great. But you know, we're not getting any younger. She puffs out her chest. Isn't this winery great?

Yeah, it's great, he says.

The AD smiles and her eyes narrow, nearly disappearing. Demon slits of black.

I'm almost positive I didn't say that aloud.

Well, guys, she says, We're having some issues with the changing rooms here. And of course, the actors think the acoustics aren't great. But we're down there in the amphitheatre and it's a great view of the lake. And I'm very pleased with all the money the winery has committed to the project. It's the first time they've had this kind of production here, Bard in the Vineyard, and we're all very excited. It's huge, you know, with the audience projections we've had and — and this will be the best thing to happen to me in a long, long time.

Great. Wonderful. Good for you. Roy smiles a big fake movie star smile. His teeth look terrible. Dipped in coffee. Gums the colour of fingernail tips. He slugs back the rest of his wine.

Oh dear, the AD says. This must be difficult for you.

No, I'm glad for you, he sniffs. Congratulations.

No, I meant about your prognosis. I heard about your illness. I could just cry.

We stand there. I think Roy teeters momentarily.

I want to give you a big hug, she says, and reaches out with her arm as if hoping Roy will go for it, but he recoils somewhat. It's very slight, but it's still a recoil.

So we stand there again, close to frozen as frozen gets.

Then another movie moment: Clouds roil and race. A sea-gull screams. Roy says Fuck and breaks his wine glass, probably not on purpose, but it's still broken, and stomps off. Through the archway, down the long path toward the lake. There he goes. Unsteady, listing to the right, then left. Over-correcting. Drunk? Yes, this is what drunks do. Toe-stubbing along the sidewalk, forcing two tourists wearing yellow Gore-tex jackets to the side.

Temperamental bastard, one of us mutters.

Watch out for the Korean bus driver with the clipboard. Watch out. Was that a shove? He's still going. Going. Watch him through the parking lot, to the far end, to the last row of cars and RVs.

Is he OK? the AD asks. Is he? God, he's changed. In 1998 he ran 10K in under fifty minutes, and there was this trick he did with a quarter for my niece. She still talks about the money coming out of her ears.

And another stumble. Another.

She continues, And he has such a nice touch with transitions, everything he does is so inventive. He's wonderful with actors, particularly sensitive ones.

Bagpipes come up from somewhere across the water. Bagpipes?

Roy fake-kicks at a silver Mercedes that managed to park in his way.

Angry, the AD says. That's to be expected. Who wouldn't be angry? And depressed, of course, my mother was exactly the same way and isn't life full of surprises.

Roy's black T-shirt makes sure that we have a lasting image of him against the blue of the lake. He doesn't look back even when he reaches my Mazda. He tries the door, realizes it's locked and that I've got the key, then sits on the hood, leans back, and lets the sun have its way with him.

The AD grabs my arm and shakes it like it's a near-dead trout. I'll make sure not to tell anybody. Believe you me, I won't. You take care of him, will you?

She turns and soft-walks away in the opposite direction, to a tent I hadn't seen before, a big white tent beside the amphitheatre, where *A Midsummer Night's Dream* will play before a grand total of ten thousand people before the summer is over. Shakespeare's best. A surefire hit. The critics' choice. And everybody will talk about it for years and years and years.

Roy's dream is the same.

Bumper sticker on the way home: Jesus loves you, but I'm his favourite.

It's on the back of an old white VW van we follow through Kelowna after two hours at a local Tim Hortons nursing double doubles, sobering up from our Mitchell Hill tasting.

Roy sits beside me wearing his shades and skimming a lit cigarette in the air out the window, the red tip glowing more intensely as we speed up. His skinny knees are up on the dash again and his feet dangle a bit, kicking occasionally like a hanged man's as we hit the bumps leading up onto the gravel side road toward the B&B.

After enduring a couple of coughs from the van's exhaust, I'm kinda hoping the stupid VW turns soon. It's dusty, I say, closing my window, thinking Roy will do the same.

He doesn't.

Dusk loves dust, twilight mixing it up with mother earth, I say. I think it's creative and interesting, almost literary, but Roy isn't buying any of it. Finally I say, God, do I need to lie down, my head's throbbing.

I don't like sleeping much these days, says Roy.

Then we are quiet for a long, long time.

I keep an eye on the VW as it peels off toward the dark side of the looming hills around us. Its licence plate reads RUHARPY.

Ha, I say. I guess happy was taken, right?

Again, Roy keeps silent.

We drive.

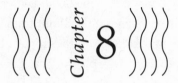

Chapter 8

The thing about depression, Helmut says. When people tell you to cheer up, you just get more depressed. Those assholes, right? He says this while making his eyes big and clapping flour from his thick potato hands. In his head, he's leading a workshop on assholes and depression. He's what you'd call an expert.

I'm back at the B&B finishing a very nice hazelnut latte courtesy of Helmut and Katrina, who make pie crusts across the kitchen behind their special table made of old railway ties. It's brown and oily. But they love their table. Talk endlessly about which line the wood came from — CPR — and how they were able to steal them because the repair crew just left them there unattended.

Helmut says, In Belarus, you know what depression is called? His voice always goes up at the end of any sentence, not just questions. He wipes at an invisible fly circling his ears with a flour-tipped forefinger. Maybe he's making the sign for crazy and I'm not picking up on it. Maybe there really is a fly bothering him. Or maybe it's an Old Country trick of some kind.

I notice his blue dress shirt under the white apron is streaked with flour, or maybe sweat stains. Apparently he likes to touch himself a lot, particularly on the upper chest.

In Belarus, he says, depression is called normal.

Katrina stops rolling with the rolling pin and Santa-laughs, holding her guts like they might spill out from behind the plain white apron that says APRON on the front in big black letters. Laugh, laugh, laugh. Forget the pies for now. Laugh, laugh, laugh. This is too much humour for the afternoon, she finally sighs.

I try, says Helmut, going back to thumb the dough.

They work like giant elves on speed, one pie after another, spitting on their thumbs — yes, you heard me, spitting on their thumbs — as they create the indentations in the dough around the pie plate, dig their wet thumbs into the dough to seal the blueberries in. Next: cherry pie. Four of them.

Are you spitting at the pie crust? I venture.

No, we make thumbs wet to aid with the design and to prevent too much sticking, Helmut explains. You bake this pie for one hour in the oven and it's OK, no matter how much you lick your thumbs. No germs. Trust me, we've been doing this for years.

I turn the handle of my coffee cup so it faces the window to my right away from them. Off in the distance, about a hundred metres or so, down by the lake's edge, Roy sits dozing under a willow tree. His laptop is open nearby.

What does he work on with that little computer of his all the time? asks Katrina, following my gaze outside.

Porn, I say.

What is this porn?

Now it's Helmut's turn to Santa-laugh, hitting the special table with his fist. This is always the question with men, he roars. What is this porn?

Is it a complex issue? she asks.

Such a complex issue, he giggles.

Does he have regular studies in this subject area? she goes on.

They are neverending, Helmut says, feigning seriousness, then wink, wink, winking at me and swaying back and forth, hands on his ape hips as if he's about to launch a salvo of testosterone at me from his oversized-cannon chest.

When men study too much, they often lose track of themselves, she continues, oblivious to the undercurrent of manly ha-ha washing through their enormous kitchen.

Roy is a little sexually repressed, I finally say. So he finds porn, let's say, easy. But it's a bit depressing too.

Katrina says, How can this be? Explain your logic.

What?

How does his sexual nature result in depression?

I was referring to the porn. That's what's on his computer. Pornography.

So, she says, if I may. Does this sexual orientation result in more or less pornography?

I speak of the depression, I try.

Depression causes more pornography?

In Roy's case, yes.

Katrina studies Roy in the distance. Are the images he studies on his computer men or women?

I have no idea, I say. Does it matter?

Holding two finished pies in each hand, she thinks hard, biting down on her plumb upper lip, letting all the past words organize themselves in nice little lines in her head, trains of logic ready for departure, which is a good thing because none of this makes sense to me, particularly with my growing hangover.

Helmut leans over and kisses her suddenly, as if the kiss will somehow help. Why I love you, he says. For your knowledge and for your quest for more knowledge. He waves his flour-smudged arms like batons at a zombie choir.

Katrina furrows her brow, and as she does her nose turns up and gives her little pig eyes.

Wonderful, wheezes Helmut. Isn't she wonderful?

Yes, well, I am a scientist by training, she says as she carefully places the pies in the ready-hot oven beside me. Thank you.

She waddles out, eyes slightly glazed over, looking for her reading glasses. An oversized penguin on a mission to find open sea.

Helmut takes the straitjacket apron off, goes to the window, and watches Roy sleep against the base of the huge willow.

I join him and feel the wind enter the room, like a lovesick ghost, to tickle under our chins, our necks too.

He puts a massive arm around me. Without love where would we men be? he says to the clouds. Think about it.

~

Life as we know it. Is it worth living?

Roy mulls his question over in the back of his mind, an armoury of doubt.

Who are we? Who the hell are we?

Feckless and indiscreet. Unfortunate and desperate. Fanciful and dripping with irony.

His list. It's a good list.

You've been doing a lot of thinking, I say.

I've been doing a lot of thinking, he coughs. His coughs are getting worse.

What are we doing next? My exact thoughts.

Down at the water's edge, particularly under the shade of the willow tree, it's cooler. I can understand why Roy won't remove his black leather jacket — occasionally my shivers mass and my arm hair stands on end, troops at the ready.

You cold? Roy asks.

A little. You depressed?

A little, he answers, finally struggling to his feet to join me closer to the water. See anything out there?

No monsters, I say. Not yet anyway. But I'm not a believer.

The lake tongues our runners. Wavelets want to be waves, but the breeze won't let them. It's slight and somewhat damp tonight. A murder of crows settles into the willow around us and starts to vocalize. A lot of them seem like angry birds. In the distance the sun settles in for the night between two mountains, the light scattering to highlight a Morse code of clouds tiny and perfect along the edges of more mountains to the left. Wow. I wish I had a camera so everyone could see how perfect this is.

What's so perfect about dying at forty-five? Roy asks. He looks at me. Well?

I'm sorry, I say.

What have I done? What? He goes on. I mean, direct a few dozen shows? Win a couple of awards? Develop playwrights, including you, and then sometimes even wonder about that? What the fuck have I really done? He says this with his hands in his pockets, jingling his change and keys. More crows show up, a convention of caw and yak above our damp heads. We instinctively duck. We're shivering a little more now because only half the sun or less is visible, the lake dipping into darkness framed by the golden hilltops, the Riesling grapes along the ridge getting the last delicious rays right in the chops.

Behind the vineyards, Okanagan Mountain — a perfect bun of rock and trees — appears more brooding with the sunset. Stony, with dozens of veins of evergreens that trickle down into the water. A perfect place to hide a body.

How's your play coming? Roy asks, taking my wine from my hand, sipping it loudly.

I think it's going to be about older people who fall in love despite approaching the end, I say. Alzheimer's disease, or maybe just madness. They keep forgetting each other's name. I'm calling it *Vertical Dreams*.

He stares straight ahead. That's a fucking terrible title. What dreams?

I put on my thinking cap. Actually, just my sunglasses. Then I take them off dramatically and chew on the tip like an English professor trying to understand something he can't really understand — like rap, for instance. Well, I say, people at eighty have different dreams. They dream of opening their fridge and suddenly finding chocolate cake, and old wedding rings making it over knuckles, and having a good, soft shit in the morning, and being able to catch the 9:32 bus at 9:32, of going home and feeling like they can do it all over again.

Roy gives me his best restrained director laugh.

You'll like it, I'm sure of it, Roy.

Oh, I doubt it, he says, accents it with a raspy cough, then spits into the lake. A little wave erases it and then another one brings in an empty Styrofoam cup.

So, you don't think it's a good idea?

I think you should write something else, he says. Something more interesting. More edgy. Life, right? Fucking life.

Right. Right.

Does that mean you're thinking? he says. When you repeat your rights?

Yes. Right.

You should never play poker, he adds, swirling what's left of my wine.

OK, I say. OK.

I sneak a peek back at the house, imagine Helmut and Katrina sitting in rocking chairs on their third-floor balcony reading books about jam-making and nuclear fission, not really worried about how many sunsets they have left, not really worried about how many sunsets they've wasted.

What is it about happy people that makes me so unhappy? I ask.

Roy says, I know exactly what you're saying.

Really, I say. Really.

Yes. He's so excited he hands back my wine and spills what's left of it over my denim shirt. Either they are living a lie, Roy says, or they want us to.

Are you saying it's impossible to ever be happy?

He pulls his coat tight, hands deep in the pockets. We have to define happy first. How do we know what it is, and then how do we keep it?

Isn't just acting happy the same as being happy?

Don't be an actor, he says. Be a writer.

One crow, the ringleader, is now very pissed off. Hopping from branch to branch, scolding the other crows for being stupid and insignificant. I think he's right.

Accomplishments make me happy, I venture.

Bullshit, Roy says. Happy is the man who fears the Lord.

OK, I sigh. Why biblical?

Devil's advocate. You keep going.

OK. When I positively affect an audience with my writing, I think I feel happy, I say.

Still ego, I'm afraid, he says.

Then having a good healthy ego makes me happy.

Then you've got problems. He takes back the wine and kills it, swinging his head back to face the noisy crows above.

Maybe doing good work makes me happy, I try.

In the end, Roy says, what difference does it make when we kick the can? Saying I'm ready to go because I've done good work just makes it sound like a sentence. A jail sentence.

It's difficult to disagree.

Well, we kinda are prisoners, I think I say.

Some asylum, he says, turning and heading back toward the house.

It's mostly dark now. The crows are finally quiet.

I pick up Roy's laptop and notice the screensaver: a young naked man, very hairy I might add, carrying a teddy bear, lying in a bunk bed behind bars. I close the laptop and carry it back, picking my way through the rocks and weeds up the slight hill to the house.

The porch light is blinking on and off, as if Katrina is signalling us to come in.

She is.

∾

The next day starts with morning, as most days do.

At the B&B, which we now discover is properly called The Swan Bed & Breakfast, we're warmly ensconced on the main floor, the ground floor actually, in Rooms A and B. We don't share a bathroom, thank God. Just a shower, which isn't in either of our rooms but down the hall, beside a third bathroom that leads into a slatted wood Swedish sauna next to another bedroom.

That room, Room C, awaits a couple from London, England. Occasionally we catch a glimpse of it and marvel at the four-post bed and the pine furniture and the giant flat-screen plasma TV along the wall over the fireplace. Ornate bronze lamps, shaped roughly like swans about to take flight, are on the bedstands.

Helmut, a committed garage sale aficionado, found the lamps

in Alberta while driving his half-ton — a late model sort-of-silver Ford F-150 — to Taber to pick up a load of sweet corn. Helmut cans his own corn because he has an immense distrust of the Green Giant, and California produce in general. He says anyone who buys iceberg lettuce these days should be taken away and shot at dawn. There's nothing good about this lettuce, he says.

Anyway, back to Room C. It's about two hundred and fifty dollars a night, which makes sense because it's technically the honeymoon suite. Comes complete with a bottle of wine, local sparkling wine, I think Chardonnay, and dark chocolate from a little shop in Victoria. Six pieces on each side of the king-size bed, wrapped in gold tinfoil. They're shaped like swans too.

At first Roy wanted to stay in that room, but I refuse to sleep in the same bed with him, even if it is a king. He sleeps like most people who can swim but haven't taken lessons, arms and legs slapping the covers, restless and damn awkward. It's not pretty, but it gets him from one side of night to the other. You just don't want to be around him while he does this. Trust me.

We've been at The Swan for two weeks and breakfast here is always the same: bread, usually dark, thick stuff; sandwich meat — ham and roast beef, medium rare; and hard-boiled eggs. Fruit comes in the form of cherries, which are in season, and some raspberries, almost out of season. Coffee, made with the French press, is a rich, creamy Colombian variety called St. Augustine Estate.

We sit on the second-floor balcony overlooking the vineyard facing the lake. Helmut and Katrina sneak up on us from behind, thrusting little baskets of food in front of us on the pine table before scampering off like Yogi Bear and Boo-Boo into the thicket of the kitchen, to argue about footwear. Apparently Katrina has bunions and lately they've been predicting a radical change in weather, although she isn't sure what kind. Could be a torrential downpour or a scorching heat wave.

This morning Roy, looking thinner than he has all week, eats only ham, with his fingers. He strings it into spaghetti, then dips it into his mouth like worms. He doesn't touch his coffee.

Why won't you touch your coffee?

What are you, my mother?

Roy, you OK?

Doesn't answer. Kicks his foot out. He's wearing his motorcycle boots, shit-kickers he calls them. He likes to wear them when he's planning to walk a lot, or when he's directing students.

The lake is ridiculously calm today, I say. A pane of glass is the cliché that comes to mind. What do you think, Roy?

Stop it, he says, I'm bored.

Boring is OK once in a while, I say. I mean, I think that's the problem with our society today: we're overstimulated. We need a constant stream of information and we're still not communicating. Right?

That's boring, too. He smiles a fake smile, then studies the blue rail in front of us and slicks back his light brown hair. It's time to go home, he says.

What?

You heard me. It's not working out here.

Wow.

Naturally, Helmut and Katrina are shocked when Roy tells them — we've prepaid for up to the end of the week, plus they apparently like us.

You should stay some more, says Katrina later on, placing her hand softly on Roy's shoulder. Give this Swan more chance to affect your insides. You are both men with old women's hearts. It will happen soon.

I want to laugh but Roy gives me the look, so I lock it up.

His hand shakes as he reaches across the white tablecloth to add cream to his coffee. It comes out in little lumps because it's bad cream. Stirs and stirs his coffee hoping the white specks of congealed cream will finally disappear. They don't.

I see that my cheese has some mould on it. Just a little. And the raspberries are mostly mushy. I push my plate away just a little, hardly noticeable. Cough. Cough again, because obviously there's this pause building up and I really hate pauses that build up because I want to fill them with blather.

Helmut says, Is it our food, is this the issue?

No, Roy says. I just want to go home.

Listen, Helmut says, the rooms will be here for you. Roy won't have it.

We pack the car. It takes maybe ten, fifteen minutes because we only have four or five bags and we haven't collected anything really, even wine. But we need more coffee so we stop at a nearby Starbucks to read the paper and watch the locals in their long shorts and hockey jerseys shuffle in to order iced Americanos. Then we drive to a winery and do a tour and taste a couple of Pinot Gris. Roy likes the one I hate and buys a case.

The tour guide talks about residual sugar and balance and, believe it or not, some people are taking notes.

Roy drinks seven samples and then wanders off to look at the vines outside. I find him sitting on a park bench dedicated to a deceased winemaker, petting the owner's dog, a cross between a beagle and a poodle. Use your imagination.

By the time we finally head out it's late, probably near six or so. We need to stop for our usual gas and road snacks, cans of Diet Coke and Spitz, our favourite brand of sunflower seeds, so we look for a gas station. It has to be a Mohawk because Roy is still boycotting Shell and Chevron over something that happened in Nigeria in 1993. We end up paying over a hundred bucks for gas, oil, and snacks. The Diet Coke was cheaper per litre than the petrol, although they probably taste about the same.

The traffic is heavy with sunburned beach bums heading back to their trailers or motels as we drive through Kelowna, up the hill on the other side toward Summerland, along the long finger of the lake down toward Penticton, and finally onto the highway to Vancouver.

The car sings about needing new tires, or at least an oil change. It's an old car. It's an old song too.

It's hot out and we have the windows wide open. Even the wind feels ancient today, adding wrinkles to our foreheads as we try to remain thoughtless while travelling. It ain't easy.

Cloudless and dull, the sky isn't worth talking about. The hills are baking. Trees too. Most of them lean away from us. Soon the lake fills the rear-view mirror as we head into the mountains.

Roy smokes most of the way. With his sunglasses down I can't imagine what he's thinking.

Why are we like this? Why? I ask, again saying aloud something I should have kept to myself.

Because we're truly fucked up, Roy says.

Doomed.

Fucking right.

We all are.

It's very Greek.

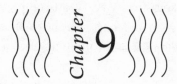

Chapter 9

What is this, Roy says, as we slow down and then finally pull over. Look at that. Look.

Point of interest: rock slide. Immense. Right up to the sky. A kick and crumble of boulders tumble-dried and then held in place, waiting for some cosmic event to move them again. Most the size of Volkswagens. Others the size of humans curled up in pain. Overall, fairly stable. Safe even for those who want to proclaim their precious high school grad year in black spray paint, third rock from the right.

Leduc Senior High School 1984!

We Will ROCK YOU Mr Roboto!

Then two rocks down in red paint: Don't Hate Me Kat!

And three more rocks to the left in green, purple, and black: Love SUCK Penus! Spelled with a U instead of an I, I mean, what is it with kids today, they seem to be really good with colours, but anything else and —

Then over there: LOST JESUS FOUND! This is in gold spray paint. Expensive for sure — excessive, I think, for rocks in the middle of nowhere.

Over there, a metal water bottle held down by a big stone the size of a bowling ball, the stone just balancing on top. Beside that, a lawn chair with a hole through it, Christmas colours, red and green fabric.

A broken hockey stick. Wood. Not composite or something exotic. Obviously an old stick because Christian Brothers is written on the side of it and I think they went out of business a long time ago.

Scattered everywhere else along the choir loft of stones: Tim Hortons coffee cups, candy bar wrappers, potato chip bags, plastic Safeway bags —

It's all very confusing. But overall, if you ignore the garbage, it *is* pleasing. Placid even. Round defined by more round. The intestines of the mountain spill down to the road and, on the other side, toward the river, widening and looking more scattered, coughing up huge butt-ugly boulders onto the stony embankment. Particularly pleasing, I suppose, for those looking for a little refuge from the perfection of, let's say, Saskatchewan.

For a moment, I wonder which came first: the highway or the big scree of stone? And if it was the landslide, what madman decided to pave over it? If it was the other way around, why did the boulders cross the road? I guess that's the question really.

Roy doesn't care. His eyes are as big as, you guessed it, stones. He wheezes excitement. Oozes it, in fact. Window down and half-hanging out, sunglasses in his fist. He's drooling. Look at this place, he says. Look at that rubble! Right up into the sky.

Yeah, it's nice, I say, turning the engine off. But we're running late. I don't like driving in the dark. You know that.

Explore? Come on. Please.

Sure. Let's make it quick. And watch your step.

Yeah?

Just be careful out there.

Immediately out the door, Roy is a hop, skip and jump away, climbing with surprising agility, picking his way up the slide to who knows what.

It takes me ten, fifteen minutes to catch up to his perch, about thirty or forty metres above the Mazda, some treetops now almost eye level. They sway a bit as the wind picks up and dies. The sweat on my forehead dries up very quickly. The backs of my ears hurt from my sunglasses. I feel a little nauseated — I've had a fear of heights since my late twenties, when I visited the CN Tower in Toronto and saw a six-year-old jump up and down on the see-through glass floor screaming WHY DOESN'T IT BREAK, DADDY?

No fear. No fear. No fear.

Grab the edge of the boulder with both hands, look straight across at the trees, don't look down, whatever you do, never look down.

You OK over there? Roy asks.

Yeah, no problem, I squeak.

What a view, he says. What a great view. Roy does his best Marlboro Man impression and lights up a fag — his word — as we dangle our legs over the rock now called The Separatist because he thinks it looks like René Lévesque's forehead. You have to give him credit for that one — up to this point he hasn't been very funny or even remotely obscure. Now he's both.

He lets the smoke out of his body in a long, steady cloud. Impossibly long and impossibly thick. A vapour snake. I wave at it. Hopeless though.

What would it take for you to jump? Roy finally says.

I'm not sure I follow.

He coughs and catches himself from coughing again. Let's say, for example: endless productions, Broadway shows, two hundred openings across North America in one year, a movie deal, a house in Vancouver.

Great reviews too? I ask.

Don't be greedy, Roy sneers, I'm being generous. It's about being produced.

Let's talk about artistic success.

Oh God. He looks to the sky for help. Can we focus here?

Let's look at your *Dream*, I say.

Forget it.

I mean, your production of *A Midsummer Night's Dream* sold out. But three reviewers thought it was overwrought and only one thought it was, and I quote, moderately brilliant. What was more important for you? The sales or the praise?

Roy flicks ashes at me. Not on purpose, I'm sure.

And what if nobody showed up? I ask. What would be the point?

I still did it, he says. Right?

Well, if nobody showed up, maybe it was both dead and alive at that same time. Schrödinger's Cat, right? Until the curtain rises and the audience looks in, who knows.

Fuck this, Roy says. I'm bored and I have no idea what you're yammering about. He pulls himself up like an aging boxer, steadying his skinny legs before gingerly climbing up toward a larger boulder in the distance. On its side in red spray paint: DREAM ON MCNEE. No punctuation.

End of conversation.

So what do I do? I pick my way down to the car, studying each footstep like a jigsaw puzzle, piece by piece, stopping only to tripod my body with my right hand, then left, as I feel my weight transfer, moving as the earth moves, the sun disappearing toward the West as night slides up my back.

Shiver.

When I look back, Roy is gone. Just rocks. Pale in the nearly setting sun, they now all look like foreheads baking in thought. The heat wallows all along the depression caused by the collapse of the mountain.

I stand in the shadow, the crook and crevasse of earth, feeling small and thinking terrible things about someday finding Roy dead, realizing that time might be now. And here I am, forty-five years old, the promise of happiness just beyond the next mountain range, the next empty field, the distant glacial lake, and so on. Unsatisfied and unloved and unfortunate, growing into bitterness and anger until it fits me like my father's old hockey sweater, and really, fuck that metaphor because I should know better, I should let the light shine or whatever it takes to live this life with dignity and wisdom and insight and COME ON, ROY! WE'RE RUNNING OUT OF TIME!

Outside the car, I huff and puff at the windshield, watch my reflection twist in the clouds.

ROY?!

Roy?

My echo, a small Roy, returns. Nothing else though.

What do I do now?

I get in the car, study the maze of broken mountain, look for the skinny black-clothed man with the big boots to come back. I want him to come back, all of him, just one more time before *his* great cosmic event. But right now the rocks have him — and they're not talking.

Then I think about how the very car I'm sitting in is made from melted rock. Most of the engine, too. I wonder who had the first idea to try to melt rock, to burn it at such an intense heat that it turned into something else, like a Mazda. And why that idea occurred to him. Or her. I mean, what were they thinking? The rock will change? I know it must? I will just make the fire hotter until it does? It will make the transition. Change! Change now! More fire! More!

I turn on the radio and listen to a psychologist on the CBC. She says we've romanticized love. We want too much, we expect too much. We don't understand pain, because we've romanticized that too. Today's music doesn't help, she adds. It's all about dysfunctional love.

I want to phone her and say, Well, if it wasn't dysfunctional we probably wouldn't sing about it. I mean, isn't that the whole point?

She says real life is about having real expectations. And that real love is often just a series of small commitments rolled into a bigger one. Falling in love is overrated, she says. Trust me.

I turn her off and slam in a tape of Prince. I know, I know. My car is so old it has a tape player. And stupid Prince disgusts me with his Purple Rain but I love it just the same.

If I were in Vancouver right now I'd be sitting at an outdoor café with my laptop, nursing a latte, checking email and hoping that somebody important just messaged me with wonderful news: We love your work. We love your writing. We love everything about you. But not this season. And not without further funding. Keep us informed. Thanks.

Some dreams have the same endings. But who's to blame for that anyway? Our subconscious? The real me under the I?

I want to blame God. But what would be the point? Why bother? He gets blamed a lot. He's used to it.

I check my cellphone. No reception. Nothing.

Roy, come on, where are you?

ROY?!

Try the horn.

Nothing.

I shiver. It's longer than my last one.

In Vancouver the temperature often stays the same even when the sun goes down. Room temperature all day. Bland, in a city that defines natural beauty. Perfect mountains all around, perfect trees and perfect water. That's why everyone wants to live there. That, and the fact that crazy people always migrate west until they run into the ocean. Then they take cover under bridges or in front of the COBS bakery.

Room temperature.

Passive audiences.

Condos.

Buses lined up on Broadway.

Starbucks.

Smartphones.

Yoga pants.

White bread.

The bland fucking preserves you. Like a caper or a pickle. But it makes you bitter too. OK, sour. But that's Vancouver. Not this place.

This mountain is seriously disturbed. Glowering, I notice now. Bigger in growing darkness. Menacing, as mystery gets added by the minute. What is out there? Every sound louder too, a kind of rubble groan. Let's face it, night is bitter here. And biting. Wind whistles at my open window. I close it and watch my breath fog up the windshield as the music slows because my tape player is too old and tired to play an entire album. Just like me, I guess.

Fuck, I think I'm seriously depressed here. It's the place. The rocks. I know it.

I take the Prince tape out. Throw it on the floor. Just sit there and pout.

Twenty minutes later, just around twilight, Roy shows up

behind me, walking along the highway with a green budgie on his shoulder.

Yeah, you heard me. A green budgie.

I'm not making this up.

Chapter 10

Transfixed by the centre line streaming out of the darkness, the bird sits perched beside Roy's left ear on the edge of the headrest, speechless, of course, and swaying a bit, tilting his yellow-and-green-crested head.

Cute, I say.

Interesting unblinking eyes, grey or blue. Notice that? Roy says.

Yes.

Fascinated by his reflection. Or the dark. Or both.

Yes.

I shall call him Chekhov, says Roy. Because he embraces the unknown.

We drive — hurtle, I suppose — toward Hope, up one mountain, down another. Vancouver. Into the mist, and beyond that, the ocean, my apartment on the edge, waiting for me to hit the light switch. Yes. We are drawing a line through our part of the world, our history, until we stop. Period.

Roy eyes the bird, who eyes him back. Wonder what he's thinking.

Why us? Where are we going?

Chapter 11

After we stopped at a pet store in Chinatown to pick up a birdcage — a bamboo one because bamboo is natural — I drove Roy to his apartment-slash-hotel and dropped him off. He was so excited about Chekhov the Budgie he left his small duffel bag in the car, the one with his dirty socks in it.

I don't find it until a couple days later, while driving to a seminar on playwrights and critics for a local theatre event called Making a Scene. I am to appear with Kathleen, a fellow writer and friend, as we face off with two local critics in front of a group of concerned playwrights. It's supposed to be an informative session.

Yeah, right, Kathleen says, taking off her enormous glasses, expensive ones, using the end to scratch behind her ear.

This oughta be good.

The seminar begins at exactly two, on a day when parking on Granville Island is a nightmare because of the sheer number of tourists wandering around looking to buy fresh Okanagan cherries. I count four tour buses parked outside the market. One of them is called Final Happy Memories Sunshine Tour. Elderly

Chinese women file off wearing identical yellow backpacks that make them look like tiny Quasimodos on a lunch break. Digital cameras in hand, they bob and weave through the locals, heading toward the anxious-looking fruit vendors hiding behind meticulously constructed berry pyramids inside the market.

No sample please. We hear a lot of that during the summer months. Please. As if the Chinese have never seen pyramids of shiny cherries before.

Finally finding a parking space on the other side of the island, I make my way up the theatre lobby stairs to the seminar and resolve to be less boring and more intellectual in front of my colleagues.

Critic number one, Mr. Big Head, sits beside me. Critic number two, Mr. Know-It-All, sits beside Kathleen. He's in a subdued mood; he's going through a breakup, and tonight he's constantly smoothing over imaginary hair on his bald head and sighing. He has the look of a tall Arab shepherd who is slightly bored of days filled with stupid sheep and nights filled with bright stars. But I like him. He's smart and funny and writes the best bad reviews in town despite being a bit of a doubting Thomas.

When I sit down, he whispers loud enough for almost everyone to hear: I really don't see the point of this. Oh, it's you. Aren't you the brave one? Then he takes a slow sip of his coffee, watching the cup as it moves across space to his lips, then stopping it in mid-motion. What, he says to me, What is wrong with this cup?

What? I say.

Never mind, he answers, his green eyes big as marbles. He sets the cup down on his lap, then pulls it away quickly after getting slightly burned. He spills some but pretends not to notice. The handsome bartender — a wannabe director and local irritant named Dave — does. He walks over with a bunch of napkins and wipes up the mess.

You guys look nervous, you know what I mean? Dave says in passing.

Thanks, Dave, I say.

Seriously, don't make my job worse than it already is. I hate cleaning up after writers and critics.

Thanks, Dave, I say, a little louder. You're a great fucking waiter.

He retreats while giving me the finger.

We finally settle in, critics on one end, playwrights on the other. Across from us, under the dark wooden rafters of the upstairs reception room outside the theatre, are approximately thirty playwrights, all very pale and anxious, waiting for the slaughter to begin. Everyone wears black and has been drinking copious amounts of free Shiraz. Very few of the playwrights have been produced recently and those that have were all killed in the reviews. You can smell the gunpowder in the room.

The moderator, Norman, drifts in like he's just slept through the matinee playing next door, a musical about starving Africans and the movie stars who want to save them. Welcome to Granville Island, he says. Welcome all.

Norman is a tall, gaunt actor who made his fortune playing monsters and aliens on *The X-Files*. Died a hundred horrible deaths and looks it, too. The actors' union sent him, but you never, never question the actors' union.

Critics and playwrights — can't live with them, can't live without them, he chortles. It's not often somebody really chortles these days. He says, Who wants to start the ball rolling?

The first question is harmless enough: What is the relationship between the two?

Let me field that one, I say, feeling absolutely presidential. There is none.

Mr. Big Head turns to me and says, Don't be ridiculous. We have history.

Although very little of it is any good, I counter.

A playwright in the back whistles. Norman tries to make peace with the old gloves-are-off comment. Kathleen just rolls her eyes.

Nine shows, nine bad reviews, I continue. It's almost personal, wouldn't you say?

Not if you've written nine bad shows, the critic says. He shows his teeth as a gag.

Kathleen gives him that look, the one that could kill, and says, I never read the critics anymore. Nobody reads them.

Why's that? asks Norman, shuffling papers on a beat-up clipboard that has the name Mike stencilled on the back in white.

Too old school, Kathleen answers. Today we have instant messaging, blogs, emails, cellphones, Facebook, Twitter, whatever. Reviews are instant and from my hive collective of friends and family. I'd rather put faith in them than a crabby critic who has little or no theatre experience. So screw them.

Somebody claps. Others join in.

Kathleen looks pleased with herself, so pleased she gets off her stool and does a little curtsy, pulling down on her oversized black wool sweater. She's blushing so much her freckles merge.

You go, girl, says a massive sweaty playwright with thin blonde spiked hair, taking notes on his iPad. He looks like a fat Billy Idol.

Kathleen grins a real grin, all teeth, gums, and pink lipstick. Don't get me started, girl, she says.

More whistling.

I notice a TV camera in the back and wonder what station would ever think that bitching playwrights and pompous critics would make for interesting viewing.

Kathleen looks over at me and mouths the words Critics suck, which for some stupid reason I decide to say out loud.

Critics suck!

Critics suck!

Half the room stands to clap, which I guess qualifies as my first legitimate standing ovation.

Right on, I say. Right on.

Norman holds up his clipboard like it might have some magical power to soothe pissed off playwrights. Please, he says in his best faux Shakespearean voice. Decorum, decorum, gentlemen.

Mr. Big Head swivels around in his bar stool to face me — stone-faced, of course, because he is still a fucking critic. No fake smile or grin. Not this time. He says, We critics will be around long after everyone has forgotten your last hopeless flop.

Your opinion, I say weakly.

My opinion, you want my opinion? Your plays have issues because you have issues. Instead of conflict you write snappy dialogue, hoping somehow nobody will notice how empty your stories really are.

Fuck you, I say. I mean, really.

Oh, good comeback, says the critic, swivelling back to face the now-quiet crowd. But the sad truth is you can't create meaningful relationships if you don't know how to have them yourself.

Come on, this was supposed to be a seminar on our relationship, not a critique of my personal life.

You started it.

Actually, I didn't.

Well, either way, the important thing is that we're creating dialogue, he says.

But apparently it's bad dialogue, I say.

Norman thumbs through his notes, his faux notes. Kathleen starts drinking her free wine. Mr. Know-It-All sobs a little, I think.

Are you crying? Norman asks softly, leaning over to talk behind his clipboard.

Mr. Know-It-All pushes him away. I just find this whole thing so incredibly meaningful, he says to the room.

What part? I ask, looking down the row, seeing him now trying to lean in a new direction.

He tries to stand up, then plops down again with little effort, and says, How we are able to just tell the truth — isn't that what good writing is all about, just telling the truth?

Kathleen downs the rest of her Shiraz in one long gulp. Norman scratches his big eyebrow with the eraser on the end of his pencil. Mr. Big Head shakes his head like he's trying to break a cobweb off the end of his nose.

Could I say something here? says Norman weakly, trying to straighten up. Could I? Could you just let me? Please?

But Mr. Know-It-All continues, listing even further to port, his right hand anchored to the round of his stool, some playwrights in the audience leaning with him. He says, We are gathered here to try to make some discoveries about ourselves as artists: who are we, what is our role, how can we make this world a better place? I mean, here we are in this room talking and thinking about theatre. Others, in other parts of the world, are much worse off. Syria. Ethiopia. Cambodia. Right? Think about it, people. They are fucking starving. And not just from the lack of any art and culture. They can't get a decent latte, OK?

He scans the room. Seeing a young female playwright in the front row tentatively put up her hand, he smiles and says, You want to say something, sweetheart?

Yeah, she says. Are you stoned?

∼

After the bloodbath we go downstairs to the bar for a drink. Or several drinks. Two glasses of Riesling later, Kathleen wants to discuss the approaching end of my career.

You're a fool, she says. A total fool.

Spank you, I say, quoting a movie from a million years ago. Spank you very much.

I'm serious, she says. No matter what you write from now on, no matter how good it is, or how interesting it is, you're going to get slammed.

Thanks, you're a true friend.

I mean, you could be Mamet and it won't fucking matter.

Thanks, but I'm not a Mamet fan.

I thought you were.

No, I just like what he says about writing.

And what's that?

Buy the book, I say.

God, you're crabby.

Well, apparently I can't form meaningful relationships.

Yeah, I know, Kathleen says into the bottom of her wine glass, then quickly orders yet another round.

I drink and try not to think.

It's then we both notice the stoned critic sitting by himself on the patio. It's drizzling a bit outside but he doesn't care because he's drinking straight Scotch and it could use a little water. Nobody else is on the patio except a couple of overweight gulls, who are hoping some nachos with cheese will show up soon.

What a sad, tall man he is, says Kathleen, watching the gulls watch us watch the critic. But at least he didn't say your writing sucked.

Whatever he says won't matter, I say, as much as what the others say. Particularly that asshole who reviews for the daily paper. I mean, who the hell does he think he is? What's his fucking problem?

Kathleen sighs and flashes the peace sign at the critic sitting outside. He begrudgingly flashes one back, then returns to his watered-down Scotch, the glass travelling to his mouth in slow circles.

How's the new play coming? she finally asks.

Does it matter? I say.

The two gulls have been joined by a flock of pigeons who crowd the rail behind the critic, their backs to him, watching a small cruise ship packed with wedding guests pass under the bridge. Long pink ribbons trail green balloons from the top deck, and a white banner whips into the wind. It reads Kate plus-sign Pete — Love at Last.

Fuck weddings on the water, I think I say aloud. Fuck 'em.

Uh-oh, says Kathleen. Uh-oh.

Shut up, I say. I'm fine.

We drink our water and shovel pretzels into our mouths, watch as the bartender opens a new bottle for us, fumbling with the corkscrew a few times before realizing the wine has a screw top. He notices us watching and does a little bow from behind the bar, bumps his head with his hand, shrugs, intones, Stupid.

Stupid is right, I say aloud.

I turn to Kathleen, who's rubbing the salt off her pretzel with the end of her thumbnail, and say, I hate my life, I just fucking hate it.

I think you should get the hell out of Dodge, she says. That's what I did when my girlfriend had her affair with that drama-turge who shall remain nameless, that bitch Deborah. How's Roy, by the way?

Recovering.

From what?

Oh, who knows, I say.

When the bartender brings us a fresh basket of Mister Salty pretzels, Kathleen pays him thirty-five bucks for our two glasses of wine and little cheese plate. She divides up the cheese like a conquistador, that is yours and this remains mine. Cheddar, Swiss, Gouda, brie.

So, she says. I have a friend who knows a friend of Roy's, and word has it he's been more than a little depressed, if you know what I mean.

I don't know what you mean, I say, running my wet finger around the rim of the wine glass, hoping for a tone.

She takes a long, slow sip, then clears her throat. Kathleen always wanted to be an actress, and her throat-clearing has a theatricality to it. There are often a series of them. Here's another one. Throat-clear. Head-tilt. Slight smile, warm but calculated. Then: Did you know Roy tried to kill himself?

I look at Kathleen, try to study her eyes to see if she's fish-ing. She has blazing eyes that look like the underside of a trout, pale blue and always watery, as if she's been sobbing for hours. With her short red hockey hair, shabby baggy clothes, and workboots, she could easily pass for that woman in the hi-viz vest who directs traffic around dump trucks, the one with the perpetual cigarette in her mouth. But with nicer frames.

Why in the world would he try to kill himself? Very sad, she says, lifting her glass in a mock salute. But good on him for trying.

A moment.

Look, I say. Don't spread it around, OK.

No problem, she says.

Who told you? I ask.

Roy did, she says.

Fuck, I say. What a talker.

I try a pretzel, but it disintegrates between my teeth, stale and over-salted. You'd think bars would do better with the treats. Maybe invest in bowls of little fish crackers — something with class, something to make us feel less horrible about paying ten bucks for a glass of fucking wine.

Poor Roy, says Kathleen. I always liked that guy. He seemed so normal. I guess they always do.

He has trouble forming normal relationships, I say. He's very introverted. Hard to get to know.

She drinks. But because I'm watching her drink, and she knows it, she stops drinking and picks up a piece of cheddar with a pickle fork. How do you define normal relationships? she asks.

Read my next play, I say. You'll see. I'm all over that one.

You're doing it again, she says, taking a gulp of her wine.

What?

Defining yourself through your work.

And?

Don't do that. It's not normal.

All of us define ourselves by our work, I say. It's just what we do. It's theatre.

So the bigger the imagination the better you are?

No, no, I say. It's really not about the size of your imagination.

Humanity?

Well, aren't we all trying to find that? Aren't we all trying to make a difference? I say even louder.

And failing that, sometimes bitterly? She flashes a smile.

Oh please, I say. Can we NOT have this discussion?

Kathleen knows I'm not having fun at her expense. We write, she says. Sometimes well, sometimes poorly. Some things we create succeed, some don't. Some people like what we do, others don't. Some lives are changed. Others not so much. Some people come to our shows just to be critical. It's their job, and it's hard to criticize that.

Whatever, I say.

I'm having another drink, she says. Her arm perches like a mini crane on the dark wood of the bar table, pivoting on the elbow slightly, and her lips slowly reach out to meet her glass instead of the other way around. For a moment, before actually swallowing the wine, she gives me a very cold, very exacting look through the bottom of the glass. It makes her one pale blue eye look like it belongs on a witch.

I tell her that.

She tells me to fuck off.

I leave the bar, trying hard not to storm out, or scurry out, or flee. I hate that bar. I've always hated that bar.

When I get back to my apartment, I see Roy sitting outside with Chekhov the Budgie caged inside his bamboo cell staring at his stupid reflection in the mirror.

What are you doing here, Roy?

I've got some good news and some very good news, he says with a toothy smile. What do you want to hear first?

Chapter 12

We are back in Kelowna, sitting outside The Swan in the late afternoon sunlight. The trees feel the warmth run down their arms, into the roots around the stony ground, and finally into the already-warm earth under our bare feet. Happy trees make me happy too. Chekhov hangs from a nearby branch, safely imprisoned in his Chinese bamboo cage, obsessed with his own reflection even when there is beauty all around, the lake, the hills, us.

Stupid bird, I decide.

Hey, Roy says. He's my best friend.

What happened to me?

That's a good question, Roy says, pouring the last of the wine into my glass. I had to twist your arm to come back here.

I'm glad you did, I say. It's incredible out here.

The willow tree above our heads agrees, waving a little at the lake breeze.

Took us five hours to drive back. Five hours before it all started again including a brief stop at the rock slide, to pee and to show Chekhov where he once lived. Then we stopped again at the lake to buy an iced cappuccino, from a local coffee shop because lately we've taken to hating Starbucks.

Hot out. The kind that makes your legs sweat. You really shouldn't wear socks in this weather. Trust me.

Heaven, Roy sighs. Absolutely heaven.

It's true. Today we're tobacco plantation owners, sweaty and satisfied with our lifestyle, wearing straw hats we picked up at a thrift shop downtown. Our sleeves rolled up even though we're wearing T-shirts. We sit on a green blanket and feel the hot wind sweep back and forth across the big lake and then into our sunburned faces. A great day. A great, great day.

Elective facial surgery, that's what the AD said, Roy says to me over a glass of Pinot Blanc. In Mexico.

So *A Midsummer Night's Dream* is yours now, I say. You're it.

I'm it. He smiles. I am it. I am directing the play.

First she produces your show in the biggest theatre in Vancouver, then she lets me direct the biggest show in Kelowna. I'm beginning to think she finally recognizes talent.

Cheers, I say, sipping my now-warm white wine. Cheers to us.

We watch Jessica wander back from the car beside the house with another bottle in hand. Oh, yes, about Jessica. The stage manager. Jessica Sara Boomer. Could be her porn name. Without a doubt the most beautiful woman in theatre, bar none: long auburn hair, blazing hazel eyes, perfect teeth, athletic body, intelligent, and very, very sexy.

Roy sees me watching her wind her way down the path to the lake, to us, her long dress fluttering like a French flag behind her, closer, then even closer, to our little picnic blanket, our cheese plate, our empty, useless conversation. She smiles at me, smiles and waves like they always do in the movies, that nonchalant, innocent wave that could mean anything or nothing at all.

Can you believe it, Roy says. What are the odds? What are the odds?

I have no idea what he's talking about but who cares. I'm adrift. Infatuation surrounds me. Wave after wave.

Snap out of it! Come on — you're old.

Hi, boys, Jessica says, looking directly at my lips. Miss me?

She throws herself on the blanket we've spread under the willow tree, making sure to adjust her long blue skirt to fall perfectly around her perfectly formed legs, legs forged by years of cycling back and forth from dozens of rehearsals and productions. Jessica is very much in demand, by men and women alike.

Are you staring at my feet? she asks while unscrewing the wine cap.

No. Yes.

I have my father's feet, she laughs.

They're beautiful, Roy says. Absolutely beautiful.

Yeah, he was a dancer, thank God, Jessica says as she refills our glasses. Paris, Berlin, Winnipeg, you name it, until his knee went. Cheers.

We drink, not really thinking about how special this day will be five, ten, or even fifteen years from now, when we are even older and hopefully wiser.

About tomorrow, Jessica says. I think we should do a line run at ten.

Agreed, Roy smiles.

A couple of the actors are still on book. They shouldn't be.

Roy smiles again. Isn't she great?

Yes, I say, transfixed by her perfect feet.

I'm so happy you're on board, Jessica says. Everybody is. Now we can finally finish blocking the show.

Roy's smile disappears.

It's not blocked?

No, not all of it, she answers with a tiny pout. We spent too much time doing table work, you know, talking about the history of the piece and analyzing and deconstructing comedic elements, that kind of bullshit, so we fell behind. Crazy, right? We have one week before our first preview and four or five scenes haven't been blocked yet.

Suddenly she jumps up. Did you guys see that?

We look out across the water, the sun-dappled water. Nothing.

Oh, it's just a skier in the water. I thought it was something else. Don't mind me, I've been drinking all afternoon. Except during rehearsal, of course.

Roy gets up, goes to Chekhov's cage, and stares down his bird. It's then I see the sweat stain along the back of his black T-shirt.

Fuck, he says. This is worse than I thought. He coughs and I notice how it sounds like a dog bark — a small dog maybe, but a dog nonetheless. The set looks like shit too, he adds. It's too much of a rake, we'll have actors falling out of their shoes the whole show. I hate that set. Sure, it's fucking gorgeous but I really hate that set. Who designed it? Was it Yvan? Was it? I mean, nothing against him personally, he's French and brilliant, but maybe he didn't think Elizabethan women should be wearing heels, I don't know.

Jessica drinks wine and says Hmm at the same time. Even her hmms are sexy.

How's our crew?

The usual gang of idiots, Jessica says. But they're OK.

Any problems with our actors?

They're less OK. Particularly Allan. He's really being a queen if you know what I mean. Oh God, that rhymes, sorry. He hates being here. It's very red-necked in his opinion, plus it's impossible to get laid. Also his opinion. But hey, this is wine country. Who needs sex when you can drink icewine on your balcony? Have either of you guys tried the Riesling late harvest from the winery? It totally rocks.

Chekhov tries to sing.

Oh, I love him, Jessica says. I hope you bring him to rehearsal. It would be so perfect. Maybe we can put him in the show. There's a thought, right?

You know the rule, I say.

Yeah, I know. No pets or babies onstage. Although if I have a baby, I'm getting him an agent as soon as he's through diapers, she laughs. She takes a moment to lean back, her long elegant hands pulling up at her perfect breasts. I think she knows, she knows what she's doing. I look away.

I wonder what it's like to be really pregnant, she moans, still feeling her body with her hands.

Yes, I snuck a peek. But I took off my hat first.

Roy circles the willow tree, head down, staring at his pointy feet poking out from his black stovepipe jeans. Then a cigarette appears.

How do we look for the opening? he asks, taking a quick puff and then flicking the smoke end over end toward the lake. Pfft as it hits the water.

Sold out, Jessica says. Four hundred and ten tickets in three days. Everybody wants to come. Including some wine reps from Ontario. I love this wine, by the way. I absolutely love it. They make a great Pinot Noir too. Very rustic. French style but with a hint of New World.

Marry me, I say, adding a little safety-valve chortle. To be clear, I'm not a good chortler.

She gives me a mega-kilowatt smile and says, I would but Ashton probably won't go for it.

Ashton?

Ashton. Yeah. He's doing props and fight choreography for the Arts Club Theatre, did you know that?

I don't think I know him, I say.

Sure you do, you taught him in college. Writing for Theatre, right?

Oh, that Ashton. Isn't he like twenty-five or something?

Yeah, but I'm only thirty-four. How old are you?

I'd rather not say, I say.

You look forty-something.

Great. Thank you.

Are you older?

No.

What's with all the grey hair then?

It's not grey. It's bleached. From playing golf.

Looks grey. You should do something about it. And by the way, there's over twenty courses within fifty kilometres of this place so I bet you're happy. I'm going to take it up next year because my dad is giving me his ex-wife's equipment now that she moved to Switzerland. Oh God, isn't this a great day? I mean, look at us here. Having wine under the trees in the most incredibly beautiful place in the world while others sit behind desks in air conditioned offices thinking of doing exactly what we're doing.

Yeah, I say. Exactly.

Exactly, Jessica says, sweeping her long sort-of-curly hair back with her long, long fingers so it catches more sunlight, even though — except for when the wind picks up and parts the leaves — we are mainly in the shade.

How perfectly perfect, I say while staring up at the branches. A lazy, hazy August day where the temperatures are higher than anywhere in Canada. Or even Hawaii. I feel exceptionally sappy, so much so that I'm happy just to be sitting down.

Roy is very quiet, I notice. Too quiet. He has taken his hat off and is studying the bottom of it as if he's looking for the number of the quality control person who checked it. His sunglasses are perched on top his head, gathering glints of sun.

You OK over there? I try.

Roy doesn't answer.

Nobody says anything.

I love smelling the lake, I say, I absolutely love it. Different from the ocean, cleaner obviously, and without that slight odour of dead fish, right?

I feel I have to fill the pause with something, anything, because silence would make my sneaking another peek at Jessica's legs so damn obvious.

Do you like the smell? I go on, discreetly passing my eyes over her prone figure, as if trying to avoid looking directly at the sun.

Yes, I like the smell, Jessica sighs, hiking her dress up ever so slightly. Why wouldn't I?

We both suck air into our lungs and then out again, slow and deliberate, as if we just finished having sex.

Shaved legs! Shaved legs, my mind screams. Don't look. Well, just a little. Look a little. Then look away. Please look away. Fast. Put your hat back on. Do something. Don't look, don't you dare.

So, what brings you here? she asks me, and I notice I have been staring at her breasts again.

I had to get out of Vancouver, I say, peering down the length of the lake at nothing in particular.

Girl trouble?

No. God no. Critic trouble.

Oh, who cares. Nobody reads them anymore, we have Twitter now.

I care.

You shouldn't. Nobody else does. So, what are you going to do — drink wine, play golf, that kind of thing?

No, I'm writing a play. A few weeks here is perfect. I brought my laptop.

Good for you. I like your writing. It's different.

I'm different.

I know, Jessica says. When are we going to work together?

Well, I'm hoping soon, I say. But who knows?

I'd love to get my hands on one of your pieces — oh, that sounded dirty, let me try that again — love to work on one of your plays, for sure. Everybody says you're easy.

Easy?

I know, I know — that doesn't sound good either. Are we drunk or what? She laughs. I like it, it reminds me of my mother's laugh after she had her kidney transplant.

Roy isn't looking thrilled. He finally stops circling the tree, sits down again, and plops the bamboo cage between us on the uneven ground. Chekhov ruffles his feathers and squawks his disapproval.

I'm not happy, Roy says.

Oh, says Jessica.

Can we run longer days?

Union rules, babe, she says. No can do. She plays with her red painted toes.

Can we cut some scenes then?

Cut Shakespeare? Blasphemy, she snaps.

Roy slurps his wine. I always cut Will a bit. It's no big deal.

Shouldn't you clear that with you-know-who? Jessica asks. I mean, it is still her production, right? You're just steering the ship home or something like that?

Well, she's in Mexico now getting her chin done, so who cares.

Although you have to wonder about the quality of health care one gets in Mexico these days.

Maybe she's just bailing on the project, I say.

Why? Why would she do that? Roy mulls. Bard in the Vineyard, nobody has done this before. It's going to be huge. It's going to be magnificent. Right?

Jessica clears her throat. Oh, I forgot to mention, she starts. The winery owner, what's-his-name, Steve-o, his wife is in the show and she can't act worth shit. But it was something that they agreed to at Christmastime during auditions. She's very — hmm, what's the word for somebody who's overbearing, in a nice way? Let's go with overbearing.

What? Roy says. Why is she — who agreed to this? I mean, come on. She can't act? Could you be more specific?

Not really. I mean, once you see her try you'll know what I mean. It's just very unfocused.

Can we replace her?

I wouldn't worry about it, Jessica says, it's no big deal. Just a few scenes — well, a lot of scenes actually, playing the fairy queen. Which makes sense because she *is* such a queen. Jessica pulls her hair back, adding a scrunchie to hold it in place, and again notices me noticing her. It's getting to be a habit.

I nod toward the scrunchie. Smile like a turd.

I know, I know, she says. A scrunchie. How very 1990 of me. I'm retro, what can I say. She laughs, then pops up again, jumping to her feet like her legs are made of car springs. Wow, she says, I'm not so sure that was a water skier after all. Look.

We all bounce up to look out at the lake. In the distance, at the far end, what appears to be a very large human head or a very small boat seems to be moving with some speed along the shore. It disappears.

Monster or myth? Jessica laughs, smoothing out her dress in the slight wind. Will it show up again? Will it? Please?

We wait until a pause stretches into a moment, and then slightly beyond.

It doesn't.

We all sort of laugh, relieved a bit I think, and then sit down again and finish the wine and talk about things not related to theatre, like why we drink even when we're not thirsty, and the people we'd most likely sleep with if morals didn't count. Who we'd kill if murder wasn't a crime. It's a long list that takes us through two more bottles. Both to die for.

Chapter 13

Marlene. The winery owner's partner. Big. Intense. Awkward. She is, as my mother would say, a queer duck. Mostly flaming red hair and cleavage, a tall woman who recklessly swings around telephone–pole-stiff arms and walks as if her knees have no joints. The meanest, bawdiest fairy in the woods. Her version of Titania, Queen of the Fairies, straddles the line between Suzanne Somers in *Three's Company* and Helen Mirren in *The Queen* — well, straddles the line until it veers off course and crash lands into a category of acting all of its own. She commands the stage like the captain of an iceberg. Or the mayor of a mirage. Or a dancer on the moon. Or —

I type OR in capital letters on my laptop, praying for another metaphor, sweat rolling down my wrists and onto my black-and-silver keyboard. Slug back some more orange Gatorade. It's warm. Salty. Barely refreshing.

Now be more creative. Come on.

But I can't think of anything to type. And my wrists hurt.

I'm writing character studies, trying to find unique personalities to squeeze into a play that is proving to defy creation.

My conflict is unbelievable, my dialogue limp, and my pacing terrible. And to top things off, I'm listening to Shakespeare over and over in the background, every line a gem, every word perfect.

I close the computer.

Sitting on the knoll above the stage on the amphitheatre under a Mike's Hard Lemonade golf umbrella, I watch the actors stumble through the play while Roy stands in front like a conductor trying to speed things up, snapping his fingers and waving his spindly arms and whispering instructions to Jessica, who sways beside him in the midday heat. Jessica makes notes in her huge red binder and then whispers instructions to Sandra, the ASM, who is sitting under another umbrella beside her. She in turn makes notes in her binder, which is blue and covered with AC/DC stickers.

Everyone is sweating. It's noon and already over thirty-five degrees. Who knew it could be this hot. Global warming, right?

The actors move like they're barely able to gesture or grimace — all except for Marlene. She does both with aplomb, all silly and futile and even a little sad, emoting for all she's worth, hoping one tiny emotion will finally mean something.

She delivers every line with great gusto, but not to the other actors — just the heavens. Roy coughs throughout every one of her lines, either trying to cover up a laugh or choking. Marlene doesn't care. She's having fun. The time of her life. The dress, purple and gold, barely holds her enormous breasts in place, and the long train follows her every wild move like the tail of a comet. Her eyelashes are enormous, cow-like even, but her eyes are the colour of the lake behind her — they're incredibly beautiful, even a bit wise.

Can you believe this scene? she shouts to the sky.

Are you talking to me? Roy asks quietly.

Yes, of course I am. Do you understand me? Am I clear when I say, Sing me now asleep?

No, says Roy. It sounds like sling me now some sheep.

Oh, that's funny, she says to the rest of the cast. They stand motionless on the steeply raked wooden stage, which is painted white to highlight the colourful costumes. Most of the actors droop their shoulders and drip with sweat, roses wilting under the constant heat.

Hilarious, I think Roy says. Right? Well, none of this is really funny when you've only got a few days before your first public performance.

The heat builds by the second.

We need to be better, Roy now clearly says. Much better.

Could you be more clear with your direction? Marlene says, throwing her train over her shoulder like it was made of salt.

What? says Roy.

Direction, she shouts. Could you direct me? I mean, specifically?

I am directing you, he says.

Marlene gestures grandly to the other actors. Really? Exactly what do you want from me that I'm not already giving you?

Roy stalls. Not because he wants to give direction, but because he wants to kill her. He lights up a cigarette and Jessica moves away from the smoke like a bee.

This ought to be good, Jessica says in my direction.

Well, Marlene bellows, holding out her hands as if waiting for rain, as Roy keeps smoking. If I'm too loud, then tell me I'm too loud. If I'm standing in the wrong place, tell me to move. But please don't just stand there and twitch.

I'm not twitching, he says calmly. I'm wincing.

Am I *that* bad? she laughs. Am I?

Roy holds on to this moment for a very long time. He doesn't need to raise his eyebrows, but he does anyway.

Somebody in the back giggles.

Marlene's face turns as red as her hair, so she turns and faces the lake, hoping for a sudden offshore breeze.

Roy blows smoke at her.

Allan pretends to throw fairy dust around the stage and does an elephant waltz in his oversized gold-leaf battle dress that looks like it was designed by a Greek sailor. Make it better, make it better, he sings to nobody in particular, dancing his way toward the edge of the stage, then stopping suddenly and pretending to teeter. Make it better, God help us all, he laments. Then he jumps with a pretend fall like he's committing suicide.

Roy nearly moves to catch him, but decides not to. Allan, who is a big guy with big knobbly legs, hits the ground with barely a sound. He recovers with the flexibility of an aged tabby and skulks away toward the winery's tasting room.

I'm on a break, he says, moving quickly down the stone path toward the bell tower. Call me in half an hour.

Nobody moves for a while. Or breathes.

Finally, Roy takes Jessica's binder and throws it after Allan. It spins to the left and hits the ground harmlessly, papers falling out like enormous snowflakes. Get back here, Allan, he yells. Get back here, you fucker!

Allan pulls up his fluttering red cape, flicks him the middle finger, and sails out of view like a disgruntled superhero.

Roy turns around and sees me see him. He shakes his head, then slowly makes his way to the actors' tent beside the stage. Stomps actually. Fuck, he says, a pistol shot of a Fuck that everyone around the lake can hear, including the row of Korean tourists standing neatly like presidential candidates in front of their enormous black tour bus in the parking lot. Some of them point toward the stage, others pull out tiny cameras.

The actors quietly disappear. One of them, a young expressionless actress, hides behind her giant bottle of San Pellegrino. A couple of them move toward the lake, I think, hoping to walk into it and not emerge until well after opening.

I finish my Gatorade, pick up my laptop and go after Allan. I have to. Who knows, they might be serving the reserve Chardonnay in there. Plus they have air conditioning.

So far, this show really sucks.

～

Susie the server sees me wander in and nods toward Allan. He's huddled at the bar, his red cape flowing neatly over the back of his tall chair.

Allan's a big guy. Naturally big, not fat or unathletic. Just big. Even his voice is big and mean. Without trying. He often plays villains but everybody still loves him. That good. That big.

Some Koreans snap shots of him in costume. Flash. Flash. Flash. They check their digital viewfinders. Re-check them before flashing again. It's a mini lightning storm in a room that loves light.

Allan never cracks a smile, just raises his glass as if warding off the light, or trying to catch it in his wine. He sees me in the mirror and pats the seat of the chair beside him. Magically, a glass of reserve Chardonnay appears to celebrate my arrival.

What a pisser, he says. Cheers.

Cheers, I say as we drink.

Susie ushers some older Korean men wearing white suits and gloves away from us, explaining in broken English that we are actors. TV, yes? You know, TV? Right? *Lord of the Rings. Gladiator. Harry Potter.* Yes?

It's then I notice Allan's wooden sword lying on the bar. Why is your sword on the bar? I ask.

Because it hurts when I sit on it, he says without smiling.

Funny, I say.

Not when you have prostate problems, he says, now smiling just a little.

I should be writing some of this down.

No kidding, Allan says. Although life always seems funnier than it really is, trust me.

Right. Right.

The wine feels like liquid flowers with a hint of apricot. Behind it all, visions of French oak barrels hidden under our feet, perfecting the wine with each passing minute. What'd you do, memorize the pamphlet? Allan sighs, and I realize I've been thinking aloud again.

Susie wanders back and lets her hair do the talking, all golden and bouncy and excited to serve us another round of —

Merlot, she laughs. Let's move on to Merlot. She pours short perfect pours in the glasses in front of us, a gunfighter so sure of her target she doesn't need to look.

The Merlot is like a nice stone house in France with pretty red shutters and flower boxes of roses and daffodils. So romantic, this wine. So feminine. So pretty.

I love your outfit, Susie giggles. It's so authentic except for the — well, maybe I shouldn't say.

What, Allan barks. What's wrong with this costume?

Shhh, she hushes back. It's the sword. You're scaring the Koreans.

Then she's off, beetling down the long bar to fill a row of stemware like they're the beaks of baby birds, the Koreans chuckling, nodding, smiling politely, holding out their tiny white-gloved hands.

Allan savours the red, swirls it around in his glass and watches the legs curl down the rim, then sips a bit. I copy him, trying to look authentic too.

Fuck, I'm bored, he says, putting his glass down carefully.

Come on, you're in wine country doing a fantastic show with other fantastic people, I say.

But O, methinks how slow this old moon wanes!

I give Allan my best blank stare, the same one I use while crossing the US border with triple the limit of alcohol in the trunk.

Theseus, Duke of Athens? Opening lines to the play?

Allan waits for me to answer. Come on, Mr. Playwright.

Sorry, I say. I haven't been watching it all that much.

Seems you were watching us all day, Allan says. Look how red your face is.

I was writing, I say.

Oh God, how tragic, he says to the room. Everyone, did you get that — writing while we're acting our asses off. We're nothing to him. Nothing.

It's then I notice the other actors now in the tasting room, all out of costume in their shorts and T-shirts, tasting wine quietly in the crooks and crannies while the neatly attired tourists line up at the bar with us. They mostly don't care about what Allan is raving about. Some have pages of the play in front of them, their lines highlighted in yellow and pink. A lot of them aren't off book yet.

Jessica wanders up to tell us Roy has released everyone early to work one-on-one with Marlene. Yeah, she says, Marlene insisted. Then she glides away waving her mountain bike seat at the others, reminding them tomorrow's rehearsal begins promptly at ten. Do you believe in miracles? she says. Tomorrow, for sure. For sure. Miracles. You watch. Tomorrow, and tomorrow, and tomorrow.

She's Moses waving the staff.

No kidding, Allan says to me. No kidding.

We watch her leave the room, pulling her hair back under a futuristic-looking cycling helmet that has COMP written in large blue letters across one side. As the door opens I feel the hot air flood in over my head, turning my ears red. I notice music, a kind of country and western tune without lyrics. I'm not entirely sure where it's coming from. Some of the Koreans are wearing earbuds, which I had mistaken earlier for hearing aids. Lots of picture-taking still, flashes going off randomly as the actors hunker down behind the tasting glasses, hiding from the light.

Flash: Susie holds up a bottle. A model smile.

Flash: A tourist holds up a sign in Korean. Red felt pen, looks like a square with a line through it.

Flash: Allan holds up his finger. His middle one.

Gladiator, someone says thickly, though it sounds a little like radiator, or even wad-he-ate-her. And many laugh. Too many, I decide, for a tasting room in the BC desert. But it is full of actors and tourists, both groups on break at the same time, drinking. A lot. And many of them are slightly pissed, I'm sure.

I eat some cheddar, cutting it off with a butter knife from a large block sitting beside me. Armstrong Cheese, says the black-and-white label in front. I let it melt on my tongue, then take a nice long slug of Merlot and place the glass neatly on top my laptop beside the cheese.

I feel thick, lazy, like I'm on an oil tanker lost in the middle of the ocean, somewhere very warm and pleasing. Noise, from people mainly, throbs like a diesel engine throughout the room, and it's all I can do to keep awake, to focus on my one ounce of Merlot sitting in front of me begging me to down it in one glorious gulp. What is it with this place? What is it?

Snap out of it, Allan finally says. It's just a lousy tasting room. It's not real.

Sorry.

We're not real.

Right. So who are we then?

Players, says Allan.

And what's our job again, I ask, noticing that I've slurred my speech a little. To bring meaning to life through a little entertainment?

And then what, he says. That's the big question.

I don't know, I say.

Even if we bring a little more meaning, it doesn't mean enough. People still go home after the shows and they still ruin their lives with indifference and boredom. We're just a ripple in the ocean of who-gives-a-shit. We're singing cartoon frogs in a cartoon nobody sees.

But we're really good singing frogs, I try again.

Allan sighs a sigh that can only be described as a drifting comma before the next boring thing is said. He absentmindedly grabs the handle of the nearby sword, raising it ever so slightly above the bar top as if raising a heavy flag.

Look around this room, he says. You think people want to come to our show for enlightenment? They're just hoping to impress their friends. We're their concept of high art, so they don't feel so guilty about buying their next RV or SUV.

Right, I say.

What's Shakespeare to them? Old English with physical comedy. How much do they understand? How much do they really care?

Right, I say.

They desperately want some poetry in their lives, but they don't even know what it is. So they wander down to the winery jingling their car keys, hoping we'll give them a brief glimpse of glory, a blink of insight, so their TVs don't hurt their eyes so much late at night.

That's good, I say. Very literary.

Well, fuck 'em, Allan says, waving his sword more than a little. Fuck 'em all!

The room seems a little quieter all of a sudden. I notice the actors have all been watching us from behind — waiting, I guess, for something more to happen.

Allan looks around waiting for someone to come out of the shadows to challenge him. Nobody does. I mean, what did he expect, really?

This is a lovely Merlot, isn't it, he says, sitting and slapping the sword down.

He stares at his own reflection in the mirror across from us: a mad Duke of Athens with a crown of tinfoil on his head, fairy dust sprinkled on his face reddened by long hours of rehearsal under the hot Okanagan sun. Look at me here, look at me, he croaks. Terribly sad and pathetic. For a brief moment, Allan presses the wine glass against his forehead, wrinkling his face slightly, a Joker grin as his lips curl to make his nose look like it's dipping below. Cheers to me, he whispers, before drinking the last of the Merlot down in one long, satisfying swig. CHEERS TO US!

Behind us, reflected in the mirror, I see a dozen others, all actors, silently raising their glasses. Nobody says anything.

Just drink, Allan says loudly, looking around the room. Either to die the death, or to abjure forever the society of men.

And so we do, without a single Amen.

～

I follow the glow of a panting cigarette down to the lakeshore and find Roy standing huddled under the picnic blanket,
drinking by himself. A sweet Riesling, it turns out, because
they're nicer to drink late at night. Less alcohol. You sleep
better. And no hangover.

What's up, I say.

Roy pours me a little, in a second wine glass he has been
keeping under his armpit for just this occasion.

I've got a few days before opening, he says. My one star is
disenchanted. The other can't act. We're not off book. The
set sucks and we have lousy dressing rooms. Other than that,
things are pretty good.

The Riesling goes down very nice; I feel like pairing it with
more of Katrina's famous apple strudel. We've just had a great
night of food, leftover baked ham with mashed potatoes, no
veggies, and apple strudel with cheese on the side. Then dark
chocolate with raisins and some Port. Helmut told us about
his childhood, I think. Neither one of us paid much attention
to him because it was too horrible — parents dying suddenly
while picking wild strawberries, grandparents losing arms in
threshers, dogs disappearing into the Black Forest, that kind
of stuff.

I notice Chekhov shuffling back and forth in his bamboo cage,
looking out over the lake.

He likes it out here, Roy says. Reminds him of home.

Where's that? I ask.

Someplace warm and dark and full of mystery, just like me,
he smirks. Chekhov is the kind of bird that doesn't push himself on you, he continues. No inappropriate squawks or feather
ruffling. Extremely polite and even a little wise.

The bird whistles.

Was that a whistle?

Yeah, he does that to warn me, Roy says. Of what, I'm not sure yet.

He listens to the waves lap up against the dark shore. There is a houseboat in the distance full of semi-drunk twenty-year-olds singing an old BTO song. Oh, you ain't seen nothin' yet. You hear that song a lot these days.

They're throwing somebody overboard, Roy laughs. Good for them. Sink or swim. Party on, dudes! He sucks the fire out of his smoke until it turns angry and bites at his lip. Then he flicks it away, always toward the water. It flies farther than any other flicked cigarette I've ever seen. Rocket, Roy laughs.

A crashed rocket ship, I say.

It's a night for nostalgia. A night for late-night journals and popcorn. The kind of evening you dream about twenty years later and think, what was I thinking, what was I doing? I try to make mental notes. The tree. The water. The stars. Roy with his head down, breathing into his chest, looking sickly even in the dark.

How are you feeling, Roy?

He doesn't look up.

Someone on the houseboat plays with a powerful flashlight, guiding it over the waves and along the shore to illuminate us briefly. We shrink back into the low branches of the willow tree.

That was close, I say, almost whispering.

Roy just grunts. We watch the boat drift away toward the opposite shore, the music trailing behind, bouncing off the nearly flat lake to echo around the hills until the empty night swallows the sound.

Finally, it's as quiet as a movie poster.

Quiet as a postage stamp, Roy corrects me.

Quiet as last year's Christmas sweater, I say.

He laughs a little. Very obscure, but it works.

We both notice some wind and shiver.

You happy? I ask.

I'm happy, he says.

Despite everything?

Despite fucking everything.

And your opening is sold out.

Love it, love it, love it. Roy smiles, then pours more wine, holding his glass up to the half moon in the clear sky, stars bending around the rim. Jesus, look at that sky, he says. You can actually see the Milky Way. Beautiful.

The Milky Way is anything but milky. Pink, green, and silver, a host of pin lights scattered like a dream above the dark heart of the lake.

You talk how you write, Roy says, poking me slightly in the ribs. Describe the stars as fucking stars and the night as fucking night and leave it at that. Jesus.

I was being literary, I say.

Well, don't. You're ruining the fucking moment.

What's with your language? I say.

What?

All the fuckings?

Just ignore them, Roy says. Like I told you, I'm fucking happy — look at that fucking sky, look at it.

We steady ourselves with our left hands against the tree trunk and look up, look way up.

How many other Shakespeares? he asks, waving with the bottle. How many other Shakespeares on other worlds? How many other *Midsummer Night's Dreams*? And why can't we ever see them?

Well, I say, physics, actually.

What?

Physics says you can't see them. Can't travel faster than light.

And the closest star, next to our sun, is what — over four light years away?

You watch a lot of TV, don't you, says Roy, patting down his pockets for another smoke. How's the writing?

I hit a roadblock, I say. No story.

Good characters create their own story, he states, as if reciting a prayer book. React, don't think. Writing is all about being in the moment. Right?

We both lean back against the cool spine of the willow. Roy fights back a cough, suppressing the urge to let it curl into a hacking fit. It takes everything he has.

Chekhov whistles again. Twice.

It's then we notice the smoke. Burnt toast at a campsite, that kind of smell. Heavier though. And then, in the distance across the lake, on the side of the Okanagan Mountain, a single orange flame as big as a Christmas tree flickers in and out of sight, fighting to crest a hill as if it wants to signal us. A slow glow.

Did you see that, Roy says. Did you?

Yup, I say. I did.

It's probably nothing, he says. Right?

Right.

Chapter 14

Shakespeare has only written six good plays, and four of them are comedies, Marlene says while sweeping red hair out of her face.

I sit in the tasting room bar with her. She orders more wine from Susie, phones the kitchen to bring up a plate of fresh oysters, tells the Filipino tourists that China needs to find democracy faster, that kind of stuff. She's good at taking over.

Right now, Marlene starts most her sentences with Let me tell you. Let me tell you, she says, Shakespeare is overrated. Here are the best plays in no apparent order: *A Midsummer Night's Dream*, *All's Well That Ends Well*, *Much Ado About Nothing*, *As You Like It*, *Macbeth*, and *Romeo and Juliet*.

And *Hamlet*?

Forget *Hamlet*, it goes nowhere fast. Plus he makes stupid mistakes and blames his mother for everything.

She looks pleased with herself, and looks around the room to see if others are pleased too. Mostly the place is full of tasters again, tiny tourists with tiny cameras saying tiny things we can only imagine.

It's five o'clock and Marlene, already exhausted from the full day of rehearsal, is bracing herself for another four hours of cue-to-cue at seven. I'm not counting her drinks, but I have noticed she's had more than four small tasters. Maybe five. I've had at least that many.

Drinking between rehearsals? I say.

Absolutely, Marlene laughs, pulling at her ponytail. Half of it comes off in her hand.

Extensions, she sneers. Like I need them.

She throws the hairpiece down on the bar and I decide it looks like a long-haired rat. A very red one. She says rabbit, but the piece is too small for that. A tourist, of course, snaps a photo of it.

How juvenile, Marlene says into her wine. How very, very, very juvenile.

Yes, I say. Very.

But she has already forgotten the issue and looks around for Jessica. Jessica isn't in the room.

She's supposed to come and get me, Marlene says. When my break is over. I'm a professional actress now, I need to be taken care of.

Marlene doesn't look the owner's squeeze, dressed in a slightly torn white blouse and designer blue jeans. She just looks like any other slightly distracted actress, except the other distracted actresses are outside, lounging around the tent smoking and trying to hydrate themselves with Diet Cokes and Red Bulls.

The day was spent trying to work out Marlene's scenes, or, as she puts it, trying to find the moment in the moment. Every moment needs something, she says, sipping Pinot Gris from a tumbler because the bar ran out of glasses after supplying the last busload of tourists, which is now being replaced by a busload of taller, fatter tourists. A moment like now for example, she goes on. Here I am sipping wine with a handsome playwright in my partner's special tasting room while he's off in France cheating on me with his personal assistant and what is it you're thinking over there right now, what is it with that slight frown on your face?

I'm just over hung, I say. Hungover, I mean.

Marlene smiles. I bet.

A Dutch tourist walks up to me and points to a cheese plate nearby. May I?

Help yourself. Cheers.

Thank you.

Marlene studies me briefly, staring at my nose, mainly, but other parts too. Why are you here? Writing?

Yes. A play, I say. Naturally.

About?

How about betrayal, I lie.

Oh God, again.

I'm sorry, I say.

Can't you playwrights think of something else to write about? I mean, really — betrayal this, betrayal that. It's getting a little boring.

Well, I'm not married to the idea, I say.

Good. There's still hope. She kisses my hand.

I smile weakly, a little lost for words. OK, I say. How about empty, meaningless love where people just use each other. Do you think that will sell?

Just to teenagers, Marlene says. What are you really writing?

I want to write something that means something, I say, realizing how stupid it sounds but unable to stop the blather. Older characters have way more depth because basically they're full of life, at the edge of something, transitioning. Or something like that.

Marlene looks at me like my hair is on fire. Right, she says. Right.

I bite my lip. Most of that sounded stupid, didn't it?

Listen, she says. You write what you write. See what happens. Explore.

Then we swirl the wine in our glasses and pretend to sniff. I spill a little because I over-swirl. Amateur, I think. Lousy amateur.

You are something, Marlene says, watching me wipe up the spilled wine with a nearby napkin.

Thanks.

What about me?

You?

Now that you know me, she says, turning her tumbler clockwise on the bar counter. When you look at me, what do you think you see? A desperate housewife-type or a talented actress? Or both? I'm waiting.

She pretends to study the ceiling, giving me the opportunity to ogle. I notice all the freckles running down her cheeks, disappearing around the jawline only to reappear on her ample chest like a star map.

Stop staring at my breasts, she breathes, leaning over to me. The tourists have cameras.

Sorry, I couldn't help notice —

Let me tell you, I get a lot of that, she says, pulling at her buttons but not really closing any of them.

You have freckles on your chest, that's what I was noticing, I offer.

And that's only the half of it, she hushes into my ear.

It makes me shiver. I steady myself with my right hand on the bar because Marlene has her left elbow leaning against my other side and I don't want to be rude. Plus she smells like cinnamon. I think it's cinnamon. Or is it nutmeg?

It's cinnamon, Marlene says, pulling out the pins holding up the rest of her hair so that it cascades down her back like a red waterfall. I like a man who speaks his mind. I find it so reassuring. You like my hair?

I — yes.

It's my second-best feature, she says. Guess what's number one?

Your—?

My personality, she laughs. And it's a nice laugh, ending with a tiny gurgle of a giggle.

Cute.

I'm not sure who said that.

Cute.

I like what's happening with us right now, Marlene says. It's decent. She stares at her own reflection in the mirror behind the bar. She *is* attractive, although my mother would probably call her a handsome woman, which isn't necessarily a compliment. She leans into me a little more, her thigh up against my thigh, her knee bumping my knee, like we're two canoes tied up at the dock and we've just been hit with the wake of a passing ferry. How do you like the water here? Marlene asks. Warm enough for you?

I haven't gone in yet, I say.

Why not? she asks.

I don't swim very well. I'm a little bottom-heavy. Bad centre of gravity. I once went down with the floor on one of those rides where the force of gravity is supposed to keep you stuck to the wall.

What ride was that? Marlene asks.

You know, a ride at the fair. When I was a teenager. I think they were playing ZZ Top and then the floor went down.

Why?

Because it's supposed to go down. We're inside and the thing is spinning really fast, and they had to stop the ride and let me and a fat woman off for safety reasons.

But you're not fat, says Marlene. I mean, what are you, six-one?

Six-two, I say.

One hundred and ninety pounds, she says.

No, no. One-eighty, I say, patting my stomach flatter.

Really?

Really.

Well, isn't life full of surprises, she says, again into my shivering ear, making the rest of me shiver too.

It's then the oysters arrive and, let me tell you, I'm happy to suck on a lemon for a while.

Susie puts the silver tray in front of us like we're suddenly Tahitian and she's making an offering. She bows slightly and shows us lots of teeth. How's Steven enjoying France? she asks.

I wouldn't know, Marlene says into her first large oyster shell. And let me tell you, I don't give a shit either.

Is he going to miss your opening? Susie asks.

Marlene doesn't say anything. Just throws a used lemon wedge down on the plate like it's a dead bug and swallows the oyster with a very reptilian gulp.

OK then, Susie says. OK then. She retreats, picking up the hair extensions on the bar and dumping them in the sink, happy to do a refill run on the new tourists — Dutch mostly — lined up at the bar smelling like wet wool and stale cigarette smoke.

I smell my hands, holding them up in front of me like I'm praying. They smell like lemons. I'm happy not to smell cinnamon anymore. Are you and Steven married then? I ask Marlene.

No. We have an arrangement.

Interesting, I say. Formal or informal?

Marlene stares at my hands.

Have you ever considering hand modelling?

Whatever you say, I say.

Sexy, she purrs. You so sexy.

I notice my nails and how dirty they look, so I wipe them down along the ridge of my blue jeans, thinking somehow that might help.

Marlene pushes the crushed ice on the silver tray around with her thumb. She singles out some nice plump oysters, then preps them with a squeeze of lemon and a shot of Tabasco. They look perfect. And the smell, oh God. A tint of crashing waves along an old fishing pier. Seagulls soaring above trawlers or perhaps small black tugboats. That kind of thing.

So, you're not married then, I say to Marlene.

Not really, she says. Just shacked up and disillusioned.

But you're still innocent, I say. Right?

Fucking right, she says while touching my back slightly.

We have a moment. The room seems to spin around the silver plate of shiny oysters sitting in front of us. The tourists circle the walls, flashing their teeth, wallets, and cameras. Nobody is miserable. Even the fat bus driver at the end of the bar slaps backs and laughs. Music is louder, yes, the music is louder. I spot Susie turning the volume up behind the bar. Why? Because everybody loves ABBA. A small rotund man with no hair dances across the tasting room floor pretending his glass of Chardonnay is a woman in a long silver gown. Other tourists, his friends I'm guessing, urge him on in a language I can't understand.

Dancing fool, I say. Look at him go.

Marlene nods. I hope this means they're going to buy more wine.

The small rotund man wipes at his brow as he spins into place at his stand-up table. He hasn't spilled a drop of wine yet, not until a friend slaps him on the back and knocks the Chardonnay across his white shirt. The friend, who I realize only then is the bus driver, apologizes and wipes it up with his shiny blue tie. He's got a wine bottle in hand too.

Should he be drinking? I say to Marlene.

She hasn't been watching any of this. Rather, she's been staring at my fingers. Can I see your hands again? she asks.

I put them back on the bar, knuckles up, fingers slightly curled, half fists, thinking maybe she won't touch them — but she does, pulling my fingers straight gently and running her fingers down the backs of them.

Yes, yes. I see.

I put my hands away like they're revolvers, jamming them into the deep pockets of my baggy khaki pants.

Marlene says, Those hands look like they belong on a magician. Do you know any tricks?

I'm a writer, I say quickly. No magic. Not lately.

We suck on oysters, taking our time with them, snapping our heads back in unison with each gulp even though I'm trying not to be in sync with her. It's not very sexy — oysters always go down like chilled mucus with a hint of lemon and shallots.

Why are we so crazy about these things? I ask. What is it about oysters? I mean, they're full of iodine and zinc and mercury and who knows what else, and here we are sucking them back like there's no tomorrow. I pick out a nice big one and finish it off, letting it slide down my throat like a little snowball slipping down a picture window in northern Manitoba. A bad simile, but it's all I've got tonight because I'm having several sexual thoughts per minute, most of them thoroughly explicit and involving me being on top.

Inappropriate love, Marlene says while grabbing her fourth or fifth oyster.

What?

It's Shakespearean, right? We love what's bad for us and oysters are really bad for us.

Right, I say, still sniffing my fingers.

But let me tell you, without it, we'd have a lot of boring stories, right?

Right.

I love your nose, Marlene says, touching the end of hers for illustration. Love the bump in the middle, it's so Eastern European. Exotic. Different.

I broke it tobogganing, I say, practically inhaling an oyster at the same time.

Can I touch it? she asks while touching it.

Marlene then places her hand on the bar as if it's the small of my back, stroking the wood slightly. It's a large, masculine hand but with a dainty, slightly freckled wrist. Red palms, not quite pink, I notice. Flushed, as if constantly embarrassed. Worker hands, maybe, but in a linen factory or something to do with cloth. She turns her hand over, slides it closer to me.

Feel it if you want, she hushes. She can really hush.

They are pillow-soft. Just about perfect for romantic walks down the Champs-Élysées, or even Broadway in a pinch.

I go back to my wine. Swirl and sniff, swirl and sniff.

I'm not a kept woman if that's what you think, Marlene says, almost in my ear.

I wasn't thinking that. Really.

Swirl, swirl.

Good, she says, because I couldn't respect a man who couldn't respect me. That's why I'm doing this play. I want my man to be in shock and awe. Has a woman ever inspired that in you? I bet someone has, right? Probably.

Marlene over-pronounces her consonants. Lips opening and closing like they're gulping. Koi comes to mind. But let's not dwell there.

Swirl and sniff. No, drink. Just drink.

Susie glides by as if on skates, bottle in hand. You need more wine, don't you?

Yes. I need more wine. Yes I do.

A Susie smile as she pours. I hope you're not driving tonight, Mister.

Leave the bottle, Marlene says, and Susie does. I top up my glass quickly, reaching across the bar to place the bottle far away so I can get some space between us, me and her. It makes no sense at all, I know, but my logic is she'll go for the wine bottle, not me.

Marlene knows what I'm doing. Oh, you are funny, she says.

Well, I don't want to get too drunk, I say. I might regret it later.

Right, right.

Drink. Swirl. Drink. Drink. Swirl. Drink. Drink. Drink.

After a slight hair toss to the right and an out-of-nowhere giggle, Marlene downs her wine too and tries to look serious. So what's your big project? she asks. Tell me about your big project. Oh, that sounds dirty. She giggles again, like a six-year-old schoolgirl. But you're not a dirty writer, are you?

Ha. OK then. Ha. Ha. That's my lame response.

Marlene pokes me. What's the dirtiest thing you've ever written? Come on, you can tell me. Go fuck yourself? I bet it is. Which really isn't all that much. Let me tell you, go fuck yourself, I say that all the time. Tell me to go fuck myself, come on, see what happens. Come on, Mr. Playwright, let's have your dirty, dirty words.

It's then that Roy walks in and, let me tell you, thank God for that. Thank God.

He sees us and marches over, Sharpie at the ready. I think he's either going to stab us or draw moustaches under our noses. He doesn't do either. He says, We're waiting for you, Marlene.

What? I didn't see Jessica. Where's Jessica?

She's not your babysitter, OK?

Marlene shakes her red hair and closes her eyes. God. Is it seven already?

It's seven-ten, Roy snaps, nearly poking her with the pen.

Really?

Yes. Really.

How thoroughly unprofessional of me, Marlene says. Will you ever forgive me, Roy?

Anytime, Marlene, Roy says. Except on opening. I'm a very bad son of a bitch on openings.

I had no idea, she says. You always look so calm and collective.

Calm and collected, he says. Not collective.

Did I say that?

Yes, you did.

Well, I'm really sorry, Marlene says. I guess I used the wrong fucking word. She gathers up her things, pushes her bar stool back.

It's then I notice how tall she is. As tall as a pirate.

I am a pirate, she says, smiling at me with just her bottom teeth. She sails out of the room, parting the Dutch tourists with ease, holding her half-full tumbler of white wine like a blunderbuss.

Roy waits for her to close the door behind her. When she does, he says to me, very quietly: Kill her, or seduce her. But make up your fucking mind.

He packs the pen away in his back pocket and leaves, bumping his way through the throttle of tourists to the door. He turns to salute me with two fingers before disappearing into the light. Warm air rushes in and I smell smoke — not just campfire smoke, but the thick, acrid smoke of a forest burning.

When I get outside I see the smoke settling around the far rim of the lake. Behind me, beside the tent, on the steeply raked white stage, an actor blows into a conch shell. It sounds exactly like it should, warning the trees along the crouching hills around the still lake, bouncing off the water and disappearing into the endless, tidy green vineyards.

Chapter 15

*B*ack at *The* Swan, Helmut and Katrina call a meeting over apple pie and coffee. It's probably nine o'clock, maybe later. Roy and I sit in the kitchen and look out the balcony window at the dark horizon.

With us are the two tourists from London, Shamir and Almeera, tiny young newlyweds on their first big trip together, driving from Calgary to Vancouver to visit friends they met while dining out one night. They wear business clothes, dark suits and starched white shirts, even when it's so blazing hot in the middle of the day. They smell clean, sit clean, talk clean. At first I thought they were related but it turns out they're just second cousins, and while the marriage was suggested it was never really arranged. Both work as dentists and are hoping to someday move to Canada.

That's all I really know about them. That and the fact that they have just started a wine cellar and were shocked to stumble across Canadian wine, which they thought hadn't existed outside of expensive icewines. They were equally surprised to find no trace of snow driving through the Rocky Mountains.

I first met them in the parking lot earlier in the morning. They had just arrived and were unloading their white Honda.

Almeera said, It was very distinctively brown in the Rockies.

We moved from India five years ago because of the opportunities presented to us in the UK, said Shamir.

The black bears were smaller and more numerous than anticipated, said Almeera.

Our perceptions of a simple English life were greatly exaggerated, said Shamir.

Both of our parents unfortunately passed away. The fortunate aspect to their sad departure was well over four hundred thousand pounds.

Opportunities present themselves.

And the future was clear.

Canada is the number one choice.

So here we are.

So here we are.

Let's face it, they both talk like brochures.

They had spent the weekend in Banff and Jasper. The second stop was their favourite.

Overwhelming in its scope and power, Shamir said.

Majestic to a fault. Terrifying in places even, Almeera said.

Certainly as advertised, Shamir said.

But colder, Almeera said.

They stood beside their car looking more than a little lost, staring at Okanagan Lake as if it somehow might make sense to them.

This is the largest lake we have encountered in our travels, said Shamir.

It is a different colour than expected, said Almeera. Darker and more mysterious. Almost menacing in nature. Although we may not agree on that concept.

Shamir nodded. Agreed.

I began telling them about the Ogopogo, but they stopped me. They had read all about it on their Mac weeks ago.

We believe, said Shamir, in the truth of myths.

Helmut scooped up their luggage — all new, but steamer-trunk-styled in old-fashioned leather, probably from Restoration Hardware — and dragged it to their room.

Our hosts told us the Indians spent the entire day on the balcony gazing across the lake looking for signs of the monster. They had visited Loch Ness with the family years ago, and a cousin from Bombay insisted something unusual had broken the surface. A small black head that looked like an inner tube was the description.

I guess it could have been an inner tube, Helmut told us. He had a good laugh over it. Tourists, he said. They never change.

Now Shamir and Almeera sit with me and Roy in the kitchen, all of us almost in a row. They politely finish their apple pie, leaving most of their vanilla ice cream untouched on their plates. When Almeera folds her napkin over the food, her husband frowns at her, but just a little bit.

Helmut stands in front of us behind the special table made of old railway ties and clears his throat. The local authorities have warned us this fire has increased in size and is along the ridge-line perhaps moving toward this very location, he announces. Of course, the flames could not advance beyond the vineyards, this is a natural firebreak, but floating embers and whatever is wish-borne — excuse me — wind-borne. And this is where we have concern. It is a glowing —excuse me — growing concern.

How bad is it? I hear myself say.

It always looks worse than it is because of the way we are situated around the lake, Helmut explains. The water exagger-ates things considerably. Atmospheric inversions, that kind of thing. But really the fire is many kilometres away, beyond the city limits.

Are we in danger? I ask.

Not at this moment, no, Helmut says. He waits for a moment before adding, Define danger.

Possible injury or death?

The tourists from London look at each other.

It is a small out-of-control forest fire, Katrina explains. We get this on many occasions through the summer in the outlying areas. More coffee, please, please, enjoy, it's Dutch. She pours the coffee into our cups whether we want any or not. Even adds the cream. In 2002, she says, we lost four cattle ten kilometres from here because they go into a burning bush and never came out.

Attracted to the flames like moths, Helmut adds. Pure stupidity.

But this is the danger with cattle, Katrina says. Worse than sheep if you ask me, so we are doing them a favour by eating them occasionally, right?

I am a vegetarian, Almeera says. So, could you please, if it is not too much to ask —

You shouldn't be vegetarian, Katrina says. Where are you going to get your iron?

I take pills.

You shouldn't take pills, Katrina says. They're artificial.

Do I smell something burning? Shamir says.

Bacon from this morning, Katrina says through her teeth. My apologies, the smell lingers.

Did you say bacon? Almeera whispers, eyes the size of eggs.

Katrina just grins.

Shamir says, Ahem.

An uncomfortable moment. Big time. Why do I feel that this might somehow be my fault? I blame my mother.

Helmut punches the railway-tie table with a gnarled fist, the kind that might have connected with a few faces in a smoky Hungarian bar forty or fifty years ago. I think he's trying to quash a bad thought, or maybe he's doing this to demand attention; I don't know. Maybe it's something they do in Minsk or wherever he's from. We have no worries, he says, Not really. Just be aware of the situation. And pack your bags and place them by your doors at the ready. There is no immediate concern though. We tell you these things because of the insurance and because we welcome your business. But, to be sure, fires will always forge their own destiny.

Yes, this is true, says Katrina.

Shamir asks, You will warn us within due course?

You will have much advance warning. Much more than the cows, that's for sure.

Shamir seems to relax a bit, puts his hand on his wife's and pats it exactly three times. It'll be all right, it will be all right I'm sure, he says with a slight lisp.

I have a recurring nightmare of burning to death in my sleep, Almeera says. You know this.

And yet I still married you, Shamir says with a very pretend smile.

Helmut and Katrina give each other slightly Eastern European looks.

When cattle walk into fires it's called stupidity, Helmut says. When people do the same thing, it's called sacrifice. What fire are you walking into with the marriage? Yes?

I'm sorry? Shamir says.

Helmut laughs, holding his chest in an I'm-having-a-heart-attack kind of way. Katrina smacks him on the back hard with her palm, the sound similar to a full bottle of wine hitting the hot dry ground. It doesn't put a dent in the old man's laugh.

He speaks metaphorically, of course, Katrina says. This is where the humour is. Yes?

Now Roy joins in, risking a coughing fit to ha-ha-ha, before standing up and steadying himself. Look, everyone, he announces. As long as we don't have to leave tonight, I've got some work to do on the show.

Katrina asks, What would you like for breakfast tomorrow?

Why don't you surprise me, Roy says, then leaves the room chuckling. It's a pretend chuckle.

Helmut brings out a bottle of schnapps and some tumblers, five of them, with tiny bunches of grapes engraved on the side. He lines them up on his special table and pours without looking down. Venezuela, he announces, I got these glasses in Venezuela. Authentic lead crystal, you bet. This is what Venezuela is famous for, not dirty politics. Yes. Tonight we celebrate. To the fire and to life! Cheers!

Knock them back. Another round. Knock them back too.

It gets easier.

We drink until we find ourselves staring off the balcony at the orange curtain along the edge of the long horizon, the flames reflected in the lake and, I suppose, our faces too.

Beautiful, says Katrina.

Outstanding, says Helmut.

Different, certainly, Almeera says quietly. She has one shoe on and one shoe off and is rubbing her bare foot along the back of her other leg as if getting ready for a race.

Nothing to worry about, my child, Katrina says. Worse has happened and we are still here.

Almeera relaxes slightly. So does everyone else.

Shamir sighs, then clicks his tongue. What is it with fire? It follows us from birth to death and then beyond, he says.

Helmut grunts, Ah yes.

Katrina grunts, Ah yes.

We drink, each holding on to the rail with our free hands, steadying ourselves. The horizon shimmers with red and orange, radiant with possibilities from end to end, the lake shivering below.

Helmut has his arm around Shamir, who now seems lost in thought — something I hope to never see from my own dentist.

I finish my ice cream, though most of it has melted.

Ah yes.

∾

Roy isn't in his room, so I wander down toward the willow tree. Our special place, as it's becoming known. Allan leans on the trunk of the tree, a movie-star pose no doubt perfected onscreen. He sees me coming and moves away so I can take his place. When I follow him, he walks away again. It's as if we're in movement class in theatre school.

I move. Hey, I say.

Hey, he says. He moves.

What. Come on. Stop. It's embarrassing, I say.

Then nobody talks.

It's dark out but you can still make out the backs of the hills, I say. Or the fronts, depending on your point of view. Sleeping cattle or giants with beer bellies lying on their backs. Look how bright the tops are with the sun over the horizon, look at that, what is that colour, what?

Shut up, Allan says. Just shut up about the hills. Save it for your next fucking opus.

What's wrong, Allan?

Why are you here, anyway, he says.

I don't rush into the response because I'm trying to think of what answer will cause the least conversation. Right now I really dislike Allan. Writing, I say. I am writing the next great Canadian play. What else?

Better than that last one I hope, he says. What was that about? Your divorce?

Yeah, I guess, I say.

Boring divorce, buddy. BORING.

Right. Why does he hate me? I ask myself. What have I done? I mean, really, I thought we were pals. I really did. Didn't we just have drinks at the tasting room? Didn't we just have a great conversation? Wasn't I funny enough? Wasn't I deep enough? Didn't I ask him questions? Come on.

I reconsider our past. A slight flash before my eyes. Not the dying kind but the minor re-evaluation kind. A glint, let's call it a glint. OK. Let's figure this out. Allan: Very talented. Very connected. One of the best actors in Vancouver. Everybody loves the big guy. But he has never been in any of my plays, despite always telling me he's wanted to be. Come on, write me something, he once said. I'm worth it, trust me, I'm worth it. Something with an accent, please.

But I haven't written the right one yet. The one that allows him to access his dark, ironic side while maintaining his humanity. He told me that when we ran into each other at a friend's wake, at the bar, over Scotch, at least five years ago. From what I remember, this is how the conversation went:

I don't drink Scotch, I said.

You don't drink Scotch, he said.

Wine, I said.

Well, you need to try Scotch, especially at a funeral, he said.

This isn't a funeral, I said. It's a wake.

Whatever, he said. Try the Scotch, pretty boy.

I tried the Scotch.

Twelve-year-old single malt, he said.

Jet fuel, I think I said.

How would you know? he said. Unless you're sucking off big jets.

Define big, I said.

Don't be funny at a funeral, he said. I'm not that good of an actor.

We knocked back the Scotch like old golfers, waved at mourners leaving the hall. Maybe they were friends, but probably they were just other theatre knobs, ones that were working more than us. A lot of them were wearing red ties or scarves. For effect I think.

I'm thinking of just doing old plays, Allan said with a sigh. Nothing new, definitely nothing trendy. I hate trendy. What's trendy right now, anyway?

Old plays, I said.

Oh, he said.

Or adaptations of. Site-specific stuff too. Like plays in swimming pools or at IKEA.

Who'd put on a play at IKEA?

People who want to save money on sets.

Is that a joke?

No joke.

Wow.

The audience wear little transmitters in their ears —

Please don't, Allan said. I just can't take it.

More Scotch. A lot more.

When did theatre become so much like real life that we ended up hating it? he asked. And why site-specific? Why a forest or IKEA or some stupid cold warehouse? Isn't a comfy theatre with real working lights and flush toilets site-specific enough? Why not build a theatre site to actually watch theatre?

Do you really want me to answer that? I said.

No, he said. Why bother?

We watched the rest of the mourners thin out.

What are you writing? he asked, sipping his single malt like an actor, which means he mostly killed it in one gulp.

Writer's block, I said, sipping on my ice cube. First time, actually.

Characters or story?

I have no characters so I guess no story either, I said.

Just write about your friends. I mean, aren't we interesting enough?

Question or statement?

Now you're being coy. Or witty. That's even worse at a funeral, he said.

Wake, I said.

Whatever, he said.

We took a good look around the room at all our remaining pathetic friends trying to connect over somebody's sudden and unfortunate end. A stroke that came out of nowhere, we were told, as if strokes sometimes didn't. Her partner, a small, tanned man wearing an accountant's old suit, was still sitting at the front of the hall, holding a large framed photo of the dead woman in his lap. His friends, the undead, I guess, moved around him slowly, holding out their hands and zombie-talking — It'll be all right, it will be all right I'm sure — hoping it some-how helped. We barely recognized anybody. Too many black suits. Too many sad, pathetic faces.

I knew the person who had passed away. She was an older actress named Doris, and onstage the light always followed her. Darling, she once said to me after a show, Darling, you have it too, you just don't know it yet.

Even in her seventies, Allan said between drinks, Doris never grew old onstage. She couldn't.

Yeah. Everything she did was important and meaningful and youthful. Everything. With great charm and innocence. What a life, what a fucking life. And then just like that, it's over.

We raised our glasses but didn't clink them. It didn't seem right.

You know what you need to do, Allan finally said. Write me something meaningful. But make sure it's character-driven. And then let me drive it home. I'll make it brilliant. You'll see. He pounded me on the back. Pretty hard actually.

Character-driven, I said. Yeah. I think I've read that before. Like in a manual or something. I slid away from him just a tiny bit.

Then we got drunk.

We were pretend friends for a couple of years after that, always hugging and saying things like You're brilliant, No, you're brilliant, Oh, shut up you bastard. That kind of bullshit. Theatre bullshit. All very sad and pathetic. Nothing is real with us except for the rejection, and we thrive on that because it develops cynicism which we mistakenly think will somehow protect us. It's the business. Eventually you stop reading your reviews, start your own blog and make shit up. More brilliance. Accolades you don't deserve. Praise from Facebook friends you've never met. Fake this, fake that. Fake, fake, fake. It's like crack.

Filthy love is still love, Allan once told me after yet another bad review. No such thing as bad press, just bad houses. He's good at that kind of BS. Sayings you could plaster your fridge with. Things like, There are five things you need to make it in theatre, and number five is talent; all actors want to be writers, all writers want to be directors, all directors want to be producers, and all producers want to be rock stars; kill your baby and find your hill to die on. Those are three of his best. They're posted on his personal webpage. And his Facebook.

But now, just after sunset here in Kelowna, he's not talking. It's all pent-up shit, the kind that destroys friendships. Allan jams his hands into his pockets but I can see that they're still fists. Shoes off, blue jeans folded up to just below his knees, he paces the slightly rocky shore as if waiting for the waves to finally stop. Wavelets, I should say; after all this is just a lake. Not much of a beach either. Hard to lie on with all the little rocks and beer cans and shit all over the place. Why are people such pigs? Why do we not love the planet better? Can't we see what we're doing here?

Oh, fuck. Let's cut to the chase. What's wrong, I say.

Allan's walking, says Roy, coming out of nowhere. I think he was lying down behind a log or something.

Threatening to, says Allan.

Why?

Marlene.

Why Marlene?

Do you need to ask, I mean, really? She's un-fucking-believable. Unprofessional. Unprepared. Unwatchable. Doesn't make eye contact with me onstage.

Not true, Roy says. She watches you when you're looking away.

Like that matters, Allan shouts. Come on, cut her loose, cut our losses.

Come on, big guy, Roy says very calmly, hoping his quiet will drown out Allan's loud, something like that. She really connects with her audience.

What audience? Allan says. We haven't had an audience. Unless you're counting you and the crew. And I know most of them hate her.

I meant to say that I'm sure she *will* connect with her audience, Roy says. She has the ability to play to the house and not look too bad about it. I mean, I think there's potential with this woman.

Allan puffs out his chest. His leg hair stands up too. Probably not a good sign. Marlene, he growls. You wanna know what I think of her? I mean, really? Amateur bullshit musical theatre acting-schmackting.

Allan. Relax.

We have yet to make it through one scene, ONE SCENE, without stopping, Allan shouts even louder. Have you fucking noticed, Roy? And she changes her blocking every time. One minute she's right in my face, the next she's turned her back on me. What was she doing today walking stage left where there's no lighting? What was that? A dramatic moment in the fucking dark?

At least she's trying shit out, Roy says. If this was an experienced actress, you'd be giving her compliments.

Not when we're opening in two days. I mean, fuck! Two days, Roy! Fire her ass! Get the stand-in to do it. She's got real potential. Whatever her name is.

Even in the growing dark I can see Allan's face is turning red. He picks up a large rock the size of a man's skull and smashes it into the water, then picks it up again with his fingertips and shot puts it deep into the lake.

KER-PLUNK! The sound it makes is the sound a body makes when it's rolled out of a small wooden boat.

Marlene's weirdly interesting and unpredictable. Just like you.

Allan turns to me. What did you say? What?

Sorry, I'll shut up, I say.

He shakes off his wet feet and pads toward me. This is not the fucking time to be fucking funny, Noël Coward.

Roy intervenes. Almost grabs Allan's collar but misses and nearly falls into the water. He catches himself, retreats, and reaches for a cigarette instead, tries to light it with unsteady hands as the wind picks up and plays with the flame.

Like I said before, Roy says, remaining calm, Marlene may not have much talent but she has stage presence. People watch her.

That's because she's always pushing out her breasts. But you know what, they're actually not part of the scene.

Character choice, Roy says.

Well, if her tits could act we'd have some scene, Allan says.

Roy thinks for a bit. Retreats. Circles the tree then avoids me. Can you just go with what she's doing, show a little flexibility?

Christ Almighty! I'm not doing this.

Things get quiet. Allan goes back into the water to kick at some waves with his bare feet. Roy finally lights the smoke successfully. I look for Chekhov in his cage behind the tree. He's not talking either.

I'll get someone to run lines with her, Roy says.

Who? Allan picks up a small flat rock and throws it at the water, not trying to skip anything. Who would fucking work with that cunt?

Allan, come on, Roy says through a cloud of his own smoke. Don't be like that.

Well, that's what she is, he says, pretending to pout, then stamping on the water like a six-year-old. She treats people like shit. And forget about the stage manager or the ASM, they're completely burned out.

Allan is really pissed. He tries to roll up his wet pants a little more but gives up. Take a break from film I told myself, he says from the water. Get over the money issue. Get over the ego thing. Do something meaningful. So here I am doing the fucking Bard thing. But it's just not fun anymore. It's just not, I'm sorry.

Yeah, I know, Roy says. I appreciate your sacrifice.

Allan keeps going. We've been through a lot of projects, good and bad, and everything — up to now — has been fantastic. Honestly. I come up here expecting to do something fun, get away from the city for a while and feel good about things, and what do I get? What?

Roy puts his finger through the birdcage bars and tries to stroke Chekhov, but he's having none of it and shuffles away, a two-step on a wooden peg — wondering, like the rest of us I suppose, how he got here.

Life is too short to work on bad projects with bad actors, Allan says. And not only is she a bad actor, she's got bad manners. She feeds me lines when I haven't asked for them and gives me acting advice. Like, Wink at me more. Wink at me more! Fuck, what's that? It's pathetic.

What about me, Roy says.

What about you?

How do you think I feel?

Allan goes back to kicking waves but misses on purpose, stabbing the air with his toes. Fuck! Fuck!

I want to say fuck too but he's doing a great enough job for the both of us, all of them landing like grenades.

A big one. FUCK!

There's a pause, equally big. I want to say something but Roy puts a finger to his lips.

OK. I get it. I get it, I think.

Roy waits for Allan to actually look him in the eye. Allan waits for Roy to stop looking at him in the eye. It doesn't last long.

I'm here with two of my best friends doing the best play in the book, Roy says first, and I'm not having very much fun either. He pulls at the rim of his cap, careful not to stand anywhere near the water.

Directors aren't supposed to have fun, snaps Allan. You know that. He says this out in the lake for effect. Nice choice, I think.

Roy coughs, a long hacking one that takes over the sound of waves and wind.

Allan turns to look at me as I look away. You OK, Roy? he asks. Roy?

Roy stops the cough with great effort, only to slump down under the tree, the bamboo birdcage hanging over his head like a raised helmet. Chekhov whistles and everything seems to stop: Allan in the ankle-deep water, hands in his jean pockets. Me holding a low willow branch chest high, I don't know why. Roy trying to slowly un-slump under the dark trunk but mainly failing, curling into a ball, a small bunch of a man, his hand shaking out the glow coming from his unfinished cigarette.

Chekhov whistles again.

We move.

Allan toward Roy.

Me toward Roy.

But Roy gets up. Brushes off his knees, which is the normal thing to do when you get up off the ground, I suppose. He steadies himself in the dark embrace of the tree trunk, hands out in a mid-teeter balancing act even though the world is pretty rock-steady here in the Okanagan, especially down in the valley of the lake where the cool, clean night breeze straightens us out every few seconds.

I take another step and Allan matches me. We've got our hands out of our pockets, palms out like we're trying to corner a cat. Roy studies us. Something not quite right. He senses this. A quiet dread. We're slightly predatory — unintentionally, of course. It's just the way we are. Don't ask me to explain it. When a guy goes down, we're mostly happy it's not one of us.

I know Allan knows more than he's letting on. The rumours about Roy's health have been floating around the set for days. Allan beat a skin cancer scare years ago. A mole that wasn't became something that was. Now Allan is an expert on death and dying, does a cleanse every six months, the usual actor bullshit you hear on set.

Roy, I say. Roy?

Boys, boys, boys, Roy says. I'm OK. OK.

Fine.

Allan wants to hold him, I sense this, but he decides not to. Circles him briefly, his wet pants making wet pants sounds, until I say something.

I'll do it.

Roy and Allan both say, What?

You heard me. I'll run lines with Marlene. What do I care, I'm not part of this production and I've got nothing else to do. And I like her.

Allan moves toward me. Stands toe to toe with me. Studies me. Say again.

I like her. Really. She's ... different.

He huffs, turns on his heel like a German officer, and marches back to his mountain bike leaning against the front door of the B&B. He puts on his little helmet and flicks on his headlight, then pedals away into the dark. Fuck, fuck, fuck, he says as he goes, I imagine, all the way home.

Chapter 16

*H*ow *to describe* the fire? Like gathering bedlam. Lull before the storm and all that. An ordinary night at the start, slightly forgettable in fact.

We seemed ready for it. We were mostly packed, mostly not sleeping that well, mostly watching the horizon for the telltale flicker of orange. The scary birthday party over the horizon, as I called it. Watch for it, watch for it. I did for a while before hitting the sack, stared out the side window up the hill, through the trees around the house, across the vineyards. Where's it coming from? Where is it? Come on, show us the magic. But I couldn't see anything.

Roy told me earlier that if we were going to go, we were going to go. God's will and all that. To be clear, he's not a religious man, just stupidly superstitious.

He slept soundly. Though he usually sleeps soundly no matter what, mainly because he wears earplugs, an eye mask, and a mouthguard to protect his teeth. He was once a grinder, not very proud of it either, but now he can sleep with the best of them.

I drifted off without too much fuss. Didn't even try reading beforehand. Just off with the lights, head on the pillow, and that was it. Drifted off. Gone. Sleepy town.

Then suddenly coughing. Middle of the night. The smoke detectors go off, I mean all of them, in the whole house, all at once. BEEP-BEEP, BEEP-BEEP! Lots of screaming and pounding on doors. Somebody is yelling fire. Total cliché, but that's exactly what's happening. FIRE!

Chaos. Pandemonium. Sirens.

I fall out of bed, bump my elbow on the corner of the pine bedstand and knock over my glass of water. Can't find socks. Pants and shirt on in record time, like the first time I had sex except in reverse. Shoes, no problem. Pop them on and don't tie them, have them pre-tied because I'm German.

What do I do now? Where do I go?

I run into the hallway, shoed but sockless, pound on Roy's door, then just burst in. He sits up in bed like a mummy, wearing his black night mask and baseball cap. Who wears a baseball cap to bed? I try the light switch but nothing happens. The emergency lights from the hallway are on.

Are you awake, Roy?

Fuck, Roy says. What the fuck.

Out now, I say. Or shout. It's time, come on. Time to go!

More running around in the hallway. Katrina clumps down the stairs with an *X-Files* mother of a flashlight, prodding Almeera and Shamir, who already have their bags with them, ahead of her with the light. Please move down there, she says. Go on, go on.

I can see the tendrils of smoke along the ceiling moving toward the outside door, wrapping us up, I think, or trying to. A very long, very thin cobra.

Everybody, says Katrina. We have terrible emergency. Please come with me.

Roy, come on, I yell into his room again. Now!

He's already mostly dressed, cap off, standing in front of his mirror to check his hair even though it's almost totally dark.

Will you stop with the hair, Roy! I grab my stuff by the doorway, throw it over my back because it's easy to do with my duffel bag; I'm a light packer and thank God for that. Roy!

He sits on the bed now and pulls on his boots, gets them on very slowly, as if he's already burned his feet or something.

Shamir and Almeera are already out the door, dressed apparently for a wedding, white dress pants and suit jackets for both, with expensive digital cameras around their necks.

Almeera is on her cellphone. Yes, no, she says. I'm OK. Yes, it's a fire all right, and it's all very exciting.

Shamir waits for his wife to leave first. What kind of guy would remember to be chivalrous in the middle of a fucking house fire? He lets me go next.

Thank you, I mean, really, thank you very much, I say, pushing past him quickly. Very kind of you.

Fire! Run! Run!

I sorta sprint straight ahead, toward the flashing lights, thinking, Why is it we always run toward the lights and not away from them?

Smoke. I mean, smoke EVERYWHERE. Out, out into the little parking lot, where I see the fire truck and six or seven firefighters in full gear, headlights giving their reflective strips lots of action so they look — I date myself here — a little like characters from _Tron_.

Where's Roy? He's there by the doorway, a sad thin hunchback. He can barely lift his bags so he waves me over. He has his baseball cap back on. Thank Christ he remembered that.

Alex, can you give me a hand over here, can you? Alex?

I run back and grab a bag from him. Jesus. Why is his bag

so heavy? Then I remember the half dozen bottles of local Pinot Gris we purchased during our first week, extremely rare and good stuff you can't buy at any liquor store back in Vancouver.

To the vehicles, men! I shout. Move it! I scramble to the car. Fumble with the car keys trying to open the doors while Roy loses his baseball cap behind me and gropes around trying to pick it up out of the dirt. I pop the trunk, throw my bag and Roy's in, then try to get back to the front door. I shove a fire-fighter out of the way, only to discover firefighters shove back.

What the hell are you doing? she screams at me through her oxygen mask. Get away from the building!

Another firefighter grabs Roy's other bag, the lighter one that I find out later is filled with socks and underwear, and tosses it a few yards toward me. I notice Helmut coming from behind the house, feebly hosing down his roof with a garden hose. He's still in his housecoat and wearing rubber boots, pretending to be a superhero by scrambling up the slope around the house with the back of his robe flapping in the wind like a cape. Katrina pushes Roy out of the way with the front end of a very large suitcase, a 1940s leather job with straps. She still carries her giant flashlight in her free hand, probing the smoke looking for an opening.

Go, please, out, out, Katrina says, as if she's shooing cats off the bed.

Roy lurches, as only Roy can, down the driveway toward me, tripping every couple of steps on the large firehose that's snaking its way around the side of the house and is obviously not working yet because it's mainly flat, like a diabetic eel or something.

The female firefighter screams, WOULD SOMEBODY GET ME SOME PRESSURE, PLEASE!

Roy manages to carry his socks-and-underwear bag to me

and I heave it into the trunk with my knee, pushing it down with both hands before closing the lid. All our shit is in there. Plus Almeera and Shamir's because they couldn't find their car keys. You'd think that would be the one thing you would remember, but they didn't. Who cares, right? Their car is a rental, plus they had parked it down the lane toward the vineyard as a precaution. They don't seem concerned, and tell me later that their credit card will cover it, which gets me to thinking that maybe the fire was an act of God. You'd think God could have been a little less showy with the flames.

God, this is wild, Roy says, staring up at the fire coming down the hill toward us. It's crackling. I mean, it's really crackling. Popping. And look at that tree, look at how tall it is with the flames and everything. And God — look at that! LOOK!

I see him open the car door. Literally has one foot in one foot out, and a hand over his mouth like he's just caught a sneeze. Another truck shows up and then three more; smaller fire-fighters jump out and try to unwind an unwieldy hose from the back. It's a boa constrictor of a hose that knocks one firefighter over when they finally get it hooked up to the hydrant nearby. Another firefighter tries to open the valve, but he loses his footing and flips over the hydrant, knocking his helmet off. Another one comes to his aid but trips over the hose and nearly falls on top of him. They get up and both yank on the big wrench sticking straight up and straight out of the red hydrant like Excalibur, pulling with all their might to unstick the stuck valve.

What the fuck, Roy says, coughing. What the fuck. Did you see that? Slapstick comedy in a raging forest fire. Hilarious.

Smoke snakes down the hill toward us, lit at the top by the flames. The willow tree down at the water looks like it's try-ing to gather its skirt up to move away, but it can't because it's just a damn tree. A helicopter pounds the air above us, a long, giant pouch of water dangling underneath. Another helicopter hovers over the lake. Brilliant searchlights. God, I forgot my watch, probably sitting on the sink in the bathroom beside my toothbrush and that expensive dandruff shampoo I got before leaving Vancouver. I mean, who forgets their dandruff shampoo in an emergency?

Roy is more organized than me. He hasn't forgotten anything. Can you fucking believe this? he yells at me, waving the smoke away from his face. It's like *Blade Runner Director's Cut* out here.

Two short, stocky RCMP officers wander through the smoke. One of them has a ponytail. It's a she.

Anybody else in there?

No, says Helmut. No.

They sprint away toward their car at the end of the driveway, and I think, Wow, they can really run fast for short, stocky cops.

A firefighter without his oxygen mask moves toward us. He's a tall man with a handlebar moustache, big sideburns, little glasses.

This your car?

Yes, I say.

Well, get the fuck in it and start driving.

Where do I go?

Away from the fire, how about that? He goes off to help hold down a hose as it snakes to life, blasting water onto the roof and making Helmut's little garden hose obsolete. Helmut looks over at Katrina loading up their car with garbage bags of goods.

Where is the table? he yells.

Forget table, Katrina yells back. Go!

The table! Helmut bolts toward the door. The table!

A tall firefighter nearly clotheslines him and shoves him back toward our car, where Almeera and Shamir sit in the back seat with the bamboo birdcage between them. Chekhov is hopping mad, bobbing up and down, screaming, GET, GET, GET.

Helmut backs up into me, studying the way the embers cascade onto his roof from over the hill. Look at that, he says, Look at that! My God.

Glowing red flakes. A thousand pairs of glaring devil eyes. With each horrible gust, more come down. Some land behind us in the vineyard below, turning it into an infernal snowglobe. Above us, on the distant ridge, the roar and crackle of the beast as it devours pine trees with ease. Each gust of wind sends embers over the edge toward us. Then even more embers.

Helmut notices I'm caught in a trance. This is tragic! he yells. Very tragic. Please leave quickly.

Time to go, Roy, I yell.

The fire truck backs up, giving us a bigger opening out of the driveway.

Another firefighter jumps out of the truck cabin and waves a flashlight at us like he's on the airport runway directing jets. GO! GO! GO!

I hear more sirens and see a small regatta of powerboats reflected in the water. Cars are everywhere, headlights turning Hollywood, sweeping the night.

The firefighter with the flashlight runs toward us in his big boots, gracefully bunny-hopping over the snake pit of hoses now swollen with water around the parking lot. What's the matter with you folks? he says. Come on. He's a kid, maybe twenty years old, but the soot around his eyes gives him age. He pokes Helmut with the end of his foot-long flashlight. Let's go.

This is my house, Helmut yells at him. MY HOUSE!

I'm sorry, the firefighter yells back. Maybe we can save it but you HAVE to move out of the way. It's not safe here anymore. Do you understand NOT SAFE?

OK, OK, I will go, Helmut finally says, pulling his housecoat closed. It's then I see he isn't wearing any underwear. He gets in his vehicle behind us, a smaller SUV of some kind, where Katrina sits patiently waiting. I think she's smoking, but at this point who the hell cares.

The back of the house suddenly bursts into flames, but just before it can get going the firefighters douse it with water. It's a lot of water.

GO! GO! GO!

EVERYBODY! GO!

I get in my Mazda, bump my head on the way in. Roy plays with the radio. I think he's trying to find a news station, but then we hear You Ain't Seen Nothing Yet by BTO. What is it with this song? Why is everybody playing this fucking song?

Crank it, baby, Roy says. Let me crank it. And he does. Kelowna's favourite song of all time right now. He turns to me. Ready to roll?

Yeah, I'm ready, I say, kicking the car into gear.

Well, let's roll, baby.

So we do. Pull out of the parking lot together, tires spitting gravel, and race away from the fire, down the hill, through the waiting vineyards, onto the highway and toward the city. Behind us, in the rear-view mirror, the crest of the hill along the lake is lined with flames, the sky losing its dark in the process, dawn coming early.

We're in a movie, Roy yells. This is just like a movie! Wow! He turns around to get confirmation from the passengers in the back, but they're petrified. He says to me, They're petrified.

Me too, I say. That was a close call.

I've never felt so — I don't know, what's the word I'm looking for? Roy says. Vibrant?

So we leave it at that, follow the suv down the road to another road.

When the song is over, I turn off the radio and we hear nothing but the hum of tires. I have no clue where we're going, mainly because of all the smoke. I just follow Helmut's vehicle in front of me now, making note of the lack of working street-lights, the number of police cars redirecting traffic down the hills, the lineup of cars growing until we are barely moving by the time we hit our first major intersection. Some vehicles go left, some go straight ahead. Nobody is coming our way.

We just sit there and wait our turn behind a bunch of suvs and vans. It seems to take forever. A lull after the storm, for sure.

A bumper sticker on a mustard-yellow Mustang says, The End is Near … If You Want It.

Some people are out of the cars, pissing in the ditch. Mostly young people, I notice, mostly doing their business along a steel fence that outlines a huge empty field slated for development. A sign nearby announces in bold type, SOON TO BE THE NEXT HOME FOR WALMART. Someone, a teenager I suppose, has crossed out WALMART and added HELL.

Roy has fallen asleep again, his head lolling into his chin a little, cap now over his eyes and askew like it thinks he should be listening to rap.

We inch forward away from the flames, toward the dark lake. We go, and go a little bit more.

In the back seat, Shamir clears his throat. Does this occur often? he says.

Chapter **17**

The next day, we drive a short distance into town to our designated short-term lodging. We're to stay at three small cabins near the water, apparently closed down for redevelopment. They've reopened them for us, they being the Emergency Measures people.

We met them at the elementary school gym that morning: tidy Muppet-like retirees with smiles glued to their wrinkled faces like they were with some happy-happy cult, like the Scientologists or something.

My name is Mabel, how do you feel this morning?

My name is Oscar, how was the smoke last night? Did you have difficulty breathing?

My name is Vern, can we give you some cash to hold you over for a day?

Roy turned to me. What do you think, hundred bucks each?

Vern pulled on his bow tie. Yes, he was wearing a skinny black cowboy bow tie and a Mennonite hat.

We're only allowed to give you twenty-five dollars. That's all we could get from the bottle drive.

I'm sorry, Roy said. Did you actually do a bottle drive for us?

Oh no, Vern said. Our grandkids did that. We don't have the fucking legs for it anymore.

Roy smiled. It lasted the whole drive down and around the lake to our worn-out little grey cabins sitting in long, off-green grass near the water's edge. At one time they were quaint, even promising, but now they're just disillusioned. The lake recedes with each passing year, leaving a bald patch of sand and small pebbles instead of a well-defined beach. But the cabins are the best we've got for now.

Our emergency representative, a compact man with a slight lisp named Glenn with two en's, tells us that the city of Kelowna was experiencing extreme demands on vacancy.

He's waiting there in the parking lot beside his car, a hybrid that I think is grey, but might just be covered in soot.

Glenn is a talker.

We don't have a lot of room because of the cherries, he says. Have you had some cherries? You should try some before the peaches start up because once the peaches start nobody touches the cherries. Then we get pears which I personally think are the best fruit we grow but tell that to all the cherry pickers, right? That's what we call them, cherry pickers. The retired people who drive down from Alberta. Or Quebec teens. The screwed-up ones. They come here by the thousands in the summer. Like locusts. Descend on us. Is that the right word — descend? Yes? Well, whatever. Those guys sure love their fruit, that's all I'm saying. I love your budgie and Chekhov is a great name. Brill. Absolutely brill.

I just love listening to you talk, says Roy from the back seat. He wants us all to sit in the car so he can hear better, but the heat in here is killing me.

That makes two of us, sweetie, says Glenn with two en's,

doing a wink-wink thingy and leaning into the open door. And by the way, I'm the only person who ever calls me Glenn with two en's, so don't get any ideas.

A snicker from Roy. A snicker? Roy nods at me. Yes.

A sign beside the cabins: Closed For Redevelopment. Bayside Park Resort Condos Start at Just Under 400.

Four hundred?

Thousand, says Glenn. But they're two bedrooms.

But they're condos, right?

Exciting, isn't it, Glenn says. I put down a deposit. In four years I'll be throwing a party on my balcony right over there. He points to the sky. Sort of, he says. Second cloud to the right. Dare to dream.

The cabins, once called Waterside Cabins, were closed last summer, but the developer was waiting for financing. Because of the emergency, the city was able to temporarily use them for lodging people displaced by the fire. So far over a hundred need new places to stay, including a bunch of temporary residents like us.

Roy finally gets out of the car. We wander around looking the cabins over, sweating a lot. Fuck it's hot. Too hot.

Glenn is extremely happy to hear about our theatrical extravaganza in the vineyard. Wow, he says, somebody should have thought of that years ago. That's exactly what we need in this town, some culture, because they've got the Elvis celebration on the other side of the lake in Penticton and what do we have, fruit and wine. It's a little embarrassing. I mean, sometimes we get a few Elvii up for the weekend but they don't sing here. Nobody does.

They've built a stage just down from the parking lot, Roy explains. You can see the lake on the other side and when the sun sets it looks like the vineyards are golden.

Oh, that's simply perfect, Glenn says. I'm coming to the opening. When is it?

Thursday, says Roy.

Glenn giggles. Wonderful. I hope there's a ticket left somewhere.

Roy gives him tickets from his wallet. I get six comps but I don't have six friends, he explains. I mean, at my age, right?

You're kidding, right, says Glenn. What are you, thirty-five?

Add ten years. About ten years.

Well, you still look like a thirty-something to me. Must be doing something right, right? You're all skin and bones.

Thanks.

Macrobiotic diet? Raw food diet? What is it?

Cancer mainly, Roy says. With lots of red wine at night.

Oh, you slay me, Glenn says, as we finally pull our luggage out of the back of my car. This is so incredible, he continues. Unbelievable. I can't believe it. I just can't believe it. I'm going to a play. Wow. Here are your keys. You fellows are sharing the middle one. Our Indian friends from the UK are in the other one. Somebody is driving them over after we feed them a decent breakfast. And by the way, that smaller cabin is not habitable because of the rodent infestation. So try to stay out of there; they've set traps. Here's the number of your host, Rachel. If you need anything like towels or something, she'll get it for you. Thank you, thank you. Break a leg. See you at the opening. And I'm really sorry your B&B burned down. Have a nice stay with us. I love you all. Bye.

He leaves in his hybrid, soundlessly. I notice that he's not wearing a shirt under his hi-viz safety vest, and that he's cut. I mean, really cut. Like a weightlifter or something.

We try the keys Glenn gave us, fiddle with the lock for a bit, finally get the door open, and walk in. It's a small cabin with stained pine everywhere. Feels like I'm standing in a Swedish sauna, actually.

Yeah, says Roy. It's a granny cabin.

Yes, it is, I say, throwing my gak down on the big queen-size bed with the tan quilt on top. I slide Roy's heavy bag off my left shoulder and push it against the wall. The bottles clink.

This place is perfect for parents, Roy says.

Retro, I say. Like '60s or '70s or something.

The linoleum is lime green or off-lime green. Ripped in places, mostly near the stove, which only has two burners. A sign on it says PLEASE AVOID USE, NO GAS. There's a smell in the air. Pine-Sol, or a combination of menthol cigarettes — twenty years' worth — and cleaning solution. A horrible side of lemon.

The TV on a small writing desk in the corner also has a sign on it: FOR PERSONS WITH DISABILITIES ONLY. It's done with black felt pen on goldenrod. This sign confuses me.

Another small table, beside us, with enough room on it for two dinner plates. It's made of pine too. Someone has etched LOVE DGL on the corner facing the counter. Probably used a small paring knife.

Roy says, Where's my bed?

Try the back room, I say.

In the back, beside a room heater, is a small bed, actually more like a cot, almost military, with a threadbare blanket on it and a very small pillow, like from a couch or something.

Roy kicks at the bed with his boot and dust billows up. Yeah, I'll be OK on that all right, he says, throwing his clothes bag on the floor with a thud. He carefully hangs the bamboo birdcage with Chekhov on a hook beside a painting of dog, I think a bloodhound of some kind.

You think he'll be OK with the dog? I ask.

Trust me, Chekhov knows the difference between what's

art and what's life, Roy says, backing up to admire his bird's plumage. Isn't he beautiful, just isn't he?

Yes, he is, I say.

Chekhov seems a little too relaxed. He cocks his head back and forth, picking up his feet like he has popsicle sticks attached to his body, walking across the bottom of his newspaper-lined cage.

What's he doing down there? I ask.

Reading the sports section. What else?

Birds can't read, I say. This much I know.

Dreaming then, Roy says. All birds must dream because of the possibility of flight, don't you think?

Almeera and Shamir knock on the open door behind us, silhouetted against the sun glinting off the water.

Angels, Roy says, shielding his eyes. Look at them.

And they are, still wearing white pants and white shirts, white shoes even. Bronze skin. Toned but not too big. Long fingers and soft eyes, golden too. They aren't even breathing hard. Or breathing, period.

Sorry to be such a bother, Shamir says softly.

No, no bother, I say. Come on in.

No. Thank you. But would it be too much to borrow some towels? Shamir asks. They have left us with only one large towel in our cabin and my wife feels we need slightly more.

Roy digs out a blue towel from his bag. Here, I took an extra one from the last place we stayed by mistake. It's yours. He tosses it across the room.

Shamir catches it cleanly in mid-air. Pulls it to his face and takes a deep breath. Beautiful, he says. Beautiful.

～

Marlene meets me at the actors' tent in the morning. I haven't slept much.

Inconvenient mess, she says. This whole thing.

Come on, the show is coming along, I say. Isn't it?

I meant the damn fire, sweetie, she says, putting an elastic in her hair to keep it from flying around.

There's a wind tunnel effect in the tent because both ends are open. One end faces the lake, the other the vineyard, and we get a gust every few seconds. Cool wind, still tainted with night, dewy even, but warming up. It throws paper around the tent — abandoned scripts I guess, because almost everyone is off book — and the effect is a little like snowflakes on steroids, or noisy, drunken bats looking for a place to hang.

Smoke in the air all the time now, Marlene says. You can see the flames across the lake all day. She knocks back an iced tea she bought at the 7-11 down the road from the winery.

What did they say about it today?

Well, it burned down seventeen houses and one small winery, the Marquis, at the top of the hill. But it's contained, unless the wind picks up again — and then who knows?

How far is it from here?

I don't know. Ten, fifteen kilometres, at least. It can't cross the lake, but it can go around, through town, and that wouldn't be good, right?

Right, I say.

Fires scare me, Marlene says. Wake up screaming sometimes. You know, sweating, fists clenched.

She picks up her backpack from the props table, knocking a sword to the ground. She picks it up and places it somewhere on the table. I hope it goes there, she says. Was it there?

Yeah.

Jessica sees us from the back, where she's sweeping up potato chip bags and coffee cups. The clatter probably got her looking. You guys OK over there? she asks.

Yes, thank you, sweetie, Marlene says, waving her backpack, a moment. She adjusts the sword on the table to point toward the lake. Perfect.

Marlene sniffs the smoky air briefly. Yes, there it is, there it is. You smell it?

I sniff, but weakly. A half-snort thing. I grew up in the country and sometimes this same smell drifted over from a nearby farm, the same farm we got all our discounted chickens from.

What were we talking about, Mr. Playwright? Marlene says. Dreams? YES! Thank you. Have I told you yet? Have I? A dream of running in the forest and falling, getting up and running again in slow motion, like your feet are caught in taffy, and the flames catch up and your only choice is to dive from a cliff except you can't swim and it's night and you have no idea how long it will take before you hit water.

Now, my Titania, I say, reading from the script, wake you, my sweet queen.

Oh please, not here, Marlene hushes. I have an idea where we can run lines in private.

So we leave the stage area where Roy is working with our Bottom, trying to get him to project from behind his ass mask. It's a hoary thing, made of horsehair and chrome, and it lends him a real sci-fi feel.

God, that thing is disgusting, Marlene says. Try kissing through all that. It's a little like trying to kiss the alien from that *Alien* movie, you know what I mean.

We walk down the path around the main part of the winery, to the back, where a guest house sits surrounded by rows and rows of new vines. Isn't this house cute? she says.

It looks Swiss, I say. With the red roof and everything.

Well, don't tell Steven that, he wanted it to look Spanish.

Inside the house it's all white. White drop cloths on furniture surrounded by white walls, and even a white painting, huge in a black frame, with a single bloody red square in the centre.

The painting is about war and what war does to our lives, please don't touch it, Marlene says, throwing her backpack down on the huge dining room table, also painted white. IKEA. Just screams it.

What is this place? I say.

Our maid's, she says, but she's visiting her parents in the former Yugoslavia. I'm not sure what part. Croatia, Bosnia, one of those, I have no idea. She's back in October after the harvest. What do you think? It cost about half a million to build.

It's very white in here, I say, sitting on the huge white couch in front of the huge white fireplace, empty and clean of course.

The upstairs is all blue, Marlene says. You should see the bathroom. Cobalt. Very vibrant, which is exactly how I would describe her. Never hugs anybody but talks a blue streak and tells everybody that she loves them, you know, I love you, my friend. I must love you. You have such spirit and beauty. It's all very Eastern European bullshit.

Right.

It's true, Marlene says. She's like that. It's wonderful.

Did you want to start with the end and then go to the beginning, I say, because Roy told me you have less trouble starting out that way.

Marlene does a ballet twirl in the middle of the huge sunken living room, pretending, I think, that she's at centre ice in a huge skating rink. Endings are always hard for me, she says. That's why I let men break up with me. I don't have the heart for it.

Wow, this is a big house, I say, feeling my way along the long white couch, smoothing out the leather with my palms.

Two thousand square feet on the main floor alone, Marlene says. Three car garage. Wine cellar, of course. Hardwood floors upstairs. Berber carpet here. Real Berber carpet, not that fake IKEA shit, and by the way none of this is IKEA so don't make any judgments, particularly since I helped with the layout and design. And oh yeah, it has a very nice Jacuzzi upstairs in the bathroom. Four jets and a built-in stereo. You'd love it.

Home away from home, I say.

Well, this is actually her home, Marlene says. Where she's from is not where she wants to go. Just like the rest of us, right? Although she's there now. You should hear her war stories. Her brother was hit by shrapnel. In the leg. Limps all the time when it rains. Something about the bone.

What's your maid's name? I ask.

First or last?

Sure, I say.

I can't say her last name, Marlene says. But her first name is Una.

Uma?

No, Una.

Not like in Thurman?

What's a Thurman?

A big star.

Are you into astrology? So is Steven, says Marlene. You're a lot alike, except for the hands. His look like a farmer's.

Uma Thurman. *Kill Bill*. Know what I mean?

Who's Bill?

God. At this point, I get up and move to another white leather couch, stare at the white wall behind it and try to imagine a painting hanging there, one with some fucking colour other than red.

I try another angle. What kind of stuff does your maid do?

Oh, she's a painter, do you like her work? It's that white thing on the wall with the red thing in the middle. The war painting. I think that's the official title too. *The War Painting!* Exclamation point. The red is actual blood. I didn't ask whose. Marlene smiles widely.

I turn to study the large painting. It doesn't grab me.

Interesting painting. What does your maid do for you work-wise? I ask.

Cleans my house and makes sure I'm eating right when I'm not, that kind of thing. I binge on cheese. It was my first word as a child. It's an addiction. Particularly aged cheddar. Una also walks my dogs. Excellent with animals of all kinds.

I didn't know you had dogs, I say, now touching the red patch in the middle of the painting. A little piece falls off. I rub it out on the carpet with my shoe. It leaves a tiny spot on the off-white Berber. Walk away, I think. Walk away. Nonchalant. Very who-cares. Don't look, never look. What's she doing?

Marlene isn't looking. Good. Now she's lying on the carpet pretending to make a snow angel, eyes closed and breathing out like she's in the water. Ouff. Ouff. Ouff.

You OK over there? I ask.

Yeah, she says. It's my back.

So, who's taking care of your dogs while you're doing the show? I ask.

My dogs, Frankie and Vibe, are at my ex-husband's for the month. They're little angels.

I didn't know you had an ex.

Everybody has an ex or two, right? Even you, right? Come on, spill, Mr. Playwright. Spill.

What kind of dogs? I say.

Australian Shepherds.

Oh.

They're smarter than most actors, trust me. They know their blocking, that's for sure. Come, go, lie down, sit, around.

Really.

Are you a dog person? Because that's important to me.

Sure, I say.

Do you have a dog?

Not yet, I say. But soon. Like when I get married and settle down.

Oh, that's so old fashioned, Marlene says. And that's what I like about you. I suppose you're waiting for the right girl to come along too.

I study the ultra-clean fireplace in front of me. I don't think it's ever been used.

Marlene sees me look it over. You're right, she says, it's never been used. Una's a neat freak, if you haven't figured that out by now. That's why everything is shrouded. But she's a maid and that's what maids do. It's a little pathetic actually. I think she needs professional help.

I run a finger along the top of the fireplace and it leaves a greasy streak. I wipe at it with a Kleenex I dig out of my pocket.

I'm very excited about tonight, Marlene says, now going to the fridge to pick out a nice bottle of reserve Chardonnay. Our preview. Our one and only preview. I hope it goes well.

But it would be a good thing to remember your lines, I say. That's why we need to run them.

Marlene drifts back into the living room, carrying the bottle in one hand and two champagne flutes in the other. Couldn't find any proper glasses so these will have to do, she says, popping the cork. We're always drinking from the wrong glasses, have you noticed? I wonder if that means anything.

We shouldn't be drinking.

Why not? she says.

Well, aren't we working?

Come on, I have a glass or two before every rehearsal, it helps me relax, she says, wiping her hands off on her blue jeans. Here.

She hands me a flute, brimming, of course, with Chardonnay. We clink. Wink. Drink.

She says, You have to maintain eye contact while drinking.

Because of the poison, I say.

What poison? she says.

I'm talking about the tradition, you know, of clinking.

She says, God, you're confusing me. Just drink.

So we do. I study the room. Where to begin, where to begin?

It's over-chilled, she says, studying her still-full flute. Over-chilled, what do you think? She pokes me with her toe. In the ribs, from the floor, where she seems to gravitate to. Splayed in an elegant way, feet up, a slight arch to her back, arms on either side grabbing handfuls of carpet like they were bunches of hair. Her toes. Pink of course. Pink like nipples. Pointed toward me, bent like question marks. Very, very sexy, oh my God.

At this point I'm sweating even though the house is very cool. Cheeks are red. Ears redder. Dry mouth. Very dry, so I gulp more wine and try not to choke. Pour more, pour it steady — don't look up at her. Don't look. No look. NO! Pretend-cough. Clear you throat. Scratch your head. Rub eyes. No, never touch the eyes. Hands on script. Hands on script!

Nervous, are you, Marlene laughs. Well, I don't bite. Well, just on occasion, if you follow me.

I open the script to the back. Page absentmindedly. Lick my index finger and pretend to look for a line or two, until finally:

Be as thou wast wont to be;

See as thou wast wont to see.

Dian's bud o'er Cupid's flower

Hath such force and blessed power.

I stop because my Queen is now doing Pilates on the floor. Why are you stretching your front? I ask.

To open up my back, Marlene says. You don't do Pilates, do you?

No, no I don't.

Marlene stretches right in front of me. Using her flute of Chardonnay as incentive, she pulls forward to take a slow deliberate sip each stretch, closing her eyes to savour the flavour in a wine snob kind of way. Finally she puts the flute on the coffee table in front of us, slides it over to the middle like it's a curling rock. Let me tell you, she says, Pilates saved my life twice. She pushes her hair back out of her face, spits some of it out of her mouth. Oh God, have you ever swallowed your own hair?

No, I say. What's it like?

Pass, she says, closing her eyes again and reaching out, reaching slowly out, to grab her left foot with her right hand. Ugh, she says. Ugh.

Can we get to work? I say. It's after ten. You have Italian this afternoon.

What's Italian?

A very fast line run, I say. Twice the speed as normal.

Yeah, let me work this out first. I need to feel centred or else I can't remember anything.

Where were we? I say, paging through the script.

Pilates, she says. For my fucked-up back. I was skiing once and fell on my ass. That was the first time. The second was when I tried to pick up my partner to carry him out of the house. We were playing this game: can you carry your one true love out of a burning building? You ever done that?

No, I say.

Well, let me tell you, someday you might have to, Marlene says, pulling her head down to her knee, then up again. Anyway,

I really fucked up my back then and told Steven that I would never carry him again period. I think he was a little upset because he's always trying to carry me. He's a little obsessed with me as you can probably tell.

How's that?

Hey Oberon, what visions have I seen! Methought I was enamour'd of an ass. She says this to the ceiling, head back and neck straining.

I'm staring at her breasts again, I know I am. I hold the script up in front of my face like a Trojan shield.

Are you listening back there? says Marlene. Methought I was enamor'd of an ass, OK?

There. Lies. Your. Love, I say, reading like Stephen Hawking, then peeking over the top of the page. She still has her eyes closed, a hurdler's stretch on the floor now. She bobs down to her knees and then up again. Bobs down, then up. Down, up. Down.

Hey, dude, I'm waiting, she groans into her crotch.

I said my line, it's your turn, I say.

Right, right. Marlene looks up and pulls at her bra under a very tight T-shirt with faded print on it. INDIAN, it says. The motorcycle company I guess.

God, this bra is painful, Marlene says. Too damn small. OK, OK — don't tell me. I got it. How came these things to pass? O, how mine eyes do loathe his visage now! Thank you, thank you. Next! She drinks quickly, first giving the wall a little toast, cheers, and then snapping her head back, the whole flute downed. Puts the glass down on the white IKEA-type coffee table in front of her, pours more wine from the bottle beside. Wow, she says. What are we drinking again, my dear?

Chardonnay I think, I say, tasting a little. I think. Keeping my eyes on my script.

I think.

Why are we doing this when we should be doing other things? I say, and immediately regret it. Because, of course, it sounds like I'm hitting on her.

Are you hitting on me? Marlene asks.

What do you think, I say.

Oh, is that the story you're going with? she says. Have you done this a lot, you know, with other actors? Run lines before? On a play like this? Then suggest something else? Something like sex?

No, I say.

Are you staring at my breasts again? Oh God, men.

Please, Marlene, I say, putting down the script. I'm not staring at anything. Can we continue? Please?

Sure. Whatever you say. She gets up. Stretches, standing. Touches her toes. Side-to-side stretch. Walks over. No, saunters. She has a runway model wobble thing going on. All hips and foot thrusts and there she is sitting beside me and smelling like, like —

Green tea.

Green tea?

Yes, Marlene says. I got it in Vancouver last month. Body Shop, you ever been? They have smells in there that take you to places you've never been and I hate perfume normally, gets me nauseated, but this stuff, oh this stuff, it's magical — really seduced me. Dab a little on your wrists. Here.

Of course she holds her wrists out. And of course I sniff them. And get more weird. And more sweaty. And —

What seduces you? Marlene whispers. Come on. What?

This time she pokes me with a finger. Not in the ribs, if you know what I mean. She leans forward as if trying to block my view with her face. I try to put the script down and it falls off the coffee table onto the floor.

Clumsy, she says right into my left eye. Or are you just happy to see me?

I stand up.

What's wrong?

Out the front room window, Jessica is waving a red towel. Waving at us? Waving at what? Down there, on the stage. What is she doing? What?

Marlene says, Maybe something's wrong? Maybe somebody had a heart attack? Who could it be? Who?

And suddenly I can't breathe.

Chapter 18

We sit *outside* the hospital on the warm steps leading into emergency. Jessica has an unlit cigarette in her hand and she's dissecting it by removing the filter. It's not hers because she doesn't smoke. She took it away from a patient hooked to an IV outside, claiming she was a doctor and that she was thoroughly disgusted. The patient, a thin, elderly Chinese man with hairless legs, just gave it up.

Yeah, that was easy, Jessica says. Just sound official, like, Excuse me, do you think we allow smoking, asshole?

Please tell me you didn't call him an asshole, Jessica, I say.

Oh, come on, you really think a patient should smoke? she says.

What if it doesn't matter? I say.

Well, it matters to me, she says. I have to breathe out here too. She jumps up and wanders down to the metallic garbage bin at the curb to deposit the remains of the cigarette, does a pretend slam dunk, then stomps back, arms crossed, pouting a little again. It's an attractive pout, trust me.

I take a swig from an iced tea I nipped from the maid's house earlier. Green tea with a hint of mint.

Where'd you get the iced tea?

Marlene, I say.

Yeah, Jessica says. You like her?

I like her.

Don't like her too much, she needs to concentrate tonight. She's barely off book. Barely. How'd the line run go?

It came and went, I say.

Did she get any better?

Yes and no, I say.

If she doesn't improve we're going to die a horrible death out there. And, guess what, Allan hates her — I mean really hates her.

She's going to be OK, I say. It's only the ending that I'd worry about. And she has all day today and tomorrow to get it down. I hand my bottle over to Jessica and she pulls back her hair to take a long, long swig. I watch her neck muscles work out each glug. Nice, nice swallows. She finishes the bottle. I mean finishes it.

Thanks, I needed that, she says, handing it back. Oh, did you want some more? Sorry. Didn't know. Oh well, what time is it?

It's ten after.

Ten after?

One.

God, we're supposed to be doing Italian right now. Everybody will be waiting. Can I use your cell?

I left it at the cabin. Sorry.

No wonder you didn't answer, I was trying to phone you when the ambulance came. Those idiots couldn't find us, I had to wave them in. Allan was freaking out and wanted to ride in the ambulance but I told him not to. I don't think Roy likes him much anymore.

What happened to your phone?

I don't want to use up my minutes. I'm pay as you go. She pulls out her phone on cue, texting like mad.

Oh my God, my friend is horny.

What?

You should see what she just sent me. Very immature.

Lemme see, I say.

Jessica grins. Oh, grow up. Then she suddenly groans, turns off the phone, and pockets it quickly, like it's a Derringer or something. Some friends, she says, are just too weird. Right?

Right. Why aren't the actors texting you? I ask.

I know, I know, she says. Are they superficial or what, God I'm hot why is it so hot out here I'm dying for an iced cappuccino are you?

I nod. Didn't follow much of that really. Oh well.

A doctor or intern, also on his cell, scoots out for a second, stethoscope around his neck like a boa. His red hair sticks out from his operating room cap like he's a friend of Bozo. I say this out loud, hoping for a laugh.

Jessica looks at me a little confused. I thought Bozo was a dog's name, she says.

It's a clown, I say.

A clown dog?

Just a clown. From tv. Or something.

I should just Google it, she says.

The doctor suddenly races back in.

What happened with Roy? I ask.

Jessica sighs. He was having trouble breathing, turning grey — well, more grey — and coughing a lot, I think because of all the extra smoke in the air, and then he just bent over and couldn't stand up, started making wheezing sounds. That's when I made the call. I don't think he was happy when I did that but I had to.

You did the right thing, I say.

Yeah, I know, but God was he pissed, she says. But he couldn't argue much because he couldn't breathe much.

It's hot, really hot on the steps because we're almost entirely in the sun, which hangs directly over our heads, cooking us from head to toe on the very warm concrete.

I'm boiling, I say. Let's go in.

Jessica pouts. Look, can we — please, I hate hospitals. They make me all weird. Plus there's a lot of really nasty germs in there, and we're about to open. I can't have a bunch of sick actors. That would be a disaster.

Right.

I steal a glance at her top, a black rock-and-roll-tour T-shirt with NINE INCH NAILS in big white letters across the top. Where'd you get the shirt? I ask.

Old boyfriend, she says. He was a roadie but terrible in bed, so I dumped him for a woman. That's when I was in my bicurious stage. It didn't last.

Another Chinese man wearing hospital blues stumbles out of the hospital, trailing an IV stand behind like it's an anchor or a kite. He moves down the slight wheelchair access ramp, making sure to keep the IV wheels from hitting his slipper heels, and stops at the end of the sidewalk to light up a smoke, throwing the match out toward an idling white taxi on the road in front. He stares at the ambulance that sits twenty feet or so away under the awning where the sliding doors open to emergency — the same ambulance Roy came in over an hour ago, holding his chest, not coughing, just holding his chest, a claw hold on his jacket.

What do you think is wrong? Jessica asks.

You mean you don't know? I say.

Know what?

He's been having some lung problems lately.

Well, that's no shocker. Smoke two packs a day and you'll end up like my old man: dead. Smoked for thirty years, my father. Thirty fucking years, and then he expected me to have kids so he could show up at their birthday parties and soccer games. Yeah, right.

I sense a little anger, I say, venturing into uncharted territory.

Yes, Alex, and that's why I'm such a good stage manager, she says with the fakey smile again. You work with bipolar, passive-aggressive actors long enough and you soon develop a good sense of anger. It's the only thing they fucking understand.

She gets up and moves toward the patient smoking beside the cab, but before she can do anything he stubs out his smoke and shuffles past us to go back in, banging his iv against the back of his bony grasshopper legs. Sighing, Jessica bends down to pick up the stubbed smoke like it's a legless white bug, and deposits the remains in the nearby garbage bin. She wipes her hands off on her very short blue jean cut-offs and stomps, yes, stomps back to me. Asshole number two, she says. No concern for the environment.

Why do you stomp? I say.

I don't stomp, she says.

Yes you do, you smack your feet down like you're totally pissed, I say.

It's just these sandals, Jessica says. They're very Roman.

I look at her feet, her beautiful, stunning feet, and yes indeed, the long leather straps snaking up and around her perfectly thin ankles make the sandals look Roman.

God, where'd you get those?

Italy. Where else?

I hold my iced tea bottle up to block the sun so I can look at Jessica's face without wincing. She's smiling for real now, and it's a smile that goes on forever. I love our conversations, I say aloud.

Jessica tilts her head and explains that we don't have conversations, we have exchanges. Look, she adds, if we had actual conversations, I'd have to break up with Ashton.

Who's Ashton? I say.

She punches me on the arm right above my elbow and it's a stinger, going to leave a mark which, frankly, I'm going to be happy about. You do this to me every time, Alex, she laughs.

The ambulance attendants, both balding and slightly overweight, come out of the building through the sliding emergency doors pushing their stretcher thingy.

What do they call those things again? I ask.

Gurneys, says Jessica.

Gurney is a funny word, I say. You'd think I would remember it.

Gurney.

Gurney, gurney, gurney.

They hear us.

Shut up, I say.

You shut up, she says.

Gur-ney.

The attendants fold up the stretcher and slam it into the ambulance van, then give us a parental look, a glare actually, and get in.

They hate us.

Could be one of their names, she says. Lloyd Gurney, ambulance driver extraordinaire. And his younger brother, Gordon Gurney, who rides shotgun.

You're funny, I say. Please be my girlfriend so I can find meaning in life.

You wish, she says, feigning another punch before rubbing my arm. It's OK, big fella. It's OK. I won't hurt you.

As the ambulance fellows drive off we notice both attendants are lighting cigarettes. Furiously even.

Typical, says Jessica. Very typical. She flips them the bird. They don't see it.

I get up to deposit the iced tea bottle in the garbage.

I wouldn't do that, says Jessica. It's recyclable.

It's OK, I say.

No it's not, she says. Here, give it to me. I'll take it back to the set. We have a blue bin there.

Oh shucks, I say. You are so mean today.

Come on, Mister. Give it to me. Give it right now or else you in big trouble, Señor.

What movie is that from? I ask.

What movie? she says.

What you were doing.

I'm not doing anything or anyone — yet, she says.

Ha ha, I say.

Right on, she says. Right on.

I saunter back, trying to be very, very casual, mainly attracted by her sense of humour and her personality and not her legs, which I've barely noticed even though she's wearing incredibly short shorts that went out in the '80s but who cares, right, she makes them work, and I'm not attracted to them, trust me. That would be very shallow. Very.

Jessica holds out an arm and I see the tattoo just below her right elbow on the inside. A small Asian symbol or something.

She notices me notice. I think it means hope, she says, rubbing it slightly with her left hand. Ashton got it for me last year when we were in Calgary.

Oh, what were you doing there?

Getting married.

I contemplate throwing the bottle down but I don't. I had

no idea, I say, giving over the bottle. She retracts her arm and the tattoo disappears. I want to sit down but decide against it, just pace a bit instead. After all, I am waiting outside a hospital, aren't I? Now I just have to think of a normal thing to say, something intelligent, hopefully.

You and Ashton, married, I say. Wow and double wow.

Yeah, well, he's very religious so we did it in a church and I was hoping nobody would find out, so please shut your trap about it, Jessica says. You have this reputation.

What?

For talking too much and then adding embellishments.

Bullshit, I say. Then I wait. But she doesn't respond. Finally: OK, what part do you want me not to talk about, Jessica, the part about getting married, or the part about getting married in a church?

I don't want anybody to know we're married, she says, because Ashton is back in Vancouver doing another show and I'm having a lot of fun here. Well, up to now I *was* having a lot of fun. Anyway, I like to think of myself as being in an open relationship.

And Ashton?

He'll get used to it, she says. Although we haven't really discussed it too much yet.

Right, right.

I mean, let's face it, she says, the reason we all get into relationships is for security, and maybe also to have a great time. I really like having security but I also want to party. Right?

For the first time ever, I think Jessica might not be as bright as I once thought. It's tragic. Is your tattoo Japanese? I ask.

I have no idea, I was kinda drunk at the time. She laughs, throwing her hair back for effect.

Confirmed.

What's confirmed? she asks.

Oh, what I was thinking, I say, and immediately regret it.

Thinking what? she asks, pulling at her ear.

I look up at the first floor windows and see a child staring out at me, a little girl I think, with an enormous bandage around her head that makes her look like a tiny Bedouin. She waves at me. I wave back and get a smile. A young mother with long golden hair pulls her away from the window and snaps down the shade.

Thinking what? she asks again.

That you're a party girl, I say.

Gosh darn, I hope you mean that in a nice way, she says.

Oh, you know me, I say.

Oh, I know you all right. I can hardly wait to hear what you're going to say if you write me into one of your plays.

Jessica, I would never do that to you, I say. I like you too much.

Even now that I'm married?

Sure, I say. Absolutely.

Good, she says. Because I like you too. You're very immature for your age. Reminds me of my dad a little. Before he left us.

Ouch.

I sit down again, plopping like a ten-year-old and immediately regretting it because my ass hurts from the hot cement. It's going to be a bone bruise, I just know it.

Jessica puts the bottle on the cement between her legs, lets the neck touch both thighs. I want to say something here but decide not to. She plays with her hair, pulling it up then letting it fall down her back, as if gravity will make it shine better. Incredibly, it does. She then whips out her cellphone again and checks for new texts. None. Disappointed, she snaps it back into her pocket.

We sit there.

What's really wrong with Roy? she finally asks. And tell me the truth.

Well, I don't know what I can say, I tell her. I mean, if he hasn't told you, then he hasn't told you for a reason, right?

Just tell me: is it serious? Jessica grabs my right wrist and pulls it toward her. I let my arm go limp, hoping somehow she'll direct it to her legs or thighs or thereabouts, but she drops it on my knee thank you very much.

Define serious, I say.

Like dying, she says. How's that?

I squirm, and why not? This is the time to squirm.

Well? she asks. Is he? Alex?

And it's at that very moment that Roy walks out holding his jacket in his arms like it's a baby, looking robust and healthy and even a little cocky.

Hi, guys, he says loudly. Waiting long?

⌒

Anxiety attack. I know, I know. Hard to believe but there you have it.

Roy tells us in the car that the doctor couldn't find anything wrong that wasn't wrong already. Jessica doesn't find this amusing. Roy also tells us that he has decided no more goddamn smoking. She perks up a little.

With all the smoke already in the air, who needs a cigarette? he says as we drive through the downtown core fighting traffic all the way.

Jessica says, I know, I know. That's what I say.

Tons of cars on the road, big Winnebagos, Airstreams, Dodge half-tons. It's hot, the air tainted with the smell of fireplaces and barbecues and singed forests. The scent of the freshwater lake is almost gone, except for along the beach, where wafts of warm, stale fish gust into the car. Most of the traffic is going one way, our way. People are moving from one side of the enormous lake to the other, away from the flames, to better vantage points, safer campsites, bed and breakfasts that haven't burned down yet. We have the car windows wide open but it's not enough — the wind is hot too, like it's from the Panhandle. No clouds in the sky on one side of the lake; on the other, a dense black plume rises several thousand feet in the air before flattening, ironed out by high-altitude winds so that it looks like an anvil. Helicopters and planes constantly butterfly in and out of the smoulder to drop dirty water and then to get out, scoop some more up out of the blue ribbon of the lake, and return.

It's a losing battle, the radio announcer tells us between songs. Tells us that the next one will be U2 and it's dripping with irony, hey, guess the album. I don't get it, but then I'm not sure I get U2 either.

Jessica turns off the radio, from the back seat if you can believe it. Fuck, I hate pop, she says, then throws herself back on the seat bumping her head a little on the side window.

Blues, I say.

Right on, says Roy.

Let's get some mo' blues.

You the man, you the man.

Jessica sighs. You boys like to banter, don't you? It's really cute for about two minutes or so. Then I want to scream. You know what I mean.

So we shut up.

A small green scooter passes us on the right. The guy driving it might be three hundred, four hundred pounds, and we're going uphill a bit. There's smoke coming out of the back.

Very unhealthy, Roy coughs. He spits out the window, a long trail of phlegm that the wind stretches into the ditch. Sorry about that, he says to Jessica mainly.

Whatever, she says. Didn't bug me.

A cop car with flashing emergency lights passes me, sound-less almost, like it's a small spaceship. Zip. Gone. On the other side of the highway, against the oncoming traffic no less.

So what's really wrong with you, Roy? Jessica asks slowly.

I told you, he says. A deep-rooted anxiety or something.

Bullshit, she says. Total bullshit.

Well, it will have to do, Roy says.

What am I going to tell everyone? I mean, they've got the right to know.

You tell them exactly that, Jessica, Roy snaps. Anxiety attack. Do you want me to give you the doctor's note first? You want to read what he wrote on my chart?

Jessica turns her head to stare out at the lake. Fuck, she says. Great. We call the ambulance, we haul you off to the hospital and you look like you're dying or something and everybody is freaking out, everybody —

Can we NOT talk about this anymore? he says. It's just making me more anxious and you don't want to see that again, do you, Jessica?

I turn on the radio again, even turn it up a little bit.

Doesn't Kelowna have any soul? Roy says. I mean, now it's the Backstreet Boys. Aren't they all old?

Jessica reaches up and turns the radio off again. I get a quick whiff of her, a splash of apple cinnamon with a slight tinge of B.O., I think. But it's gone as quickly as she smacks herself back on the faux leather seat.

I'm not done talking, Roy, she says. Can we address the issue? I mean, can we? Please?

I've never seen you like this, he says. I thought you were pretty stable. Level-headed. But now you're just pissing me off. Yes, I'm not well. Yes, I went to the hospital. But I can still handle this show. I can still handle our opening. Do you understand? Do you?

Yeah, sure, she says. I get it. Don't yell at the stage manager, ok?

We clear the last of the heavy traffic and get on the highway, driving in silence because Jessica knows better. Down the road we go, up and down the soft plop of land, the blacktop snaking through the suburbs out toward the winery nestled in the crook and crackle of sun. Motorboats crisscross the water, leaving our minds to give them metaphors, whatever each of us wants to believe from the safety of the car. Blue on blue, water as far as the eye can see, the sky wide and perfect, without so much as a blemish until you see the other side, in the east, where the dark, puffy scar meanders with the wind, the thing we try not to imagine as we chase our *Dream* until opening.

I wish somebody would say something, but nobody does. It makes me drive faster.

As we pull into the winery, Roy says the doctor also told him to cut back on his hours and to drink more fluids — both excellent ideas, but I know he is saying this just to placate Jessica, who sits in the back seat pretending to sleep.

What about Italian this afternoon? Jessica says as we park the car in the enormous empty lot behind the tent and stage.

You can do it, Roy says. I'm going to take the afternoon off.

But what about Allan and Marlene? I ask.

They'll just have to work things out, he says. And by the way, can you drop me off at the cabin?

Sure, I say.

Jessica isn't happy. You know EVERYBODY is going to be asking about you, she says loudly.

I know, I know.

What am I supposed to say, then? she asks.

I'm resting, how about that, he says, suppressing a cough.

We leave Jessica standing at the curb with her arms crossed. Because her hair is pulled back into a tight ponytail, and her frown gives prominence to her nose, her face looks slightly pointy. But this is a minor flaw. Minor, minor, minor.

We drive away.

OK, I say to Roy. You want to hear something funny? Jessica's married to Ashton. It's all very hush-hush.

You're a little jealous, aren't you, he says.

I'm not the jealous type, you know that, I say. I'm very normal. Very normal and very stable and I happen to be attracted to very normal and stable women.

I think when women first meet you they are somewhat normal and stable, he says, but when they leave, they're not. Notice a pattern?

I don't make women crazy, don't you dare say that, I say.

Why not, you make me crazy, he says. And I've only lived with you for a few days. I mean, look what happened. I just had an anxiety attack, whose fault is that?

I'M FUCKING NORMAL, ASSHOLE, I say, honking the horn by accident.

Roy grins. Too easy, he says, giggling. Way too easy, hombre.

You can stop laughing, Roy.

But he laughs all the way home. Asshole's right.

When I drop him off at the cabins he's still laughing, but now mostly under his breath, I'm sure because he respects me.

You got a thing for Jessica, he says, leaning into the car through the window before I can take off. He says it in singsong, like a taunt from a nine-year-old. Got a thing for Jessica, got a thing.

Shut up, Roy.

What did you think, she was your last great hope? Come on, she's way too young. And way out of your league.

Roy —

Time to grow up, he says, slamming the passenger side door. You're getting old now, dude, try thinking with something other than your dick.

Come on, Roy. I'm not like that anymore. You ever hear of true love?

Oh, you want true love in your forties? Get a pet, he says. That's what I did.

I wave him away, say Up yours or Give me a break or Screw you, something like that, and then watch him ignore me to wave at Almeera and Shamir standing in front of their cabin wearing identical oversized white skirts. I know, I know. White skirts.

Chapter 19

The winery is doing a special tour of barrel tastings, led by one of the winemakers, Mr. Murdock, who was flown in from New Zealand to add commentary on the process of properly aging Cabernets.

I have prepared for this little event. I made sure to leave the car at home, to wear loose-fitting clothing, to turn my cellphone off. Being drunk requires planning, right? I mean, really drunk.

We can all hope to be Cabernets, Murdock says in closing, his voice echoing in the limestone cave surrounded by French oak barrels. Yes, Cabernets — gaining depth, sophistication, and value as we age in the dark.

This draws laughs from the mostly American tour group, an equal number retirees, wine aficionados, and assholes.

I am one of the assholes because I simply refuse to spit. Samples from bottles that would eventually cost over forty bucks each at your local liquor store? No way. I'll drink that shit.

By four I am fully loaded. By five I am wandering around the winery in a daylight daze, looking for sunglasses that I eventually find perched on my head. How is it that with a little alcohol abuse we turn into our parents in their eighties? Right down to the excessive peeing and bad jokes.

I tell the guy beside me a knock-knock, only to realize it's Murdock himself. A large man with a silly laugh, he says, You're a little tipsy, Mister, maybe you should drink some coffee. He gently shoves me toward a door. Out you go, Mister. Tee-hee, ha. So out I go, into the blazing daylight. And the heat. I can't see. I can't see a thing. I walk, no, stumble toward the stage, my vision getting clearer, and there she is, the AD.

Isn't she supposed to be in Mexico letting her facelift settle? Yet she's here, wearing a tensor bandage on her head, a skin-coloured balaclava with openings for her eyes, nose, and mouth, complete with a white baseball cap on top with a bank logo on it, BMO.

She isn't happy: one, the director isn't here. Two, Marlene is unwatchable. Three, Allan is pissed off and he's her second-best friend. Four, the show sucks even at twice the speed. Five, it is way too hot outside. And six, the understudy, Emma, is apparently better in Marlene's part.

The AD stands there in her bare feet, swaying slightly. Or maybe I am. She addresses the actors like they're about to be loaded onto a boat and sent to actor's hell, which is probably somewhere along BC's coast, somewhere like Vancouver in the summer: a place where actors quickly learn to play golf and wait on tables. And starve.

What was that? she says from the stage, looking down on the poor actors nervously sitting on the grass. With her tensor bandage she looks a little like a Taliban soldier without a gun. What the hell was that?

Allan, lying prone, smiles. I know he's thinking, Here we go, yes, here we go indeed. His eyes are closed, like he's basking in bullshit or something.

That was the worst blocking I've ever witnessed, the AD
continues. It's the worst Italian I've ever witnessed. And when
you actually slow it down it's clearly the worst interpretation of
this play I've ever witnessed.

Marlene, wearing a green tank top and running shorts, moves
out of the ranks of actors sitting down in the grass in front of
the stage. I thought it was good, she says. I finally got it.

Got what, dear, the AD says.

What the point was.

Well, good, maybe you can enlighten us.

First of all, Marlene starts, I'd like to say to everyone here that
I'm sorry I was late, but my partner wouldn't shut up on the
phone because he thinks I'm having an affair, which I'm not,
but he was calling from France so what could I do, really — anyway, what was obvious to me, from being in this show, is that
it's about false romance and the relationship between what's
real and what isn't. And I thought we nailed that part for sure.
Thank you.

She finishes her speech by pulling down on her tank top so
that her breasts flatten out and then bounce up again, as if to add
an exclamation point, though I'm unclear how it does so.

Thank you for that clarification, Marlene, the AD says. I don't
think any of us here would have guessed that.

Marlene isn't sure she's been insulted, but doesn't sit down
either way.

The AD sees me now, even though I have my sunglasses down
and think I'm in disguise. Where is Roy? she asks. Where?

He's sick, I say. Sick.

Where?

At the cabin, madam.

Are you drunk, Alex?

No sire, I am not!

Everybody leave, she says, Except for Jessica. We have our first run tonight in front of an audience, I want you to be ready to go on — even you, Emma. Be ready to replace Marlene, OK?

The actors scurry off, except for Marlene, who hangs around looking for her shoes.

Ass imprints are left in the grass. I pick one, not Allan's, and sit in it, thinking this is the right thing to do when you're drunk.

Marlene gives me some sort of signal before moving away, pointing a forefinger to her lips and then swirling it a bit in the air.

What? I say to her. What?

Over there, Marlene says. I'll be over there.

Then she walks away over there, which, really, in my state, could be anywhere. I guess it's probably the tasting room but it could be her bedroom too. Drunk thoughts are like lazy cats on the couch watching TV. Yes sir, that is a good one indeed.

The AD slings her short stubby legs over the edge of the white stage, pulls her bank cap back as if to let the sun play with her bandaged face. Then she pulls out an enormous pair of white-framed Fendi glasses and puts them on with theatrical flair, as if ready for her close-up.

This is a disaster, isn't it?

I think I said that aloud. Uh-oh.

It might be, Alex, she says. It might be. She waits for Marlene, who searches for her sandals by the far edge of the stage, finds them, and is gone.

Jessica meanders over, script bible clutched to her chest tightly as if it's sewn onto her top.

Is Roy getting worse? the AD asks.

I nod my nose at Jessica and say, very loudly, Roy had a minor chest thing, right? Jessica? Minor, that's why we took him to the hospital, right? Jessica?

What are you talking about? the AD says. His cancer?

Jessica's mouth opens. Facial fenestration. Eyes windows too. Big and getting bigger. Cancer? she says. Did you say cancer?

The AD looks at me, then looks at Jessica. Back and forth. She says, You didn't know?

How would I know that? Jessica says. How?

Oh my, the AD says. Who else doesn't know?

Just everybody, I say.

Oh my, she says. Please, let's keep this under our hats. Please, Jessica. We don't want this to get out to the masses.

What kind of cancer? Jessica says.

I think we should stop here, the AD says. I think we should just stop and re-evaluate the situation and, yes, the show is in trouble but now I can see why.

No, no, Jessica says, I think we should talk about this. I mean, this is serious.

No, says the AD. I don't — I mean, not without speaking to Roy first. So let's just pause this discussion, OK?

Jessica doesn't move from the grass, caught in the shock of it all, caught squeezing the play into her breasts, the script wedged open between act one and act two, her legs quivering a bit so I can see the slight thigh hair standing on edge. She says, This is unbelievable. This is unbelievable. This is unbelievable. She kneels down.

I finally push myself up from the grass, losing my sunglasses on the way, and walk over to Jessica. When I haul her up, she hugs me with her one arm, the script jammed between us so I can feel the rings of the binder.

Jessica lets go of me, bites the bottom of her very cute lip, and says, What am I supposed to do next? Should I tell the cast?

No, no, no, the AD says, stretching out her short legs in their black karate-type pants, stretching them out in front of her off the back of the stage so that she can count her thick red-painted toes. I don't want any unnecessary tension with this cast, she says, considering how bad the show is right now. She takes off her sunglasses, clips them over the side of her top, then pats them. Well, what do you think, Alex, speak up. Come on.

I like Marlene, I say.

What?

In the show, I correct myself. I like her in the show. I've been working on her a little.

Thanks for your input, Alex, but you're drunk. And I'm going with Emma.

Jessica picks up my sunglasses and gives them to me, says, I think you should go have a coffee.

I take them from her, drop them again, then step on them by accident. I turn to look for the nearest coffee thingy but can't quite seem to find my bearings.

The AD says, Are you still staying with Roy?

Yes, I am, I say very loudly. Yes I am.

When you see him, could you please tell him to contact me as soon as possible?

Don't you have his cell number?

I do, she says. But he's not great at returning calls. And I've tried a few times already.

I will do as bid, I say. Adieu.

And off I go, adjusting my pretend hat, down the path toward the tasting room in the winery, hands in my pockets acting as ballast against drunk walking, looking for a coffee to save my life, a double Americano preferably, without sugar and with just a touch of cream.

Adieu, I say again, to myself, and to the non-existent wind. I think that went well. That went very well indeed.

⌣

An hour of coffee and cheese and I think I've got my old self back again.

Susie glides down the tasting room counter, hovers with coffee pot in hand. Another one or not, she says. You decide, dude.

I don't know, I say. My stomach is bitching.

Try some cheese. She holds out another tray of cheddar, mostly Old Fort, but some mild white stuff too.

I groan. What are you, a cheese pusher?

Ha, ha. That's funny — cheese pusher — I'm telling the Germans, she says as she leaves.

I don't bother checking for the Germans. They're somewhere in the bar, I guess, somewhere down the long table huddled over a couple of bottles of white, tasting and re-tasting because they can't believe Canada could produce any wine comparable to theirs. Instead I try Roy's cellphone again, scrolling carefully through my contacts, reading glasses perched on the end of my nose where my sunglasses usually sit.

The phone rings. Nothing. Just his voicemail.

Who you phoning, big boy?

I turn around and see Marlene standing behind me. She's changed, is now wearing black jeans, a red blouse, and a cowboy hat. God knows why.

I'm trying to call Roy, I say.

Yeah, I'd like to talk to him, too, says Marlene.

Why?

Because I'm worried about him. Everyone is.

Just anxiety. An attack of it, that's all, I say.

Marlene sits to my right with an audible thud, taking the last bar stool. She drops the script on the bar with a slightly less audible thud.

Let me tell you, right now I'm getting slightly depressed, she sighs. This is just the first of a series of sighs. The AD's going to put Emma into the show, I just know it, she goes on. Why did Glenda have to come back? Why?

I've never heard anyone call the AD by her name, I say. It's always just been the AD.

Oh, I Googled her, says Marlene.

Well, Glenda can't, I say. What would your partner Steven say?

After today? He'd say go with Emma.

Why?

Marlene looks to the ceiling for help and instead gets a cup of coffee from the robot called Susie. Because, like I said, Marlene says, he thinks I'm screwing around on him.

Why would he think that? I ask.

Because I'm overly happy on the phone, she says.

Hmm, I say. Hmm.

She sips her coffee like an Egyptian, avoiding the handle, using two hands as if it's a bowl. Finishes. Sighs.

The room is practically empty except for the Germans at the other end of the bar, standing and sniffing Rieslings from their own personal tasting glasses. Sommeliers from Hamburg — I guess they're always packing. That was my first joke to Susie earlier. She laughed out loud and said, You keep that up and I'll sleep with you.

Do I look overly happy to you? Marlene asks.

I look at her looking at me in the mirror behind the bar, the mirror with empty wine bottles in front of it, and I think Marlene looks a little happy indeed, albeit mixed with a certain dose of anxiety. Although it could be because she's looking country and western. Blame the wide-open skies and green pastures. And distant gunfire.

I say, I think you look happier. How about that?

I think I *am* happier, too, she says. Except for the fact that I might get replaced. Glenda can't replace me. She just can't.

Look, I say. You enjoy what you're doing and it shows. You're an intense, bitter, sometimes funny Titania. The AD won't replace you. So get rid of the anxiety and keep being happy. It's going to be great. Despite the fire. Despite Glenda. Despite Emma. Despite everything.

I think this little pep talk of mine is actually pretty lame.

Yeah, Marlene says. It is. Lame.

I drink. Sorry.

Marlene pushes her cup away as if it's filled with lard. OK, I'll be honest with you, she says. I've never acted since high school. And even then it was in *Grease*. Second girl on the right with the big eyes, if you know what I mean.

Uh-oh, I say.

Uh-oh is right, she says, pulling off her cowboy hat and letting her hair fall down her back and across the red blouse.

I'd drink more coffee but it's bitter and turning cold.

Susie, Marlene barks, more java, please. She plays with her cowboy hat, covers the script and turns it over so it can spin a little on its crown. It's a white straw hat, not felt. Cheap, the kind you would buy at the dime store when dime stores existed. Let me tell you, she sighs, this was supposed to be it, this show was going to be my big chance. I know I'm the winery owner's girl and I know he's paying for the production, but do you really think I'd have a chance?

You're improving, I say. Every time out.

You're lying, she says. Every time out.

I drink what's left of the horrible coffee. All you need to do is have a good preview tonight, I say.

If I am in the preview, Marlene says.

You'll be in the preview because Roy will put you in the preview, I say. He likes what you're doing out there.

What part?

Well, the last scene is interesting, when you find out your Oberon has dropped something in your drink and you've fallen in love with an ass.

Oh, I hate Oberon, Marlene says. He's such a predator.

Yeah, I say. I love how you stare him down even though you're supposed to be looking at Bottom. It's like you're really pissed off.

I am pissed off. If Oberon was around today he'd get charged with date rape or something. I mean, how funny is that: spiking a girl's flower hoping she'll fall in love with his asshole friend.

That Shakespeare, I say. What was he thinking?

Love isn't about being obsessed with losers just because you're half-drunk, know what I mean? Marlene says.

You're talking to a guy, Marlene, I say. Plus I'm in a bar, so —

Susie hears me and skates over. Was that a joke? she asks.

Susie, Marlene sneers. Don't. Listen. To. Us.

Slightly rebuffed, Susie glides and spins away, trying to keep her face neutral, though when she faces me again I can see it's not. Crestfallen, I guess that's the word for it. She speaks German to the Germans. They don't laugh but look over at us with some concern. One of them puts down his wine goblet and puts on his glasses. Down his nose.

Susie speaks German, I say. Did you know how talented she is?

Yes, says Marlene. And French. And Spanish. Even a little Japanese. That's why she was hired. Where were we?

Shakespeare?

Yes. Titania. My Titania. How do you see the part?

I see you playing it. How about that? You have that smoulder-ing anger thing going for you. And you're funny without trying to be funny — it's different. Yeah. And I'm thinking, What's going on there? What's with this fairy? And what's she going to do next?

No answer from Marlene at first. We watch the Germans pour wine from their fancy goblets into a large plastic spit bucket on the bar, then help themselves to another round while Susie digs up some reading material for them. Pamphlets or something, I suppose. Then I see it's actually info on the show.

Marlene sighs. This was going to be my big break. I was going to be a somebody.

Keep going, I say.

Let me tell you, life is short. We're fucked up in our twenties, barely coherent in our thirties, so what does that leave us with? Our forties. Maybe ten, fifteen years before the curtains come crashing down, and where am I now?

Keep going.

What am I doing? Have I played the part? Or have I just pretended to play the part? I want to be seen as an artist. I want to live like an artist. I want to affect people. I want to change some lives.

Do you honestly believe that you're going to add meaning to meaningless lives? I ask.

I want to believe that I'm on this stupid planet to do something that will benefit people, Marlene says. And I honestly don't think I've done that. I mean, look at me. I'm somewhat educated, somewhat well off — but I'm afraid I'm sort of insignificant. Know what I mean, jelly bean? She pokes me.

I drink. Try to gather thoughts, but at this point it's not that easy, because most of them are of the useless drunken variety and they disgust me. Why are you with Steven? I ask, finally.

What?

Marlene looks like a vampire cowgirl right now — her lips are very, very red and she's drooling just a little bit. I continue where I shouldn't and say, It seems to me that being with Steven means you can get him to buy you into these productions. I mean, have you come into this part honestly? Have you paid your dues?

No, Marlene says, of course I haven't. But that's beside the point. I'm still doing it. I'm still in it, whatever it is. And it's my one chance to find ... redemption or something.

Redemption for what?

She sighs. Redemption for my lousy, boring, stupid life.

Look, I say. Look, you're putting a lot of pressure on this artist thing. I'm not sure you can actually find meaning in life with it. In fact, you'll be lucky to find love there.

Well, at least the two of us can talk about it, she says. And that's more than I've ever had with Steven. I guess I can be overly happy after all. That's what he hates. Please tell me I'm not weird. Please.

All right, I say. But, if Steven's so unhappy about you being overly happy, why are you happy with that?

Because he's what every girl wants: a biker who owns a winery.

That's a funny line.

That's the truth, Marlene says.

What kind of biker? I ask, pulling my coffee cup back.

Hells Angels kind, she says, but not officially affiliated with any known outlaw group. They're independent. Call themselves Vintage Devils because a lot of them work in the wine biz. They have a clubhouse down on the coast and they go there a lot on weekends. Some of them own pit bulls and sell dope, that kind of thing. But Steven is really the most successful of them all. He's really into wine and cheese, not just dope. Although I'm not sure if he's actually killed anybody or not.

You must be making this up. You must be.

No, I'm not.

I start a tiny coughing fit. Not sure if I'm faking it or what. Christ, I say. Christ. I grab a napkin from the bar.

You're not going to write this down, are you? Marlene asks, just slightly aghast.

No, no, I stopped writing on napkins at the same time I stopped drinking rum and cokes, I say. Now that's a funny line.

She doesn't laugh. Just sighs. Again.

I wave the napkin at Susie, who is down at the other end, leaning over in her tight jeans and whispering something to the Germans. When she finally sees me waving at her, I stop and use the napkin to wipe the sweat off my brow.

She glides over. Does a lot of that. Let me guess, she says. Coffee?

Yes, I say. Can you make it an espresso?

Susie fake smiles at me and says, I can make it anything you want.

Marlene puts on her cowboy hat and stares at Susie, who now retreats, smile gone. Well, well, well, she says. What is it about her that you find so fascinating? Is she your type?

She's my type, yup, I say. University-type. Funny and cute. Perky. Yeah, absolutely perky. And she has that confidence, you know what I mean, that absolute certainty that life will be grand. It seems like she doesn't have a lot of regrets. Loves what she does and loves life. I think.

Marlene says, Really. That's all you get?

Yeah. I guess. Sorta.

And young. You like them young?

I sit on my hands and turn to watch myself in the mirror. Squirm, squint, squeeze my ass cheeks tight, generally look uncomfortable. Let me tell you, it is not particularly attractive. I look away. Steven is coming to your opening tomorrow, right? I finally say.

I doubt it, she says. She picks up her script, pages through it, finds a spot, and clears her throat. I want to act, she declares to the room. I need to act.

I dread what's coming up, but it doesn't stop it from happening.

Head up, chest out, Marlene swivels to face the nearly empty room.

Come, now a roundel and a fairy song; then, for the third part of a minute hence, some to kill cankers in the musk-rose buds, some war with rere-mice for their leathern wings to make my small elves coats and —

She spins around and slams the script down on the bar. OK, aren't elves always small?

Susie saves me from laughing by arriving with the espresso. I quickly put it up to my lips. Drink, man, drink! Don't look at Marlene. Do NOT look at her.

But she's on a roll. The Germans sense comedy and move closer, wine glasses held at their waists like six-shooters. I smell aftershave. Mint or menthol or licorice or something European mixed with the slight stale stink of garlic. Or it could just be me. I can't remember what I had for lunch.

I stare the Germans down briefly and they drink slowly. Ja, ja. Busy themselves with low, menacing small talk, like they're pit bulls or something. They have no idea that I can understand portions of it — my grandparents were Eastern European, and they would fight in German because they thought we wouldn't understand.

Cankers, Marlene says. Did Shakespeare have an oral fixation?

I concentrate on keeping the glazed-over face.

And what are rere-mice? Do they fly or something? She pulls at my sleeve. Cankers? Rere-mice? Alex? Do they? Are they? Please —

Tug. Tug.

You would be correct, I say without any emotion because I must NOT lose it. Rere-mice. They are bats.

Drink, you fool. Drink. I go back to the espresso which is, oh my God, mostly gone now and I've burned the tip of my tongue a little which is exactly what I deserve. Fake gulp of coffee. Fake it, come on. Gulp. Gulp. Not too obvious.

I'm right about rere-mice? Marlene takes a moment to smooth out the pages of the script. OK. And leathern wings are —

Wait for it, I mumble into my empty cup. Wait for it —

Made of leather?

Yes!

She smiles, and I can see how perfect those teeth are, capped in front, expensive probably, but I'm no dentist. I appreciate your help, she says. You're amazing.

Thanks, I say.

We should do this more often.

Nod, nod, nod.

Marlene celebrates, takes off her cowboy hat and jams it on my head. It quickly sinks down to my eyebrows, until it must look like there's just a hat with a big nose sitting in my place. For a guy with such a big brain, your head sure is small, she says.

Thanks, I say. Then I finally let myself laugh.

And thank God for that.

The smoke now wraps the lake in thin grey linen. Distant crackling comes from the horizon, the sound of orange flags flapping, an approaching army of flame swallowing pine trees on its way. The boutique winery on the far hill, known for its off-dry Riesling and rustic Merlot, is easily overrun. Flames as high as forty or fifty feet signal the overthrow as stacked wine barrels burn and burn and burn. It is turning into a rout.

When the taxi drops me off at our three little cabins by the lake, I see a small crowd gathered along our mini-beach taking pictures with their glowing cellphones. Mostly tourists, I think, because when I join them I hear accents, English, Australian, American.

It gets worse every day. The smoke covers half the lake, cloaking the far side. Some boats drift in and out, slowed by the spectacle. Kayaks are everywhere, low to the water like surfaced mini-subs, their fluorescent paddlers also snapping photos, both arms above their heads as if in surrender. Even fat guys on inner tubes take it all in, beers balanced on their sunburned bellies.

Disgusting, somebody says.

Sad, somebody else says.

Where will it all end, says another.

It smells more acrid, less like an out-of-control campfire than a house on fire. Or a warehouse. Maybe even a school or college. Something big. Something rotten.

My eyes sting. Lips sting. The inside of my nose where the hairs are stings. Yeah, I know. Gross. But it's there, and it's not going away.

I shoulder my way to the front, stand on a flat rock with both feet, teetering a bit from the view. The smoke rolls over waves like clouds on vacation, riding the surf toward the middle where houseboats safely gather, full of other tourists taking more photos. No music this time. I mean, what's the point?

I follow the sound of an airplane with my head, trying to pick it out of the sky with my radar eyes. Where is it? Where? Because the grey is everywhere over there.

Then I see it. Big. Very big.

A water bomber, all silver and orange, dips low out of the clouds and skims the water along the far side of the lake, swallowing as much as possible before tilting up and into the wind. It turns toward the burning trees along the far hills, engines whining.

I think dragon. Dignified, enormous, beyond that metaphor even. Noisy. An aura of roar as it shudders loose its load of lake water over the smoke and trees, engines screaming. Beautiful though. Outstanding. Graceful.

That's the Mars water bomber, says a tourist. World-famous. Carries seventy-five hundred gallons of water. Can you believe it. If it can't stop the fire, nothing can.

I balance better, turn slightly to my left to look at the tourist, a tall skinny retiree around eighty, with a US aircraft carrier baseball cap on. It's black and silver and says USS Nimitz on the front, which I decide is a funny name for an aircraft carrier.

Nimitz. Nimitz. Nimitz —

You an aircraft buff? he says, looking at me look at him.

Zah? I say.

Military man?

Huh?

You in the military?

Uh, no. Theatre.

Oh. He seems unsure of himself. Turning to scratch his long red nose, he bumps me and I lose my balance, almost falling into the water. I grab his plaid green shirt to steady myself. You OK, son? he drawls.

Sure. No problem, I say. But really, I'm still a little drunk and I know it shows.

I push my way back through the throng, wander toward our cabin, and stand in front of the door. I think briefly about life itself before deciding to knock. Three times, of course. I'm being polite even though I live here.

Roy opens it. His shirt is unbuttoned to his waist and I see he's got thin white chest hair around tiny nipples and a small round belly that looks like a volleyball with fur. There's a grey to his skin that makes mine crawl. It's everywhere, right down to his belt, which is also dark grey.

Behind him, on my bed, sit Almeera and Shamir, legs crossed, still wearing white, pants and shirts now, eating sushi from identical green TV tables with pictures of orange songbirds on them. They have angelic smiles, white teeth, beautiful skin, those two. But I don't think they ever blink.

Do you have any idea what's going on? I ask.

Roy waves me in. Yeah, I heard, he says. Jessica phoned me, she was pretty freaked out — you know, about everything.

He finishes buttoning his shirt, fumbling mostly, jamming the front part into his pants.

Are you going to the preview? I say.

He stifles a cough, or tries to, then recovers. Yeah, I am going, he says thickly, mucus clinging to every sound. Why wouldn't I?

One cough escapes. It hurts to even hear it. Roy puts a hand to his heart, then moves back toward the bed very slowly. Almeera hands him his black leather coat.

Chekhov is perched on the headboard, his green-and-yellow head bobbing up and down, agonizing over the sesame seeds sprinkled on some of the sushi rolls. I haven't seen him outside of his cage before. Roy is always too worried.

What's going on in here? I say.

Roy coughs again. Another ouch. Nothing, we were eating, he says.

Right. And Chekhov?

He's having fun, Roy says. With the company.

Almeera and Shamir give me a little wave with their chopsticks. Hi there, they say. How is it going with you today?

Not great, I'm pretty loaded, I say, my head starting to pound from the developing hangover even though I still have a good wine buzz going. You heard about Marlene? I say to Roy, trying to usher him out the door.

He pulls back, pats his coat looking for his cell. No, he says.

The AD wants to sit her out, I say. Might go with the understudy. Emma-what's-her-name.

Roy freezes. What?

I know, I know, I say.

She can't do that, this is my show. Fuck! Now he moves fast, stumbling past me out of the cabin, ignoring Chekhov as he flaps toward the door. I quickly swing the door shut behind us, hoping not to hear the thud of his tiny feathery body on the wood.

I will never let that bitch run my show, Roy says. Never in a million years.

It's all very melodramatic. Perfectly normal for theatre people.

He marches to the idling taxi sitting in front of my cabin. The driver is leaning out the window to snap shots of the fire.

Can we go please? Roy says. Or are you here just to take photos like the rest of them? He points at the gaggle of snappy-snaps huddled at the water's edge. The big old retiree with the Nimitz baseball cap holds court in the middle, waving at the passing helicopters whoop-whoop-whooping their way to do battle over there, over there.

I am here at your service naturally, my friend, the taxi driver says, putting his camera phone away.

We jump in the back seat and Roy already has an unlit smoke in his mouth. Drive, you bastard, he yells. Drive like the wind.

The driver, Ali according to his licence, crawls in, turns around with a shit-eating grin, and says, Do you not know how long I have waited to hear someone finally say that, dear sir?

He jams the car into gear and we're off, spitting gravel as we hit the road to the winery. We make it there in fifteen minutes flat. Never got my seat belt on.

෴

An hour or so before the show, as we move toward dusk and then dark, the actors' tent is even more medieval than before. The soot from the fire dusts the white in patches from top to bottom, and at the peaks the greenish flags are dirty and life-less. On the stage, actors in full costume prance and vocalize, spitting out Shakespeare like half-eaten pieces of steak, hoping that somehow it will all make sense in the end. The audience is somewhere back there, hiding in dark houses, looking at the ash snowing down on their perfectly manicured lawns, tomato plants, and leased Acuras.

Three actors hold hands centre stage and practise screaming, their heads held high, eyes closed. The word is Here, or Whore. At the top of their lungs. Here! Whore! Imagine that, over and over again. This is the usual routine, the cabal of theatre. Trust me. It happens every time, and it's just as weird every time.

Here! Whore! Here! Whore!

At the front of the stage is the AD, now minus her tensor bandage, wearing her trademark all black: track pants, baggy sweatshirt, and shawl. Birkenstocks with no socks. Pencil behind her ear. Pacing, hmm, studying the script like she's the manager of a baseball team, one that's losing a lot. Who we got here? Who's doing what? What time is it?

She spots Roy at the same time he spots Marlene sitting on the grass in her faux cowboy outfit, hardly looking like she's ready to go on.

Roy, the AD says, Roy. How are you feeling? Please tell me you're OK.

Roy takes bigger steps, each one seemingly more difficult than the last, but all are calculated: this foot here, that foot there, here, there, here, there, don't look up, never look up, a straight line through the neatly arranged rows of plastic audience chairs that appeared this afternoon out of nowhere. He's puffing, sweating too. Odd, because it's not that hot out and it's all downhill. There's a thin smear of white around the corners of his mouth. Dried saliva, I guess. Sweat maybe. Either way, it's not complimenting his ashen face.

The AD moves to the edge of the stage and leans over, hoping we'll lunge toward her for hugs.

Roy doesn't. Instead, he stops a safe distance from the

waist-high front edge of the sooty playing area. What's going on? he says.

Going on? she says. With what?

With my show.

The show I left in your hands?

My show, says Roy, hands moving out of his pockets to form fists. Tiny ones, but fists all the same.

Well, she says slowly, it's about who's ready and who's not. That's all. Her consonants are perfectly clear, almost staccato, rifle shots even. This show needs big help now, she says. Right?

I thought I was the director, Roy says, now reaching toward the stage, only to grab the script from her hands.

The AD just smiles.

You were directing my show, Roy. *My* show!

Roy punches the script a little. It's not very accurate, a slight jab to the corner that sends the paper clip — big, industrial even, more like a clasp — scuttling across the dirty stage.

Emma, the understudy-slash-stand-in, picks it up. I don't know much about her. Roy never mentions her, she's never onstage, and she never rehearses. She's just graduated from an acting school called Studio 58 and is doing the show for credit — that is to say, for free snacks, beer, and connections. She usually watches from the wings, hiding behind a huge Pellegrino water bottle and sucking on lemon wedges. Completely forgettable, with a face that defies definition — it just looks anxious, round, and bland, if that's possible, all the time. Kinda like the back of a mixing bowl with bangs.

Right now she's wearing a long white gown that looks like a wedding dress from the '50s, something my mother might have worn. She hands me the clasp, then backs off.

Fuck! Roy now shakes the script as if it's a chicken that needs its neck broken. Whose name, he says, is on the program?

The AD looks very calm.

Whose fucking name?

Still calm. She's been through this before, with board members so rich and powerful they help form provincial governments. She has a calming smile on, no teeth showing. Well, she says, I got back here and heard you were in the hospital. So I had to take over. The show must go on, right, Roy?

Not without her, though, Roy says, waving the script at Marlene, who stands nearby hanging her head. A page falls out. He picks it up and nearly loses his balance, steadying himself with his left hand on the stage. Shit, he says. Shit.

I know his world is swirling. Happens when blood rushes to the head, or away from it. I hope he's not thinking about death or dying. But he probably is. I mean, why wouldn't he be? I am.

The AD waits.

He straightens up, slowly, as if his back is killing him, and waits for normal to return. Better posture, clear mind. There. Done. He glares, hands on hips.

OK, the AD says. For tonight, Emma is taking her place, just to give her more time to prepare. I'm talking about Marlene, of course.

Marlene is ready, Roy says.

I feel ready, she says, I do. She gets off the grass, camel-like, slowly unfolding into her bigness, and saunters awkwardly over with her hat in hand, jeans straining to keep from bursting out along the seams. She has a nice ass, and I really hope I kept that to myself.

Look, you two, the AD says. I don't want to make a scene, but I've decided. After all, it *is* my show, right?

You can't do that to me, Roy stutters. I've worked with these people. I've worked the show.

Well, it isn't working, is it? the AD says, pulling her hair back to make her eyes bigger, though not necessarily more attractive. We have this one preview to see how we can make it work. That's what previews are for, Roy. Right?

No, Roy says. No —

Just give it a try, she says. Trust me.

No way. No!

Yes. I'm afraid so.

Roy wants to scream, I know it, but he ends up coughing instead. Not just his usual hack job; but bad enough to make him look horribly ill. Everyone stops doing what they're doing and waits for the hack to finish. When it does, he looks as grey as the ash on the tent, as lifeless as the flags at the peaks.

Allan moves stage right, toward us, pulling his great red cape behind him. Roy, he says. Roy?

But Roy just turns and walks away, no, stumbles again, hands jammed in his pockets, or on his hips. His eyes are closed or maybe half-shut. Not sure he can see. What is he doing? He bumps into chairs and kicks at non-existent cats, swearing under his breath like Fred Flintstone.

Roy, I say. Roy.

Ignores me too, drifting ghost ship that he is, sails slack, shirt looking way, way too big as it billows out behind. No ass, just baggy pants that weren't baggy before. He sits in the sound booth at the back with Jessica, who's been watching the whole time, then lights up a cigarette that she immediately snatches from his mouth and tosses into the seats below. Lights another that Jessica tries to grab but misses, and takes a huge wilful drag, before tossing it into the seats himself. The seats are red. I think I mentioned that, didn't I?

Everyone onstage shuffles a bit, looking for a place to hide. Like Europe.

Jessica waits for a bit, stares Roy down even, then cups her hands around her mouth and yells: One hour, everybody! One hour!

The stage empties. A cliché, I know. But it does empty, sadly.

Emma is the last one to leave. She makes sure to give us a nice exit: head back, arms out, wide white dress shushing the stage. She's desperately trying not to grin, but it's there, and who could blame her, really? What is she, twenty-three, twenty-four? At that age it usually shows no matter what. So she grins. Who gives a shit?

Marlene doesn't seem to notice, fixed on something in the air I suppose. She fingers her cowboy hat, bending the sides over so it looks like it's been worn a lot. Then she steadies herself on the edge of the stage, running her hand along the dirty playing area. Drops her hat, bends over to pick it up, drops it again, probably on purpose, just to buy herself some time and maybe even some dignity. It's probably harder to cry when you're bending down a lot.

The AD catches me staring at Marlene's ass and holds out a chubby hand. Make yourself useful, she says softly. OK? Help me down, Alex. Please.

I make sure she swings down as gracefully as possible, bracing her hip a little so that when she lands it's not catastrophic. It's like I'm Dad and my child has had enough of the merry-go-round. OK, there you go. Take it easy. Everything is going to be just fine. Down you go.

Oomph, she says as her feet hit the ground, Birkenstocks flipping off in the process. Oomph. That hurt a little, she says in my ear.

Sorry, I say. Sorry.

What happened to all your big muscles anyway? she says a little louder.

I don't respond. What's the point? I've been drinking a lot for the last few weeks. Eating bad food and basically goofing off. I'm embarrassed. I'm in pathetic shape.

Marlene flees to the actors' tent, cowboy hat on, red hair flowing behind. She stomps her feet.

The AD fishes for her sandals in the long grass, using her toes as bait. I notice that her face is puffy around the edges, like she's just gone three rounds with a light heavyweight named Roberto. And her lids are shiny, as if dipped in Vaseline. Her neck too.

The rest of the actors have already made their exits, waiting inside the tent to console Marlene in that fake actor way. You know: I love your work, it's so honest. You'll get your chance. Stay grounded. It will all work out in the end. Be strong. Be strong. Love you. Love you. It's what actors do, even when they hate each other. It's nauseating, but in a nice way.

Having found her footwear, the AD makes her way to her black coat, which is smeared across two seats in the centre of the four-hundred-or-so empty chairs in the amphitheatre. She places her bottom down carefully, as if warming some invisible dinosaur eggs, and says with a micro smile, Be a sweetheart and get me a nice cup of coffee, Alex. I'll save you a place, OK?

OK, I say. No problem. And then I just go and look for a coffee. Somewhere.

Chapter 21

Emma was good. Not outstanding. But solid. Each line delivered with efficiency, on time and at the right place. A FedEx performance, I guess. As if Emma had been practising every line in front of a mirror, which we found out later was exactly what she'd been doing while she was in the back waiting.

Nonetheless, the AD was pleased. A fat grin was on her still-swollen face for the entire three hours. Genuine, but in my humble opinion totally uninspired — I speak of both the smile and the show.

The audience, all four hundred of them, applauded at the end. Enough, in fact, for two curtain calls. But it felt forced, like most of the action in the play. The actors filed out in a tight line as if facing a firing squad, pretend smiles plastered on their pretend faces. They knew it was a lifeless show, even if it was a tight one. The funny bits were funny and the romance was sometimes giddy, but mostly it was full of shit, lacking any genuine moments of humanity or transformation. Or as my mother would have said, it was merely adequate.

Marlene, sitting in the control booth in the back, said it was the first time she had really followed the show. She was trying to be generous. I could see she'd been crying.

Later, in the tasting room, she says bravely, Wow, that show has potential. I liked how everything came together at the end. Funny stuff, with the play within the play. Funny, funny.

I'm trying to avoid Roy at the bar. Boycotting wine, he is hitting the Scotch pretty heavy. Hunched over in black — a big crow springs to mind here — protecting his two fingers of Glenmorangie, a serviceable ten-year-old Highland. His coat up at the collars, the top of his head barely visible as it slowly sinks into the leathery depths.

Allan stands across from me near the exit, empty beer glass in one hand, Merlot in the other, two-fisting it, just waiting for his chance to flee as the AD makes her congratulatory rounds. Each actor gets the mandatory fake hug and wink-wink-wasn't-that-a-show comment.

Fuck, we were godawful, says Allan. Embarrassing even.

No mistakes, I say.

Right, he says. Just the whole boring show.

Lots of laughs, I say.

Not for me, he says, and I was working my ass off.

We drink our cheap Merlot. It has that plush, slightly jammy taste of a patio wine served with Cheezies. The reserve Merlot is being saved for opening night. This stuff, not that it's bad, is just bland and uninspired. Like the rest of our night. There, I said it.

What did you think about Emma? I say.

Allan puts his wine glass up to his mouth to hide this comment: Adequate.

I'm surprised.

Well, don't be, he says. Marlene was a nightmare, but at least she was interesting.

You've changed your mind about her, I say.

I guess I have, Allan says.

We drink quietly.

You were good, though, I finally say.

Boring, Allan says. Completely and thoroughly. And that's the one thing that fills me with terror. That, and dying onstage.

I like the atmosphere, I say. I mean, the lake and everything. It's a nice view.

Charred in the Vineyard, Allan says. Cheers.

The AD goes to the bar to console Roy. Allan and I move ahead too, just in case Roy turns violent, which won't happen because Roy is one, a pacifist, and two, weak and frail.

But you never know, right? When you're not in it for the money, you think the difference between good art and bad art is life or death. This is the delusion of theatre artists: we think we are actually changing lives. But we're not. We're simply distracting people for one short night.

Look, the AD says to Roy loudly, tomorrow is another day. You saw what happened tonight with Emma. Very tight. Very professional. But tomorrow is your day. Your opening.

Beautiful case of reverse psychology, I say to, I hope, myself.

Roy doesn't move. Takes a gulp and his Adam's apple jumps.

The AD pats his black leather coat as if trying to straighten out the bulges in it. It doesn't fit Roy all that well anymore. She kisses him on top of his head, then turns on her heel — a dance move from a show thirty years ago, I suppose — and sashays out of the room.

Allan retreats to find Jessica, who's stuck in the back doing what all stage managers do the night before opening: drinking highballs and writing soul-destroying notes for actors on her Macbook.

I sit beside Roy. He is very quiet, not really moving much.

Hand frozen around the tumbler of Scotch with exactly two cubes of ice in it. It's a fist with a glass for a brace, basically.

So?

Fuck, Roy says. What a night. Coughs.

You OK?

He nods, but also says, Not really.

I think, then ask, What about the show? What did you think?

It was what it was, says Roy.

Yeah, I say. It was, wasn't it?

He sips on the Scotch, letting the ice cubes filter the liquor so it doesn't burn on the way down.

And Marlene? Let's get back to her.

What about Marlene, says Roy.

How is she doing?

Haven't seen her, he says. I think she went home.

Oh, I say.

To cry, he says. Or not to cry. That is the question.

Right. Well, I'm sure she's OK, I say.

No, I meant me, he says, now looking at me with very droopy bloodshot eyes. A show with no spark is like apple pie without cheese, he sighs.

Cute, I say.

He nods. And drinks.

But it was competent, right?

It was mostly that, Roy says. Yes.

I finish the Merlot, thank God, because that's what it needs, to get out of my fucking glass. I tap the bottom of it on the bar very absentmindedly and Susie waltzes by with a Shiraz.

Shiraz? she asks.

Yeah, yeah, I say, then watch her pour and notice how she never looks where she's pouring, not exactly. Right now she's looking in my eyes, that's where she's really concentrating, and

I feel slightly violated because I'm in a weird mood, you know, with the show and how my life in general is going. I haven't written anything decent for weeks, having concentrated instead on developing a serious drinking problem. Trust me, it's a lot of work to be a lousy drunk.

Good times, Susie says. You like them, right? Party on, dude.

What? Reading my mind?

You're funny, she says, spinning away, blonde hair flouncing, yes, flouncing behind.

I smell more smoke. It's everywhere. I smell my sleeve. It's there too. Sniff my pants, or try to. There too. It's in my hair for sure. I smell it when I turn my head. I turn it again to try to get another sniff in, trying to make sure none of this looks stupid. Sniff. Sniff. Hands on the bar. Lean a little to my left and then to my right. What is that? A fine layer of soot on the bar too? You can feel it with your fingertips, shows up on your napkin, even at the bottom of your drink. My God, it's everywhere!

I sip the wine and it's much, much better than the crappy Merlot. Deeper and more complex, full of black cherries and plums and other fruit I've read about in wine magazines at London Drugs. I go there to buy computer paper and toothpaste and to wander around in their special electronics room taking in all the wonders of flat-screen TVs, the colours always, always better than real life.

Where did I go wrong? Is it the writing? Or my lack of it? One play, one movie, one novel — one hit and then my ship will come in. I will become more organized. I will pay my back taxes. I will take cooking courses. And then a European vacation. Then hire somebody to clean my place, do my laundry, and then finally find out where my precious time has gone.

Then, I'm certain, I will fall in love.

I know I'm saying this aloud, but I don't give a shit. It's all about finding clarity in life. Maybe not peace, I know that's too much to ask. I mean, birth is a stressful thing and it only gets worse: your first bus ride to elementary school, puberty — enough said — then finally screaming at your parents that you'll kill them if they try to stop you from going out with your friends.

Yeah? Roy says. Really?

I don't know, I say. Maybe I'm just talking crazy here.

The dilemma, though, he says into his glass now, is never about becoming clearer or more organized. Right?

Yeah, I say, having no idea where this is going.

It's about ambiguity versus confusion, and how we as humans must find that line between.

Yeah, I say, still confused. So — tonight's show was where in all this?

Right, he says. You got it.

Wow, I say.

Roy drinks.

That's — interesting. Sure it is, I stammer. Do you mean that once we've figured everything out, it's too easy? Or do you mean there needs to be some mystery? Could you be more specific?

Roy, snuggled up with his smugness, starts teasing the ice cubes in his tumbler with his off-white tongue. Not that attractive, believe you me.

I swallow more Shiraz and ogle Susie, though I'm now convinced she knows I'm not her type and never will be. It's not just an age thing — it might be a drunk thing. And a fact-that-I-haven't-showered-in-two-or-three-days thing.

Emma walks over wearing a long, white dress, so close to her actual costume I could have sworn it was in the show. Hi, she says.

Hi, Roy says. Or coughs.

Hi, I say.

She ignores me. I'm just a playwright without anything on the boards, therefore unnecessary, a waste of time. Young actors have so little of it, ten years or so, before the good parts go to other college grads who are much more perky and employable. It's important to be new and exciting. It's very now.

She asks, About tomorrow?

No answer. I'm not sure Roy has actually heard her. He concentrates on the ice cubes, studying them for clues, I suppose.

Emma sways a little, firmly living in that young girl fantasy that innocence is always more attractive than cynicism. Her round, round face radiates Buddha love. But it's already tainted by life in the theatre. You can see it in the corners of her eyes. I love your jacket, she says to Roy. Is that new?

No. He drinks and Emma waits and waits.

So — about the opening?

I'll let you know, Roy says. Or coughs.

OK, Emma says.

OK, he says. Or coughs.

She leaves, hiking up her dress with her hands jammed in her pockets in an aw-shucks kinda way. It doesn't make her look any more mature. To me it looks clearly calculated, like the rest of her performance.

After she's gone, the bar seems to pick up energy. I think some actors laugh in the back, though it might actually be the tourists laughing. A busload of Dutch teachers saw the show and are now discussing the true nature of fairies with one of the props guys named Howard. All very passionate about reality and how Shakespeare just knew we needed an ethereal world to balance things out.

Why live without dreams? Dutch guy says.

To dream is to die, says Howard. Come on, don't be so naïve.

Howard, I decide, is stupid. He's joined by Raph, another props guy. They are both bald and keep meticulous beards. The Dutch are tall and loud and wear plastic clogs in a variety of colours. Neither group is imparting much wisdom, in my opinion.

His visions are unparalleled, says another Dutch guy.

No, says Howard, his visions are our demise.

Our real demise started with cellphones and email, I say, mostly aloud — a clear sign that alcohol has been abused. Then blogs and bubble tea. Followed closely by Facebook and Twitter.

Roy nudges me. Look, he says, for you, where does art live?

With his mother, I say. Probably downstairs with his own cable hook-up and hot plates. Ha!

Roy doesn't laugh. Instead he starts a lecture about how I should try to respond to him in a non-performance mode, and, dammit, I really should have better timing. It's a long speech full of coughs and finger-jabbing and fuck, I don't know what else. Friendship, I suppose.

But what is friendship? Right? And what are the limits? I mean, I am with Roy, right? And he is dying, right? Why should I go through this trauma? Do I really need this? Is this going to make my life more meaningful? Or more painful?

I think of my first serious relationship. It was a marriage to an actress who shall remain nameless until she appears in my next play as an unsympathetic character. She insisted true relationships were meant to be friendships even after the inevitable breakup. That's what made them true, that they could survive almost anything. Like rats after a nuclear holocaust.

I told her this theory was naïve and a little irritating. Anyway, I said to her, what is this, a breakup? Come on, we're perfect for each other. Your craziness, my inertia. Sorta works, right? Go ahead, do something nutty, see if I care.

Yes, she told me to fuck off. Yes, she moved out. Yes, she was seeing somebody else the whole time. Yes, she married a realtor-slash-carpenter-slash-loser who broke it off with her to be with somebody else, and yes, they remained friends afterward. We still talk about it. Well, others talk about it. I don't have contact with my ex. I guess it was never meant to be.

Oddly, to this day, I still imagine we laughed at the same time during movies or episodes of Friends. But maybe she didn't laugh. Maybe she was seriously fucking angry and I was seriously fucking disconnected. I don't know. Can't remember everything. Or don't want to. After all, I was in love.

I'm in a haze, I'm in a haze. Must NOT drink any more. Put the glass down. Put it down now! Everything collapsing into words piled on top of more words. Actors arguing over there. The TV blaring over there. The tourists shouting over there. Roy still telling me I'm full of shit. I should respond, but I hate fights. I just don't have the energy. And I'm not sure I want to work at a relationship. I used to believe it should just happen. You should have it and it should be easy. And no fights. At least not over things like who's doing the dishes or sorting the recycling. Maybe sex and money, but really, that should be about it.

Life is too short, my mother would say. Right.

This is what I think, and I think it very rapidly: Roy, you and I have been through this before. A million times. We're like a married couple. I know I can just wait you out and you know I'm doing that right now.

I watch the fancy TV screen above our heads and hear about the fire closing in on us. I mean, it's coming. It really is. They've evacuated another subdivision on the far side. Over thirty-six homes and two businesses, one of them a bread factory, so everybody knows it's toast. I only hope it's insured.

Roy puts his tirade on hold. Drinks some cold water. Good.

I clear my throat, hoping it will also help clear my mind. OK. I have a question for you, Roy. If the choice came down to being safe and having a successful but uninspiring show, or being risky and having a horrible bomb onstage, what would you take?

I'd take the one that sold out, Roy says.

That's selling out, I say very cleverly.

I get another big speech about what makes theatre so special. Roy changes sides in his argument. Proposes, in the end, that most art is a useless exercise. Theatre isn't that extraordinary — really, seeing a white-tailed deer run across the highway and not get hit by a logging truck is much more life-altering than anything onstage.

When Roy finally runs out of gas, he puts an arm around me and says, Do me a favour, OK? Somebody needs to check in on Marlene.

Jessica, I say. Isn't that her job?

Jessica is trying to figure out what happened to the blocking in the second act, he says. That's why she's on her Mac. And she's a little bit preoccupied with my cancer thing too.

Right, I say. How about one of the others? Howard? Allan?

Nobody really likes Marlene, he coughs. Except you.

Is she going on tomorrow? I ask.

I think — well, from what I've seen, probably not, he says, clearing his throat in the process.

You'd have energy in the piece, I say. I guarantee that. She's unpredictable. There's your fucking chaos.

I'm not asking for chaos, Roy says. Remember?

Then what do you want, Roy?

He pulls out a smoke and uses it as a pointer. Well, he says, I want people to remember this show, think about my ending, wonder what it all meant. Ambiguity, remember?

Aren't you being just a tad bit egotistical? I say. I mean, come on, your ending? After all, it is just a play, right?

Roy puts the unlit smoke in his mouth. This seems to make him think harder. He wrinkles his forehead hard, rubs at it with his left thumb. Yeah, it is just a play, he says. But it's my play. He swirls his ice cubes and finishes his drink like he's in a movie scene, dramatically bangs the glass down, then slides it over toward me.

I stop it with the side of my wrist, push it back just a little. I really don't like the smell of Scotch.

You want another one? I ask. I'm buying.

No, I've had enough, he says. But you can pay for this one if you want.

Right.

Ten bucks, he says. It's fucking expensive. Sorry. But after tonight, I had to. That show was awful.

He gets off his chair, slides off it actually, and then lists to his right once he's settled on the floor. He shouldn't list, he's a thin man. But parts of him hurt that he won't talk about. His lungs, probably. Every fucking breath.

What do you want me to say to Marlene? I ask.

Nothing, Roy says, just make sure she's OK. He thinks for a bit. Tell her she's good.

Is she though?

Yeah, sometimes. Yeah. He shuffles his weight, what's left of it, from side to side, as if testing out his balance, and scans the bar to see who he can avoid on the way out.

It's after midnight. The actors know tomorrow's going to be the big day, so most of them are just a little bit drunk. It seems to give them added insight about the play, particularly the ending where they all lie on the stage and pretend to sleep, yes, as if it was all just a dream.

Despite what Roy says, I think it's obvious. Not ambiguous. Or confusing. But that's just me. My point of view. I'm jaded, even a bit cynical. Theatre will do that to you, especially after twenty years or so.

I notice Susie isn't pouring as fast in here — hoping, I guess, that patrons will figure out bad service will soon lead to no service. She needs to wash her hair anyway, I'm sure.

Roy blows his nose, coughs into the linen. He's using a handkerchief, probably one he got from his dear old mom. He never talks about her. They were too close for too long. She saw every show of his, went through every relationship with him, then one night, while fighting pneumonia, she went in her sleep, a half pack of cigarettes at her side. Menthol Lights, I think. The healthy way to smoke.

The smoke from outside slowly seeps in through the cracks, big time whenever the door opens. The TV above the bar shows the fire at night, flames almost as high as the helicopters trying to fight it, certainly higher than any tree it hasn't consumed yet. A wall of fire. Hell coming to greet us. Or already here. In fact, those exact words — HELL IS HERE — are on the screen in big white letters. CBC News carries it.

I'm incredibly impressed with the quality of the images, the flat-screen TV so clear you can see the firefighters' sweat running down their smudged faces. Or maybe they're crying. I don't know.

Everyone be aware, the situation can change, the announcer says. Meaning from bad to worse, or from worse to horrible, or from horrible to something unfathomable. It all depends on the wind, right? I can't really hear because Bryan Adams is spilling from the bar stereo, Cuts Like a Knife rattling the stemware that's hanging upside down above our heads like icy bats.

Susie pulls at her hair, stares up at the screen. I think she's crying too, or trying not to. Her hair is pulled back into a miserable-looking ponytail, matching her face perfectly. She knows I'm watching her so she disappears into the back balancing a tray of dirty coffee cups.

Roy goes out the door and into the smoky night. A cab is waiting outside, yellow of course, and idling, adding noxious fumes to the noxious fumes already in the air.

When Susie comes back, she glides by and snatches up my empty glass. It's time, she says. Time.

Then the music stops. I'm actually sad when it does.

Chapter 22

I had no idea what was behind the big fancy house behind the big fancy vineyard. So when I saw the big fancy heated swimming pool complete with two sets of big fancy diving boards and the big fancy rainbow-coloured cabana, I nearly fell over.

Wow. A huge, huge pool. The kind of blue you only see in lovers' eyes.

Susie led me in here after feeding me the last dregs of the coffee in the tasting room. Don't be too shocked about Marlene, she said.

I was ready for the worst, ready to give some sympathy to, or at least drink some more excellent wine with, an excellent, slightly depressed buddy.

I wasn't ready for this.

She stands in the waist-high shallow end of the pool, steam rising around her, wearing, I think, one of her costumes from the play. All white lace and gold trim, it billows naturally around her in the sapphire water like an enormous jellyfish. Her plastic gold crown pins her hair back, giving her face more definition.

She's like a silent screen star, really white and full of expression, although it might just be the runny mascara. Her blue eyes blaze up at the smoky sky as the moon peeks around a cloud to see how the fire is going, and I guess to also see what the hell we're doing.

What are we doing?

Me, standing and gaping by the side of the pool.

Her, half-submerged.

Marlene doesn't see me. Or sees me and doesn't care. Hands held out, I guess like Jesus would do, as if to still the waters — except they're already still. I mean, it is a pool.

I continue to hold my empty wine glass from the tasting room, running shoes in my other hand because I didn't want to walk through the house tracking dirt.

I think I hear rap from somewhere. Probably behind me, from beyond the vineyards, bouncing off the hills, deep bass like a heartbeat popping from car speakers. Thud-thud, thud-thud. A helicopter adds to it, buzzing through the sky across the water, its searchlight piercing the dark backside of the lake. A bug in the black, looking for what?

My ear itches. I want to clear my throat. I'm dying for a drink.

Another roar. A powerboat, I suppose.

Everything fades, centring me to this silence, here, at the top of the hill, in a manicured backyard overlooking the rows and rows of vines and perfect dirt.

With the house lights dimmed, the underwater halogens give the pool a 3D-screen feel. Twinkling vacation homes dot the shores over there. The fire adds orange trim along the far ridge.

It's definitely a movie moment.

Instinctively I want to take out my cellphone and click a photo, thinking somehow my memory will never do this justice.

But I can't. No power. Dead battery. And even if I could snap now, it would never get all of this in, especially not the green pot lights around the outside edge of the pool, or the planters bursting with red and yellow roses which droop somewhat in the dark.

I should say something here.

Hi, I say. Because what else can I say?

Nothing. She ignores me. Takes another step deeper into the water.

OK. Pocket the phone, put down my shoes and glass on the white patio table, get closer to the water. The lawn is slightly damp, my toes feel it. I have a dry throat, like I haven't swallowed all day. Itch behind my ear now, getting worse. Fingernails hurt too. A throbbing between my eyes, which sting like hell.

God help me. Help me please.

I think all visions get this response. What is she doing? Is she crazy? Am I?

At first I think Marlene is praying or mumbling to herself, but when I stumble by the diving boards to move alongside, what she's saying becomes clear:

If we shadows have offended, think but this, and all is mended: that you have but slumb'red here, while these visions did appear. And this weak and idle theme, no more yielding but a dream, gentles, do not reprehend. If you pardon, we will mend.

She says this to the water, all of it, and then it's gone, into the smoke and mist and —

Fuck me, this is great. She's great.

I shiver. Think. Shiver. Think.

Marlene is incredible.

Act.

ACT!

A moment passes like the wind behind a freight truck.

What do you say? What can you say, when you know everything will change when you speak?

But there she is, a beautiful fairy queen. In her element, I suppose. Onstage she's awkward and gawky with no sense of blocking. Here she drifts and drifts into the centre of the pool and my universe.

Fuck me.

Perfect.

Those aren't your lines, I finally say. Are they?

No, says Marlene, not even looking at me. But aren't they great?

Yeah, I say, sitting down beside the pool, feeling the damp of the cement seep through my blue jeans. It's not uncomfortable.

Marlene now studies me, sinking deeper into the water until her breasts go under, her long hair forming a red train along the back of the white dress. I'm certain she's treading water, but it's effortless, as if her head is held up with strings. Why are you here? she asks.

Why are you? I say.

I live here, remember? Marlene says with her chin now dipping into water. Did Roy send you?

Yeah, I say. He did. He's worried.

About my mental condition, Marlene says.

I suppose. Yeah.

He's not going to put me in tomorrow night, is he, Marlene says, her voice bouncing off the surface of the pool.

Well — not in that costume, I say.

It's not a costume, Marlene smiles. It was my mother's grad dress. From high school.

And the crown?

Tiara, she says. Homecoming queen, wouldn't you know.

People still did that in the '70s. All downhill after that. Married three assholes in a row, then killed herself last year.

She spins in the water.

One.

Two.

Three.

I'm sorry, I say.

Marlene smiles again, says, Well, didn't actually *kill* kill herself, just drank too much and ate tons of bad food. She weighed two hundred and eighty pounds. Big woman, small dreams — or big dreams that, you know, became small. Over time. Always over time. Know what I mean?

Yeah, I know, I say.

She floats toward the deep end of the pool, the steam of the water giving her that movie veil of soft focus. She's beautiful, more beautiful than I ever could have imagined.

Why are you in the pool? I ask.

Because I still like to dream big, Alex.

Good one. An excellent answer that makes no sense whatsoever.

I want to say you're crazy, I finally say.

Yeah, I bet, Marlene says from the other side. When I come out here, in the pool, I remember my cues.

You mean your lines, I say.

Whatever, she says. Give me something. From the play. Anything.

All right, I think. Out of this wood do not go —

No, no, she says. You got it wrong. It's, Out of this wood do not desire to go: thou shalt remain here, whether thou wilt or no. I am a spirit of no common rate; the summer still doth tend upon my state; and I do love thee; therefore go with me.

Marlene opens her eyes and it's very, very nice. Her expression. Innocent, and motherly, and sexy too, I guess. I got it right, didn't I? she says, spitting out some water.

Yes. I think so.

She slips away a little more, head lower in the water so that her eyes barely break the surface. Then she pops up somewhat and spins, a slight churn of water signalling it. A vortex. Why don't you come in, she says, her back turned toward me. It's warm.

Why would I do that? I ask.

Why wouldn't you? she says back.

Then I have one of those life-defining moments, you know, when you consider the odds of this ever happening again, or anyone believing it did in the first place. But there she is floating just in front of me, some of the dress now clinging to her body in all the right places, and her lips still so red and soft. Even her freckles sparkle with, I don't know, fairy dust. Or something.

God help me. Why am I here? Why are any of us here?

Marlene points at me and waves her forefinger. It's oddly parental, but still, I drop my pants, toss off my socks, and ease myself into the warm, warm water, realizing only then to remove my shirt, which I throw behind me up on the deck like it's a skinned wet seal.

Maybe that's not the right simile. Maybe I'm so drunk that this is just a haze of alcohol-related imagery. A fuzzy mind made fuzzier. A manic playwright exaggerates. Desperate lies to give my life some fucking poetry.

But it *is* real. And I'm having some sober thoughts, too. Like: I'm naked in somebody's pool. It's very late. And there's this woman, this amazing woman wearing a fairy costume, waving me in, deeper and deeper. She has beautiful hair and red lips.

And she's with someone else. Living with someone else. Repeat that one for sure.

How deep is this anyway? I'm in up to my chest. My neck. Finally my chin. I toe the bottom of the pool for balance. Steady. Steady —

It's warm in here.

Perfect.

What a time this is, Marlene says. The two of us here, right now, under these stars. We could be anywhere and would it matter? Would it? Her mascara runs a little more. From the water, or from tears. Her hand is flat on my back. The other one too.

We spiral each other. Slowly. Closer and closer —

Maybe I shouldn't be doing this, I say, now fully embracing her, our lips inches away, inches away, circling and circling, treading water so efficiently that we never kick each other. Bodies, warm and soft and sensuous, and under it the hearts, our hearts, keeping it all so perfectly perfect we finally need to kiss. And when it's done, another one, and another one, until we both start thinking about where we need to go next, and then realizing at the same time that we are exactly where we should be.

Hmm.

What happens next? I think I say.

Marlene laughs and leans her head back gracefully, dipping her ears in the water. She bites me slightly, here on my lip and then here and here. I bite back and one of us gurgles bubbles, me I think.

Very immature.

Or endearing, one of us says.

Another kiss. Shorter but perfectly formed.

I'm confused.

Why, she says, now running a hand along my face, her shrivelled fingers slightly witchy, but in a good way.

You're with someone, aren't you? I say.

You mean Steven? she whispers, her red hair clinging to her head like little snakes. How came these things to pass? O, how mine eyes do loathe his visage now, she whispers into my right ear so that it tickles me all the way down.

What do you think you're doing? I mean, come on. Visage?

Shhh, she hushes, a finger on my lips. It moves slowly to my cheek and then to my neck. I quiver. We both do. Even in this warm water. A quiet burst of pent-up shit: love, romance, horniness. Danger. We kiss again and it all starts up again, this love; we're spinning slightly in the water with no sense of time or place because our eyes are closed and the water suspends us.

Under the perfect smoky sky.

A fire behind it all.

This really is.

Some.

Moment.

Hmmmm.

Let's not ruin it.

With any more words.

Promise?

Later. In bed. An empty wine bottle sits beside us on the table with both our cellphones and a green office lamp that's been on all night. The sun crests the hills to lay down a coat of morning, the kind that makes you overheat and throw off the blankets and sheets to lie naked in bed and feel your skin on hers. Shoulders and hips and legs touching. Every pressure point ecstatic.

This is a good feel. A full-body one that goes down all the way to our feet, also touching. Every twitch gives me pleasure, especially when our hips bump. Neither of us has spoken for a while, because why ruin it?

And I know I would. With something stupid.

Maybe she's asleep. If she is, it doesn't matter. I'm OK with that. OK with everything as is. Yeah.

And then I realize I'm happy. Almost completely. Even though my mouth is dry and I've got a growing hangover. It suddenly occurs to me that shallow, self-centred people can have moments of redemption. Here I am, and here she is, and the world is over there, and everything is really wonderful.

Look over her naked freckled body and see that she's smiling too, at my smile. Happy? I ask.

All good, she says. Very good.

Never had that before, I say. Trust me. It's crazy good.

She kisses me on the cheek, then my eyes, says, Oh, you, always the playwright.

I'm serious, I laugh. This is all new territory for me. Cheating with somebody else and then discussing it in the morning. I wish I felt more guilty. I wish I felt more remorse. It's all very confusing.

Another kiss, on the lips.

I want to say I love you. I think.

Uh-oh. Marlene twitches. Leg moves away, just a bit. Uh-oh again. Her head turns, feel her breath on my neck.

OK. What did you just say? she says, leaning over me to touch my nose.

I know what I said, I say. So do you.

She leans back on her pillow and closes her eyes, thinks. Yeah, she says, I know, I know.

I wait her out. Stare at the sparkles in the ceiling, the pattern on the walls, her plasma-screen TV above the antique Amish dresser.

Where did I go wrong in my life, she finally says, to only now realize what I've missed?

I know what you mean, I say. But it's a gamble. Life is, isn't it?

She doesn't answer, because really, I'm full of shit and we both know it. I shouldn't talk when I'm emotional. My mother told me when I did it sounded like complete blather. Silence is golden, she said. Try it sometime.

So I try it now. Tell the voice in my head to take five. Or ten. I turn and smell the chlorine in Marlene's hair, mixed with a slight tinge of sweat and perfume, vanilla and tangerine I think, and say: About tomorrow —

She kisses me, says, Please, don't speak.

This could be a performance. Both of us using each other, and to what end? Then it's gone and we're left with snapshots and clever dialogue. We are always much more interesting when love creeps around.

Stop it, she says. It's about other things with us. I know it.

The kiss continues.

Wonderful, I mumble.

No, you, she mumbles.

Both right. The kiss continues.

When I first met you —

Me too —

Shut up.

Shut up.

Very, hmm, very —

Yes, hmm, yes —

Our mouths feel no room for words now. I want to focus on her eyes at least, but it's all a blur. What are we doing and why now, with each other? Stop it. Just Zen the moment out and enjoy. Can you do that? Yes? Please?

The kiss continues. I relax. Lean into it. Let it wash over me. No songs, no poetry, no slogans, just the lips, just the lips.

Very nice.

And that's when we hear a motorcycle approaching.

It's like a gunshot to Marlene. She bolts up in bed, tits flying a bit, and screeches something like, Christ Jesus, shit on a stick!

What? I say. What?

It's him.

Who?

Him. Steven.

Where?

His motorcycle. Marlene points down the vineyard in the distance, along the highway, at a slowly approaching bike, its rider all black leather and helmet with red stickers. Yes, he's that close.

He's back early, Marlene says. Fuck! Already on her feet, she grabs not her clothes but mine and jams them into my arms, my shoes falling to the floor. Pick them up, she shouts, Go, go!

Wait a second, hold on, I say. Why can't we just tell him?

Don't be an idiot, he's crazy, Marlene says, yanking down the blinds.

I have my pants on now, my shirt next, socks are confusing me. Grab my cellphone. That's important when fleeing the scene of an illicit affair, right?

Stop talking and go! she yells.

Could you call me a cab? I say.

What?

How am I getting back to town? I was drunk all day yesterday so I was using a cab and, just so you know, I'm very responsible —

Are you crazy? she says. RUN!

But these aren't my good running shoes, I say, holding up the right one which clearly has no tread and virtually no support either.

Go, go, go, Marlene barks, unlatching and then sliding open the glass bedroom doors leading to the pool. She pushes me out into the warm air toward the vineyard. Steven is insanely jealous, she says, slamming my other runner into my hand.

This isn't fair, I say. You should have told me.

He wasn't supposed to be here, Marlene says, pulling on a brilliant bright-red housecoat and then shoving me again, hard, with her elbows.

I need to get my running shoes on.

The vineyard, go, she says.

Where? What?

It leads to the road. Hurry!

I jump over the little cement wall around the outside of the pool area, shoes in hand.

Run, stumble, fall because the first row of vines have wires suspended below them that I don't see. Pick myself up. The motorcycle man is maybe fifty, sixty metres away, his head swivelling, as if picking me up on his radar. I duck instinctively. Didn't see me. Didn't see me. Positive. Absolutely didn't.

Run hunched, a rat through the vines, in bare feet, shoes and socks in my hand, turn to see Marlene sans housecoat jump into the water to swim, the logic of this escaping me. Duck. Run. Serpentine. Go. Go. Go. You're a rat. A fucking rat!

Past this row, then cut across and down that row. Low and almost drunken run. More like a downhill lurch, feet stinging from sharp rocks, almost tripping on the wire. My heart pounds, eyes water. Where to go, where to go.

I try a lope, doesn't work. Lurch. Just lurch. You're doing

well with the lurch. Calm down. That seems to work. Here and there. Go. To where? Where?

There to the paved road. Behind me I hear someone screaming, Hey! Hey! Or maybe I'm imagining things. Maybe it's just me, inside my head. Or Marlene in trouble. Not my problem. Well, yes, it is, but it's all downhill from here, right?

Run, you bastard! Run!

I'm getting away. Unbelievable. Yes, I am in better shape than I thought. Not really out of breath. But my knee hurts and I think my foot is cut and ok, I might throw up.

Thank God for nice organized rows of grapes and the tilled ground and the downhill route. Really not so bad. Just through here and then over the wire and toward the ditch. Go to the ditch! Go fast! Skip it. Come on, skip the ditch. In one leap. One glorious leap. Just build up more speed. You're only in your forties. Yes! Look, I'm nimble. Over it! Get over it! All right, run down one side and then up the other. Not so hard. Keep the speed up. Lift your knees. Pump your arms. Chin up. Chin up.

Burst out of the vineyard, not looking behind, not daring to, until I realize I'm on the edge of the highway. I sit down huffing and puffing, thinking I'm safe, I'm not on the property. It seems logical to check my foot. No blood, good, put my shoes and socks on, good, and while I'm doing this a cab — yes, a cab — pulls up.

The driver leans out — it's Ali again. This time he's wearing a baseball cap with the Angels' logo on it. How appropriate.

He says the words I'm dying to hear: Need a lift, my dear friend?

Nobody will ever fucking believe this.

I slump into the back seat like a tall man at the cinema. I am barely sweating now, barely out of breath. I give Ali the address, hunker down just a bit under the seat, and stifle a laugh, a

244 IIII Aaron Bushkowsky

sigh, and a nervous giggle. Do not do that, you are not a child, do not bring bad karma upon yourself, believe in God again, and make sure to be kind for a while. Jesus. Thank you, Jesus. No atheists in foxholes, my father always said. Or among cheating bastards in fleeing cabs. Does that make sense?

Drive on, my good man. Drive on. Onward and upward. To the finish.

After a moment I sneak a glance behind me, thinking I'll finally see my enemy — the man I've wronged, the man who has every right to punch me in the mouth — see him run out onto the road, black helmet in hand, screaming, I'll kill you, or You bastard, you. But I don't see anything, just the empty vineyard and the empty road. The morning sun in my face gives me shivers. The world behind stretches out. The sky widens as the highway thins out. Everything is so blue and bright. Hurts my eyes. A pounding in my temples.

I wonder if Marlene will be found naked in the pool floating face-up.

This is what us writers do. Especially the crazy ones.

Chapter 23

An oxygen mask is hooked to a small portable grey tank beside the bed, DANGER printed across the bottom of it in bold red letters. Almeera and Shamir stand like bedposts on either side, white shirts again, looking concerned, tired, but resolved. Roy struggles with each breath.

Yeah, I know. Shocking.

When did this happen? I say, holding my coffee, sweating and shaking still from my morning run through the vineyard.

Early this morning around six, says Almeera. We took him to the emergency, and this is their solution. We phoned you. Several times.

My cell was dead, I say, watching for Roy to signal to me that he's OK.

He does. A wink, I think. So I move closer, watch as he pulls off the mask with an eagle claw of a hand. He rasps above the slight hiss of forced air, I'm fine. Or I'm fried. I'm not sure I heard. His eyes flutter like he's just waking up.

The smoke in the air, Shamir explains, has made the oxygen a necessity.

For how long?

This is what none of us really know, Shamir says. When air becomes unnecessary.

Almeera smiles and says, What he is saying is that the condition will continue to decline until transformation is inevitable.

What transformation?

Shamir clears his throat and doesn't look at me. Again, this is the great mystery, he says.

Roy's eyes open wider, as if he's just figured out what this stupid conversation is all about.

Hey, I say.

Hey, he says.

How you doing, I say.

Not so good, he says.

Yeah.

Yeah.

Can you walk?

My legs are fine, Roy groans. It's my lungs that are shot.

What about the show tonight? I say.

The show always goes on, Roy coughs through the mask.

There's something I should tell you, I say. Something I know you'll find important.

I back toward the cabin door and open it for Shamir and Almeera.

We'll find some tea, says Almeera on the way out.

Shamir says, Not too much excitement for him. It's best that way.

They disappear into the light. Yeah, I know how that sounds. I partially close the door to keep the heat out. It's getting hotter earlier, probably because of the fires, probably because it's the apex of summer, probably because I'm dehydrated from all the drinking. I can't entirely trust my own perceptions anymore.

The sound outside is a cacophony of helicopters and planes. A drone. It's irritating. I cut it off with a slight slam, making sure to lock the door.

I pace a bit to get warmed up. Roy watches me from behind the plastic. It takes a moment to get used to the sound of the air filling Roy's mask, the slight wisp of shhh. Even Chekhov doesn't like it, smacks his left talon on the cage floor over and over again, shaking his little head with his eyes closed. Maybe he can't grasp the seriousness of the situation, Roy leaving this world with every second breath.

Roy finally pulls the mask off. Fuck this, he says. It's not really helping.

Just pretend you're a pilot in a jet fighter and it's the Korean War. Just let it hang around your chin or something, I say.

Yeah, cool, he says, and does exactly that, looking a little like a thin, weedy John Wayne piloting an F-86 over the always-cloudy skies of Pyongyang, North Korea on a Friday afternoon. Bombs away, he says

Yeah, funny, I say.

He hasn't shaved lately. The stubble doesn't add fullness to his face — most of it has gone grey, adding pallor where pallor isn't needed. His eyebrows are even bushier than before, and his Adam's apple works its way up and down his neck like a busy mole.

Are you shocked? Roy asks.

Yeah, I say, a little. I mean, look at you.

I've stopped looking, he says. Whatever this is, well, it's not me, and I'm not interested in seeing it develop, if you know what I mean.

Yeah, right, I say. I take a deep, deep breath and sense that Pine-Sol cleaner has been used recently. Our cabin looks exceptionally clean and tidy. All of Roy's clothes are neatly hung over the backs of the two wooden chairs of the small dining room table. Black jeans, black shirt, black shoes hiding below in the chair spindles. The floor is clean, maybe even waxed, and some of the chrome handles to the kitchen cabinets practically glow. Someone has folded the one red-and-green dishtowel over the edge of the sink. Two white coffee cups stand upside down on the counter, also clean.

It's nice in here, I say.

Yeah, they cleaned it while I slept this morning, Roy says. Shamir and Almeera, they're the best.

I thought they were on vacation. Don't they have somewhere to go?

No. Plus they're waiting for the insurance to settle over their car. The fire got it.

They seem to be taking it pretty well, I say.

He nods. Like I said, they're the best.

Well, they sure replaced me, I say.

What?

Replaced me, I say again.

Bombs away, he says again, then laughs.

Are you on medication? I ask.

Yup, he smiles. It's good. All very good. By the way, I hope you don't mind that I took your bed. But you haven't been around lately.

No, it's fine. All yours.

I sit on the bed and notice how warm the sheets feel. Comfy sheets too. Like three-hundred-thread-count cotton ones. Like sheets you might get at The Bay or something. Very, very nice.

I put my coffee down on the bedside table, the one with the Gideon's Bible on it. You reading the Good Book now? I say.

Almeera is using it to press flowers, Roy says. She found some pretty yellow ones outside the hospital.

I pick up the bible and page through it. No flowers. I put it back quickly because I don't want anything to rub off on me — almost say it aloud but decide against it. Instead I say, Can you go to the show tonight?

I wouldn't miss it, says Roy. Not on your life.

And who's in the show? Have you figured it all out?

Yeah, he mumbles. Sure.

Who?

I guess whoever was in it last night, he says. Go with that.

Why. Why go with that?

Because it's safe, Roy says. And I know it will work.

Look, I say, fully aware that starting a sentence with look always means something important is about to be said. Look, you know what you're going to get with Emma. But I have to tell you that Marlene is the one you want.

Is this your big important news? he says. Or is there more?

It's all about the show, I say. Your show.

Roy watches Chekhov peck at his reflection in the little mirror. He puts on the mask and grabs a couple of deep breaths as if he's about to go on a dive.

Marlene is not an actor, he says. And that's the truth. Sometimes she gets it right, but mostly she flails about hoping to get lucky. It's like directing a person picked at random from a crowd.

You're wrong, Roy, I say. I'm going to tell you something about what I just did last night and one of two things will happen. One, you will see me as a cheating, arrogant bastard who takes advantage of a bad situation, essentially a dirty dog — or two, you will see me as somebody who now believes in miracles and fell in love with the right person at the wrong time.

Roy pulls the plastic mask down to his chest. This isn't going to get weird, is it? he says.

Fuck, I don't know. I take a sip of my now-cold coffee. Put it between my knees. Sigh.

Tell me you didn't sleep with Marlene, Roy says. Please tell me you didn't. Shit, you did. I know you did. God help us.

Chekhov nods his head over and over, like he's a devout Jew at the Wailing Wall. I take another sip of coffee because I know it will help me swallow.

Roy puts his mask back on, looking like he's just seen the end of a very bad play. Mumbles. Well, he says, I'm waiting. Why did you sleep with her? What were you thinking in there? In that big stupid head of yours?

I have some words coupled like boxcars on a very long train track and I think about re-ordering them a little to start with the more loaded ones. But in the end, it just comes out like I knew it would — hardly logical, a flurry of words.

I'm not going into details with you, Roy, I say. But I gotta tell you, she's the one you have to go with tonight. She is. I saw her run lines that made every moment real. I mean, I was naked in the pool with her but it was amazing. She's the real deal. Trust me. A fucking artist if I ever saw one. And she'll make this production special.

What's in that coffee, he says.

Yes, I slept with her, I say. Yes, her partner nearly caught me. Yes, he's here for the opening. And yes, she showed me she can act while floating in the deep end of her heated swimming pool. And no, this is not about her breasts…trust me.

Jesus, he coughs. Oh my Jesus.

It was amazing, Roy. Totally. She's an amazing actor.

Oh God help me, he wheezes. Fuck me. Fuck me good.

We take a little time to contemplate my sanity. I keep sipping at the coffee, Roy fumbles with the loose blue elastic on the mask.

Why should I care if she's that good? Roy says. I didn't see it. Why risk complete failure? Why not go with what works?

Look — no, listen. Listen to me, Roy. You're slipping off the proverbial edge here. You're getting worse and worse. This is going to be it. This is the big one. The big one. Because it's probably going to be the last thing you direct. And you've worked your ass off. In the smoke. With a bunch of sketchy borderline-actors and a meddling AD who thinks she's better than you. We've been burned out of house and home, embarrassed by our lack of commitment and artistic integrity, we've drunk too much, and you've smoked about a thousand cigarettes. We've fought over trivial things and damaged friendships and made up again and drunk even more. Well, what are you going to leave us with? What's going to be your statement? How is your show going to change anybody or anything? What's going to be your fucking legacy? What will you leave us with? What?

Roy rubs his eyes, smothers a cough or two. I don't know, he says. I just don't know. This is all very dramatic.

Well, yes, I say. Life-changing, dude. Come on.

He breathes, squeezes his mouth into a very false grimace, like he's just sucked on a lemon or two. What a way to go, he says. What a way to go.

～

It's after seven o'clock and, as they say, we're about to rock. As we walk down the knoll toward the amphitheatre, searchlights — yes, you heard me, searchlights — probe the smoky sky even though it's still light out. Whose fucking idea was that? All they do is show off the smoke, the dark edges puffed out and rolling across the whitecaps of the lake, smothering houseboats on the way to the opening of our *Dream*.

How much farther will it spread, before we can't see what's going on and the audience coughs their way home, charred programs in hand?

What happened to all the seagulls? Why aren't there seagulls around?

A crow sits proudly on the top of the nearby power pole, ruffles his feathers, watches the fools line up for the show, sees me picking my way around them toward the entrance.

Slightly behind me, Roy, all in black, leans on Shamir, all in white, all in linen, while Almeera, also in white, carries the portable oxygen tank in a backpack. They walk as if in a funeral procession.

I move ahead to look for the AD, with her oversized sunglasses and squinty eyes, who said Roy could decide his own fate though I know better. I know what lurks in her heart. She's worked in theatre for over twenty-five years. There's nothing there but stone.

The tent looks spent. The edges along the sides are all covered in grime and ash, like somebody's shaded it in with an HB pencil, a nice big one. The opening night crowd, mostly wealthy locals and winery employees, line up around the side dressed in the mandatory black. Everybody has a glass of wine in hand. Plastic goblets. Reserve Merlot. The good stuff. Muted conversation. Bits and pieces I barely understand. All about the fire, of course. The thing that brings us together. Catastrophe and disaster.

Did you see the back of the lake, did you see the news, the way those ten houses went up, what about the winery, that little one over there, what happened to all their barrels, isn't this incredible that we are here and the fire is just over there, just over there.

I know, I know.

In front, three large ladies with red aprons are handing out programs, keeping the crowd orderly, and telling stupid jokes.

They see us coming and wave us through. We make our way in through the front by the stage and see some of the chairs marked with coloured bits of paper, names on them like Joel, Cathy, Lorne, Miriam, Kristen, Eunice — Eunice?

Another Eunice exists who isn't my sister? Must be in her eighties.

Marlene and Emma are onstage wearing identical costumes: long, pale sleeping gowns, no frills, bottoms frayed slightly. Marlene's looks dirty and wrinkled. Not a good sign. Emma has too much rouge on her cheeks, too much mascara, and she looks a little like Cleopatra. Marlene looks like she's in a trance, like she just waded out of the deep end, red hair still wet, curling at the ends around her shoulders. Both stand away from each other and vocalize like grieving Arab women at the bright lights above, where I see tendrils of smoke snaking around the extension cords and lamps.

Roy groans. Not good, he coughs. Not good. What are they doing onstage? The house is open for Chrissake.

Don't worry, Almeera says. Everything will work out. Please, one step at a time, my friend.

We stumble up the steps toward the sound booth in the back where Roy wants to hide during the show. I pick out a seat near the three-quarters mark, on the aisle, and put my jacket on it. Assess the situation. Scan the room, as they say. A couple of worker bees, also large women wearing red aprons, guard the entrances.

Jessica appears onstage with her headset around her neck. She's all businesslike, her hair done up in a bun, wearing the traditional black jeans and black T-shirt. It looks like she's drawn black circles under her eyes with that stuff baseball players use to help them deal with bright stadium lights. Later I find out that's exactly what it is. You can buy it at Walmart in the sports department beside the leather gloves and aluminum bats. She moves to centre exactly between Emma and Marlene and checks her clipboard, as if studying the starting lineup. Motions to both actors to please leave. They do, but not without looking up at the back where Roy settles in, his oxygen mask on now, his ball cap pulled over his eyes so he looks a little like a sleeping pilot.

Jessica sees me and quickly jumps off the stage. I have this effect on a lot of women, I joke to myself, and then file under Not Funny as she approaches.

Why is he here if he's like that? she snarls at me, making sure to stand directly in front of my face so Roy can't see her.

Come on, Jessica —

Shouldn't he be in the hospital?

He's OK, I say. Really. He just needs the oxygen because of the smoke in the air. It's making things worse.

She doesn't look like she's buying it. Chews on the end of her pencil, scans around like she's sensing something in the air other than the smoke. This is not a good night for an opening, she says, nodding toward Roy. I can feel it in my bones.

He's got help. Almeera and Shamir. They're dentists from England.

Jessica says, Great. Dentists too.

Where's the AD?

Jessica looks past me, to Roy in the back. She's back with the actors spreading her poison, she says. Where else?

She's not deciding who's going on, is she? I ask.

I doubt it, Jessica says. And oh, by the way, you look nice, what is that, a new shirt?

Yeah, it might be. Sure, I say. I flex my chest muscles. It *is* a relatively new shirt, a black silk short-sleeved number I've been saving for a day like this.

Jessica is trying to be nice even though she's really, really worked up. So, she asks, Can Roy speak?

He can speak, I say. He's not dead.

Don't talk like that, she says. It's bad karma. And here's a scary thought: we open in half an hour.

Are some people coming in? I ask, noticing a gaggle of over-dressed wine snobs, big guys on either side of a smaller guy, pushing their way past the red-aproned guards to claim front row seats.

Jessica barely looks. Yeah, that's the owner. Steven. He gets to do that. It's his fucking winery.

You know the owner? I ask with a tiny shiver.

No, I don't know him personally. I know who he is because I was told to watch for the guy because he's a psycho. So now I know him, OK.

I peer past Jessica's bun head and there he is, smaller than I thought, but wide. Fills out a tux very nicely. Has the perpetual five o'clock shadow, short cropped hair à la Justin Timberlake, with some sort of tattoo on his neck behind his pierced left ear. He carries a bottle of red in one hand and a couple of glass wine goblets in the other. His friends, three taller men with facial hair, also wearing tuxedos and short haircuts, carry wine glasses and full bottles as well. They look like boxers: square jaws, bent noses, large protruding fore-heads. Two chatty Kathys follow them wearing very tight black cocktail dresses and carrying tiny sparkling black hand-bags. They have nice legs, complete with cute tattoos, and teeter expertly in stilettos like cranes in a shallow swamp. Steven hands over a wine glass to one of the gals with blonde hair extensions and pours her a big one, then sees us in the back and waves at us with a grin. He raises his glass, probably in mock salute.

He seems like a very happy guy for a jealous boyfriend, I say.

Partner, Jessica corrects me. Because, you know, they do live together.

Steven then recognizes Roy in the very back of the open sound booth and flashes a peace sign or something. It might even be a rapper thing, a secret gang signal.

Wow. He's cut. I'm dead. I am so dead.

Jessica sees me wince. I wouldn't worry, she says.

What? What do you know, Jessica?

That's the question, isn't it, she says. By the way, I think you should be taken out at dawn and shot for what you did.

What? What did I do?

Oh, come on, Alex. Don't act so innocent. If you wanted to get your rocks off why didn't you just come and see me? I would have fixed you good.

What? What are you talking about?

You are a dirty stick, Alex. And you haven't just fucked the star, you've fucked this show. Thanks for making my job so much easier.

Does Steven know?

Jessica smiles. Well, that's the million-dollar question, isn't it? She makes her way up the stairs toward the back, her headset cord dragging behind, a very long cartoon fuse that leads to her cranium.

I sit down and pretend to read the program. Blah, blah, blah. Lots of typos and spelling mistakes. Typical. Fold it up into quarters and slide it into my back pocket. Then I decide to follow Jessica to the rear, careful not to turn my back entirely on Steven and his gang, who are engaged in a lot of loud back-slapping and fuck yous.

When I get to the booth Almeera is massaging Roy's skinny shoulders, while Shamir adjusts the oxygen tank, making sure it's leaning just right against the plywood panel that makes up the table. Roy has a happy-opening grin splattered across his ashen face. If he died now, the death mask would be comical.

Jessica pretends not to notice the three extra bodies in her control booth, four counting me on the edge, but I know she's pissed. Puffs out and bristles, doesn't look at us, throws down her clipboard. She busies herself with getting the computer ready, the colourful grid grabbing her attention as she goes through her pre-show routine, talking softly to invisible elves scattered throughout the venue via her headset. Glares at the stage with death ray vision. The show must go on.

Fifteen, she says. We are at fifteen. And who's watching the back entrance? Where's my ASM? Talk to me. Somebody talk to me.

Jessica sees me staring at her. What? she says. What do you want?

Where's the AD now? I ask.

She quickly points to a video monitor and I see the AD backstage, helping the dressers straighten costumes and adjust wigs. She waves at the camera.

How does she know we're watching? I ask.

Oh, she knows because I told her, Jessica answers.

Then I see the AD's wearing a headset just like Jessica's.

She's not coming out, Jessica says. Going to watch it from the wings.

Wow, that's weird, I say. I thought she'd be up here at least. Trying to run things.

Well, it's my fucking show now, don't you know, Jessica says. Right, Roy?

Roy, hunched back into his leather coat, his body shrinking by the minute, gives us a little wave. He holds a Styrofoam cup of tea, the bag still floating, hooked over the rim with a plastic tab of some kind, and sips it with agonizing, slow moves, as if he's suspended in Jell-O.

My head hurts. Not just from the days upon days of drinking red wine, but from the smoke and lights. I haven't eaten since noon, and then only stale pizza, ham and pineapple I think, with copious amounts of coffee with extra cream in between.

Roy hands his tea to Almeera, who removes the bag and gives it back.

So, who's going on? I ask. Who?

That's another big question, Jessica says, and God the suspense is killing me. She flashes her teeth. They look sharp. I can't imagine running a tongue by them now.

Roy, I say. What's happening? Who's going on? Emma or Marlene?

Almeera smiles at me. He has made many critical decisions over the past twenty-four hours, she says, and now he wants to close his eyes and watch the program. It will, no doubt, be a wonderful evening of entertainment for all. It occurs to me now how nice her accent is, a blend of Indian and educated English. He is very contented, as you can easily see, she continues.

You sure that's contentment? I mean, he *is* medicated, right?

Almeera flashes the angel smile again. Stress is his enemy right now, she says. Do you understand?

This is bigger than his stress, OK. Roy, do you hear me? You know what has to happen. You know.

Roy's eyes flutter open, just a bit. I told her, he says, barely audible. I told her.

What? You told who what? Roy? WHO?

He waves a very bony hand at me and concentrates on his next difficult breath. With that, Shamir ushers me down the stairs to the middle of section G, seat 13, where I will sit and not cause problems for the rest of the show. His words. Very professional. Very stern. Almost lawyer-like. You must be here, he says. And please. Think kind thoughts and positive energy. Enjoy the entertainment.

It's then I notice his hand on my shoulder. For a little guy he's got a great grip. He looks like he belongs in some Bolly-wood movie singing about his mother. He's practically glowing. Loving it, absolutely loving it.

This will be transformative, my friend, Shamir says, and it's like the words are appearing in front of him as subtitles. We will remember this for all time.

He gives me a quick friendly squeeze, a nod too, as if we both know what might happen next. I will attend to our poor friend, he says. Please, the important decision has been made — and as they say, the show must continue on.

And then he goes back to Roy.

Before long, the audience drifts in. Some are dressed ele-gantly in suits and summer dresses, but most are in beachwear: flip-flops, Hawaiian shirts, khaki shorts with lots of pockets. Everybody is laughing and pointing to the empty stage. Bryan Adams fills the room with Summer of '69, booming from the huge black speakers perched at each corner of the tent like knights' shields. Most people carry drinks, wine of course. Some munch popcorn.

The show is already a hit because they can see, beyond the raked stage and exposed by the open back flap, the scenery of the scorched hills and the approaching flames. The lake edge is barely visible, and what's left is a wide-screen Technicolor shot of the worst of the inferno cresting at the city limits on the other side, marching on through the twilight. I imagine we're about to re-enact the burning of the Parthenon here in Kelowna, at an over-designed winery where the wealthy mingle with the

common man over Merlot and Chardonnay and caramel popcorn, where the mundane will soon meet the extraordinary and
time will stop as the story is retold, our story, our *Dream*. And
afterward maybe things will go on as they do, maybe we will
all go home to our pets and lawns and gardens and telephone
bills, and maybe we will continue to be bored and stupid and
desperate, but you never know, you never know.

Four hundred people sit. And wait. A hundred conversations turn to whispers as the lights on the stage dim and the
music fades. I notice how dark the shadows cast by the hill
behind us have made everything. We remain in the shadow line
of the penumbra of initial inspiration, to quote Joseph Conrad,
who probably knew that it isn't the story we live that really
counts but the stories that remain long after we're gone.

And then a trumpet flourish begins the adventure. French
horns too. The audience leans forward as one. Lights up,
brightly, and the stage glows as if made of molten lava. The
blood orange canvas, lit by gels in the lights, throws the actors
into relief, all of them dressed in white nightwear, all of them
pretending to sleep in various positions of dreaming. I scan
them quickly, looking for Marlene, then see her and feel some
sense of relief — but then I see Emma too, in the back, also pretending. Everyone in a trance, everyone everywhere, right here,
right now.

Who will rise first, I think? Who, tonight, will give us that
moment? Who will begin our journey toward the end? Who?

Chapter 24

The fire shut the show down two weeks early. The run was supposed to be four weeks, but in the end it became too dangerous. Too many embers in the air, too much smoke, too many insurance problems. The winery balked at a longer engagement. Everyone working on the show was treated, mostly with cheap red wine. Anyway, the audience had dropped off considerably. No matter how good the show was, most didn't want to see the horizon in flames. Oh, there goes Naomi and Randy's house, and Cindy the lesbian dog breeder's house and animal barn. Look at those homes burn. Look at the height of those flames. Stunning. What are we watching again? What is this play? What are they saying now?

The fire was a little tough on the actors too, although the lighting designer was ecstatic.

Here's the thing: it was a good show. A great show. A fucking fantastic show. Even the last one, when only one hundred diehard theatre buffs showed up in the heat and smoke to see a play they never thought would make sense in the twenty-first century. I found out later this last audience was mainly young people from Quebec, transients who came out to pick fruit for the summer. Lots of tattoos and pot. Long hair and beards. Beaded beards. Braided hair. Big smokers. Heavy on the water bottles, I think because most of them were on Ecstasy. Later they came backstage and told the actors it reminded them of Robert Lepage, Quebec's best-known theatre artist. It was, yes, beautiful. Of course. Poignant. Yes. Well-crafted, my friend. Très bon. Yes. We enjoyed. Very much. Merci. Now we smoke some weed. Yes.

Helmut and Katrina came on the last night, too. I went just to see how the show had grown, and there they were at the actor's tent talking to Jessica. When they saw me, I immediately got two bear hugs.

Exceptional, said Katrina. With the ending. It is full of ripe ambiguity.

Helmut said, I was looking for you, thinking you were acting but now I find out you are only interested in writing. Congratulations. This is much better. Much better.

They then invited me to stay with them soon. They had their eye on a new B&B close to where our cabins had been.

Beachfront, said Helmut. This is what people from Germany crave. So we will provide. Of course.

The view of lake is always better than just rows and rows of grapes, said Katrina. They already have that in abundance in Europe.

They didn't mention Roy, but I think they knew. Of course they knew. It was in the papers.

I walked them to their vehicle in the parking lot and we talked about tragedy in general. They said they had friends in the arts that always seemed to find more life in life. A painter who had Parkinson's. A singer who couldn't get out of a wheelchair. You know how it goes.

They hugged me again, less enthusiastically, then left for Denny's. Said they were famished and had I lost weight over the past while?

Yeah, nice folk, as my dad would say. Nice folk.

The show had its problems. The venue wasn't great. Dressing rooms were too small. Washrooms stank — they were portables and some teenagers had knocked a couple over for fun late one night after a show.

The soot was like a skin disease. Every seat in the house needed to be wiped off with a damp paper towel before the audience got in. It got worse and worse, even after the fire was sort of under control. The Mars water bomber did that, almost singlehandedly, because the pilots were starting to get pissed off at the news reports saying they weren't doing their job, which I guess is putting out forest fires. When they left, over two hundred locals gathered at the airport to see them off. Appropriately, it was at dusk on a cloudless night. The higher the plane climbed, the more it gleamed.

By the end of summer there were spindly black trees everywhere, like stubble on the chin of the lake, the far dark side. Beautiful still. Rugged. Even handsome.

I took some photos. They really didn't do the scene justice, so I touched them up on my Mac, and even then people said they looked fake, like a volcano had passed through and left a thick layer of lava. The few untouched firs, however, looked exceptionally green and stoic. Proud even.

It didn't rain much. Four months later and the place is still much drier than usual. Charred too. Christmas in a few weeks and the surrounding ski hills closed, still waiting for the right front to move in. At least that's what the TV guy said.

The winery, though, thrived. The show helped with the profile, naturally. It even made *The National* on CBC. They sold out of their icewine and reserve Chardonnay. And a reviewer from *Wine Spectator* gave their Merlot a very high rating. Eighty-eight, I think, out of one hundred. And this wasn't even the reserve Merlot. Close to perfect for a product made so far north, said the review. The best you could hope for given the place.

The winery didn't ask the theatre company back for another year of Shakespeare. It was just an experiment, said the PR guy. Don't get us wrong, we like theatre, and we liked that humorous play, *Midnight Summer's Dream*, he said. His first name was Rivers. He was a pretentious, skinny twenty-something ex-model turned spokesperson from Toronto who always travelled with his golf clubs in the trunk, wore mint green golf shirts and jaunty hats made of felt. He had a communications degree, a new BlackBerry on his designer belt, and a Saab convertible. And he never saw the show.

The critic did, though, Mr. Big Head himself. Drove out from Vancouver in his Prius hybrid. This is a direct quote from him: This dream is worth the drive, and is a worthy adversary for the forest fire that announces itself in the second act after the sun goes down. Epic, profound, and visually arresting, this production rethinks Shakespeare's *Dream* and gives us a fiery vision we won't soon forget.

No mention of the director, but what does it matter?

She was magnificent, the review goes on. Marlene. A star is born. Ravishing, extraordinary, and sexy, you can't take your eyes off her. A performance somewhere between chaotic and genius.

Another direct quote, from a different reviewer who had flown in from Toronto: She stopped my heart several times.

That's all it took for Marlene to become a star — that, and what she was able to do onstage for two weeks, every show. The power to stop time. To transport the audience to another place. To hold them there against their will. And then to release them at the end of the night, so utterly transformed they are unable to watch another crappy Hollywood movie for months. That takes talent.

So she moved to Vancouver in the fall. Steven didn't follow. Afraid to, after he found himself in tears in front of his biker friends on opening. He found solace later with Emma, who moved in and helped Susie run the tasting room. Said she always wanted a rich boyfriend who loved the arts — Emma did, just to be clear. Susie, it turns out, is a Jehovah's Witness.

I liked Emma in the end, because she told me Marlene was amazing. She came up to me at the opening night party, wearing a dress with a faux fox fur collar, and said, God, that was special, the way Marlene held on to her moments.

That was the key. The moments.

As always.

You need to hold on to them, Emma said, or else nothing much matters. Then she gave me a little princess wave, a limp-wrist sort of gesture I guess, and left with Steven, who was wearing aviator sunglasses even though it was close to midnight.

Marlene saw them leave together. Wasn't upset. She sat at her makeup mirror in the back and stared at herself for a long, long time while the rest of the cast slowly got drunk. Pensive, I thought, what a pensive woman she is. Turns out she was terrified, but with the kind of terror that makes life worth living — at least that's what she told me weeks later.

About Roy.

Yeah. About Roy.

I guess this is the tricky part. Endings are always hard. You get into your story and then hope like hell something profound will occur to get you out of it — something that will transform an audience, something they will take with them long after the lights have gone down. Something significant for God's sake.

Yeah. Right.

Roy.

What happened was this.

He left after the opening. The next day, in fact. Said he always wanted to see the most-photographed place in Canada, decided to drive out to Lake Louise with Almeera and Shamir. Call me romantic, he said, getting into the back seat of the car, dragging his oxygen tank behind.

He left me with a lot of stuff I was to take back with me to Vancouver. The trip was supposed to be three days, enough time to wander around on the Athabasca Glacier, then around Lake Louise, then a day in Banff to take photos of the elk downtown.

You sure about this? I asked him, still nursing a hangover.

Yeah, absolutely, Roy said, waving away a cough he couldn't stop. We're going to party like it's 1999. His eyes were watering over, making them look like they belonged on a Basset Hound, or, I suppose, an angel.

We didn't hug. Which I regret now. But Roy wasn't exactly the huggy type. Plus, I was afraid of squeezing more air out of him.

Almeera and Shamir were in the front seat, wearing all white, of course. The usual for them. Identical linen suits with expensive white cotton shirts, Panama hats, sunglasses, gold watches.

Until we meet again, Shamir said from the driver's side window, his hands at the proper ten-and-two.

We will remember you fondly, said Almeera, leaning over from the passenger side and showing her perfect teeth. She reached out and touched me on the cheek as if I had some glitter there.

Then off they went, with Roy collapsing into himself in the back seat listening to Mozart on his new iPad, nodding his head to the violins, directing French horns with his nose. He gave me a little soldier salute from the back window, half looking back at me, half smiling, I think.

There it is. Wave. Wave back.

Going, going, gone.

Into the horizon they went — happily, I'm sure of it. They made it as far as Moraine Lake, Valley of the Ten Peaks. Actually the sister lake to Lake Louise, encircled by a group of perfectly serene mountains, the same as the back of the old Canadian twenty dollar bill. Google it. The Great Divide runs across the tops of the jagged peaks behind the lake. I don't think he made it up there. Actually, I'm positive he didn't. He didn't have the air.

Roy passed away in the back of the rented Honda, Almeera on one side, Shamir on the other, the oxygen mask dangling from his face as if his jet fighter had just been strafed, downed behind enemy lines.

Yeah. That's some image, I'm sure.

I don't know how much of that is true and how much I'm now inventing. Don't know if it matters.

The fact is he's gone.

Shit.

No real surprise, I guess, given his condition. Although he didn't last six months as promised. Either he lied about that, or the doctor did.

He left me an email. Got it the day after he died because I was too upset to play around on my computer and hadn't checked for a while — plus I had a feeling that wouldn't go away, a thin wedge of dread in the back of my heart. Fuck, it was all just so depressing. Death is. He said: Damn good show.

Especially with Marlene. Take care of the little green bird. Whatever you do, don't set him free. That would be a cruel gesture. Plus budgies hold grudges. Thanks for the trip. It was the best ever. Love your pal Roy. No commas.

There wasn't a funeral. He wouldn't stand for that. Something low-key was his thing. Jessica helped arrange a memorial weeks later at a half-filled theatre in Vancouver, where actors cried a lot and said sad things about Roy. We had a couple of laughs too, although Roy probably would have thought the jokes about his smoking and drinking habits were forced.

Marlene was there. She went up to the front, threw back her long red hair — which was by then mostly in braids — and said very loudly into the microphone: Roy didn't really direct me, but he pointed me in the right direction. Although now I'm stuck with all of you.

That comment got a little laugh, but not necessarily the right kind. A lot of theatre people thought she was too brash. One old friend of mine, Bill, the actor-slash-director who starred in my last play, said she could have used more tact.

Marlene, is that her name? he asked. That woman with the great red hair? Who does she think she is, anyway? I mean, really. Who would want her? Who?

Later at my place, over expensive Spanish wine and stinky white cheese from Quebec, I told Marlene that I loved her.

She smiled and said, Yeah, I figured. Gave me a little kiss on the forehead. I'm sure most couples do this before making big decisions. Right?

Shortly afterward, we talked about moving in. I was being very optimistic. She said she wanted to take some time to think about my offer.

In the meantime I got a little house off Fraser Street. Renting, just like everybody else in Vancouver who works in theatre.

From the set designer, Yvan, a great guy who lives on the other side of the cemetery. I can cycle there with his rent cheques. It's all very convenient.

The house is a bungalow with sparkly stucco. Huge picture window. White picket fence. Very 1950s, very old school. Fresh herbs in the front yard. Rosemary. Thyme. Some other kind of thyme, lemon, I think. In the back the plum tree is recovering from bug problems — ants and their stupid slave aphids. Plus I have drainage issues. Like my mom would say, it's always something. But I have tons of room. I know Marlene's used to bigger houses, but this one is comfortable, even nostalgic.

I got a dog, just like her old dog back home, an Australian Shepherd named Frank. Two cats I haven't named yet. Chekhov the budgie. The animals actually sort of get along. The cats admire Chekhov's bravery. They sit outside his bamboo cage and occasionally slap at it, as if to make sure he sees them. He does. And still prances. Fuck you, I think he's saying, fuck you stupid cats stuck on the outside without a mirror.

Funny bird.

Roy's bird.

I also got a load of debt. I spent way too much, not at IKEA, setting this all up. Leather and chrome. Lots of art. A painting from Una, Marlene's former maid. It's all red except for a black spot in the middle titled *Me*. Don't know what it means. But I love the house. Wish Marlene was here, but I suppose she needs more time.

In the meantime, I guess we're a regular couple. Absolutely. We do regular couple things: take walks, go to shows, rub feet, laugh. Occasionally we throw dinner parties with copious amounts of the great wine we discovered while in Kelowna.

Friends come and go. Some for good. That's OK.

Sometimes we fight over friends. Sometimes we fight over laundry. Or her acting. Or my writing.

You're bigger than me now, I tell her.

I know, she says. How does it feel, Mr. Playwright?

Yeah, that bugs me.

But the truth is we're all a bit irritating on occasion. And brave. Shallow. Brilliant. Insecure. Crazy. That's the nature of the business.

Anyway, I'm sure she loves me. Positive.

To pay bills, I teach actors how to write plays at a small college down the road. Marlene, when she's not doing a show, which is rare, reads to seniors at a retirement centre. Many of them are Chinese and have no clue what she's saying, but they can't take their eyes off her and her magnificent blazing eyes.

Marlene has her own place on Commercial Street, a one-bedroom over a gelato store. I think she should just give it up. Why not move in, why not with me? I'm a nice guy, we're a nice couple. We get along. And I'm writing again. I'm more focused. I'm more responsible.

I've stopped fucking things up. I have. Really.

I finished the play. A romantic comedy with drama. Or a dramatic romance with comedy. Write what you know, right. Ha. So I did. It was called *Soulless*.

It was OK. My little theatre company produced it. Joanna directed. Solid production. Tiny theatre. Nice lighting. Good performances. Funny, a little sad, and slightly ironic. Somebody died in the end, of course. My kind of story. Somebody always has to die, right?

The critic hated it, of course. I read his review on the packed city bus, wedged between a wheezing old Italian guy in an old black leather jacket and a young mother holding a sleeping bald baby.

Life More Interesting Than Story. That's what they went with.
That was the fucking headline.

For a moment, I was upset.

And then, before I knew it, another moment appeared.

And I was happy again.

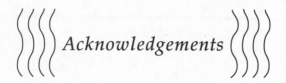

Acknowledgements

There are many other people within the world of literature and theatre who influenced and inspired me to write this story. Roy Surette and Norman Armour both inspired the title character of Roy. I consider them great artists and good friends. Thanks to Bryan Jay Ibeas for editing the book and making the story stronger. Others to thank for the inspiration that helped forge my characters in the book: Vern Thiessen, Emma Slipp, Andrew McNee, Lindsey Angell Jespersen, Sara Rodgers, Allan Morgan, Colleen Wheeler, Bill Dow, Colin Murdock, Jessica Chambers, Scott Bellis, Jay Brazeau, Glynis Leyshon, Johnna Wright, Del.Surjik, Susie Codin, Almeera Jiwa, Kathleen Oliver, David Hudgins, Yvan Morissette, Rodger Cove, Harry Hertscheg, Colin Thomas, Jo Ledingham, Deborah Williams, Rachel Peake, Una Memisevic, Stephen Miller, Josh Drebit, Celine Stubel, Alex Zahara, Naomi Wright, Chapelle Jaffe, Ami Gladstone, Dawn Brennan, Christopher Gaze, Bard on the Beach, Solo Collective Theatre, and of course, my lovely partner in life, Diana Lyon.